A nail-

JUST CAUSE

She wanted the truth. It might come too late.

CAROLYN ARNOLD

A Detective Madison Knight Mystery

HIBBERT & STILES
PUBLISHING INC.

2021 Revised Edition

Copyright © 2014 by Carolyn Arnold
Excerpt from *Deadly Impulse* copyright © 2015 by Carolyn Arnold

All rights reserved. No part of this publication may be reproduced, distributed, or transmitted in any form or by any means, including photocopying, recording, or other electronic or mechanical methods, without the prior written permission of the publisher, except in the case of brief quotations embodied in critical reviews and certain other noncommercial uses permitted by copyright law. For permission requests, contact the publisher.

Hibbert & Stiles Publishing Inc.
www.hspubinc.com

This is a work of fiction. Names, characters, places, and incidents are the products of the author's imagination or are used fictitiously. Any resemblance to actual events, locales, or persons, living or dead, is entirely coincidental.

Names: Arnold, Carolyn.
Title: Just Cause / Carolyn Arnold.
Description: : 2021 Hibbert & Stiles Publishing Inc. edition. | Series: Detective Madison Knight series ; book: 5
Identifiers: ISBN (e-book): 978-1-988064-20-8 | ISBN (4.25 x 7 paperback): 978-1-988353-10-4 | ISBN (5 x 8 paperback): 978-1-988064-18-5 | ISBN (6.14 x 9.21 hardcover): 978-1-988353-11-1

Additional formats:
ISBN (6 x 9 paperback large print edition): 978-1-989706-31-2

JUST CAUSE

PROLOGUE

Eight Years Ago

If only there were a way to turn back time. Then he'd make different decisions. Depending on how far back he went, he never would have taken on the Russian as a client. But he'd been blinded by his hunger to make a real name for himself in the law community, to bolster the family name to new heights. Instead everything came down like a house of cards. He'd gotten in over his head, and one bad decision became several.

At least Jessica had Mason there for her. She wasn't alone. He was though—now dead as Bryan Lexan and resurrected as Jayson Nash. He was building a life from scratch because he'd had to.

He hadn't planned on returning home, and he certainly never expected Jessica to be there. Now she knew he'd staged his death. But really, what damage could she do? The answer was likely nothing. Besides, he was already on his way out of town for good. No sense wasting time worrying or letting the regrets fester.

Everything would be okay.

As he stepped outside, the warmth of the sun was magnificent. *At least I'm alive,* he thought as he flicked his sunglasses in place.

He reached his car, and his legs froze. There was an envelope tucked under a wiper. "What the hell?" He snatched it. His name was scrawled in messy handwriting—his *given* name.

He went cold and looked around. No one within sight. The only sounds those of birds singing.

He took a deep breath. He was being paranoid.

The envelope wasn't cooperating with his efforts to open it, his fingers quaking, and he ended up ripping a slice off the top that fell to the driveway. Inside was a single sheet of paper.

So much like a threat he'd received before.

His hands were shaking almost too much to hold the paper still, but once his mind registered the message, his breathing sped up. He clutched the sheet as if that would protect him from its encoded message, but the words were very clear. He might never be able to hide, and he'd always be looking over his shoulder.

He hustled to his car and stopped. His skin pricked with goose bumps. Someone *was* watching him. Then the soft patter of approaching footsteps. They were closing the distance to him rather quickly. He turned. As quickly as he recognized the horror of his fate, it rushed to meet him.

The man raised a gun. Pointed it right at him. A *pfft* and pop of light.

Then searing pain.

He looked down. He'd been shot in the chest.

Time came to a halt as his legs gave out, and he crashed to the ground.

The man stepped closer and pressed the barrel to his forehead.

There'd be no coming back to life this time.

CHAPTER ONE

Present Day

The bullet pinged the metal step just above her head, barely missing her, and fell to the floor. Madison had lowered in time—barely—but slammed her knees into the concrete.

She spun and returned fire on her attacker.

Anatolli Belsky, one of the Russian mob's consiglieres.

A noise now from behind her, at the top of the stairs, had her heart thumping. She was flanked, right in the middle of Anatolli and another assailant.

"Stop!"

Madison quickly faced the man, Sergey Evanoff, and pulled her trigger at the same time Anatolli got off another round.

Sergey cried out. He'd been struck and gripped his side, blood pouring between his fingers.

She froze. She could have been shot from behind. She was panting, trying to figure out her next move, but she hesitated just a second too long. Anatolli had moved in on her, and his gun was pressed to her head. The heat from the recently fired weapon was almost scalding.

"Drop the gun!" Anatolli barked.

She had no choice but to comply—for now. She set her Glock on a step.

Anatolli pulled her up by her hair, his fingers digging into her scalp.

"Let me go!" She squirmed and struggled against his hold, to no avail. He was much stronger than she was.

"Get up now! Or you die!"

She hesitated, then struck fast. She kicked the heel of her shoe into his instep and went to retrieve her gun. "Go to hell, you son of a bitch!"

He recovered quickly and jammed his gun against her harder. She stopped all movement.

"Just give me the word, Sergey!"

"No!" Sergey eased himself off the step he had perched himself on.

She swallowed hard. The delay in killing her meant only one thing—they would make her suffer until a bullet to the head seemed like a welcome escape.

Sergey inched toward her, nostrils flaring, teeth gritted, like a raging bull charging at a matador's waving red cape. Her only chance was to make another move for her gun, but there was no way she'd be able to get to it without securing holes in her head.

She began to lift her arms in surrender— A blinding pain raced up her left arm from her wrist and had her crying out. She must have slammed it on the stairwell. She raised her right hand.

Anatolli eased the pressure off the barrel.

"Get to your feet," Sergey hissed, then spat in her face.

An act meant to humiliate only fueled her rage. She'd personally see their entire operation come down. She rose to full height.

"Do you want me to kill her, boss?" Anatolli moved the gun barrel to her lower back. "Or I could aim for a sweet spot in her spine and watch her flop around like a fish."

"Enough!"

Anatolli lowered his gun.

Sergey spoke more words in Russian, and Anatolli linked her arms behind her back, holding them with his hands. Bile came up her throat as his meat hooks got ahold of her left wrist. Maybe she'd broken it.

Anatolli guided her up the stairs, with Sergey leading the way and grunting as if he struggled with each step.

She was taken to a fairly large office, but nothing about it was showy or meant to impress. Though it was unlikely many visitors were welcome here.

She took in the space. Only the basics. A simple executive desk, computer, monitor, wheeled chair, filing cabinets. On the wall, a framed map of the world and three clocks, set to different time zones.

Anatolli nudged her across the room, where Sergey opened a door. Anatolli shoved her inside, and she stumbled forward but caught her balance before falling.

A switch was flipped, and darkness morphed into blinding light. But as her eyes adjusted, fear coiled through her body. It was a concrete, windowless cell with a bloodstained floor and a drain. People had been murdered here, but not before they were violently tortured.

There was a chair in the middle of the room with shackles attached to its arms and legs, and a metal clasp at the top of the back that would fit around a person's neck.

She was already finding it hard to breathe. If she got into that chair, she'd die in that chair. "You're never going to get away with this," she ground out. She was a Major Crimes detective with the Stiles Police Department, and if something happened to her, the Russians would have the full force down their throats.

The Russians laughed.

"We get away with murder all the time." Sergey gestured toward Anatolli.

He took her phone, then proceeded to secure her wrists. Again, a fire of agony shot through her arm, and she winced. As he bent to slap the shackles closed around her ankles, she lifted her leg, connecting her knee with the cartilage of his nose.

Retaliation came swiftly. Anatolli smacked her across the face, torquing her neck. Her spirit so badly wanted to fight back, but her vision faded to black.

CHAPTER TWO

On Monday morning, Detective Terry Grant had been all over the station looking for his partner, Madison. He'd tried her cell phone a number of times. She was a master at leaving the paperwork to him, but he couldn't imagine her ignoring his calls.

He stopped at the front counter. "See Detective Knight yet today?"

Ranson, a young woman who handled the phones and walk-ins, shook her head. "I haven't. You check with your sarge? Maybe she called in sick."

Terry highly doubted that. She would come in puking before she let a little bug kick her ass. Besides, he was quite sure bacteria and viruses were afraid of her.

He pulled out his phone and tried her again. Like before, it rang to voicemail. He might as well leave a message. "Where are you? I'm not doing all the reports." This wasn't good. Something was wrong. She'd never hidden her efforts to ditch paper shuffling in the past.

He selected her home number, and her machine picked up. That left him with one person who might know Madison's whereabouts—Cynthia Baxter. She was the head of the crime lab for the Stiles Police Department and Madison's best friend. Cynthia answered on the third ring.

"Have you heard from Maddy?" he asked, skipping the pleasantries.

"Ah, no." There seemed to be a mark of irritation in her voice, as if she wasn't Madison's keeper.

"She hasn't come in, and she's not answering her—"

Cynthia cut him off. "You can't reach her?"

He flailed a hand. "No." He hated it when people interrupted him or finished his sentences. The latter was something Madison did periodically, and his wife quite a bit, but outside of those two women, he found it hard to tolerate.

"She could have just slept in. She's done that before."

Maybe he was being paranoid, but the fact that he couldn't reach her niggled at him. She was the type of person to live next to her phone, and the only reason she wouldn't answer was if she couldn't. The more he tried to come up with a logical explanation, the more reason he had to worry.

"I'm sure she's fine," Cynthia said as if sensing his darkening thoughts. "She's tough and can take care of herself."

"I just have a feeling something isn't right."

"She's rubbing off on you."

"What?"

"It's just you're not normally the feely, gut-instinct type."

He groaned at the accuracy of Cynthia's statement. Madison was changing him. "Not sure her rubbing off on me is for the better."

"Trust me. It is."

Leave it to the two women to stick together. "But even looking at this rationally, there's no answer on her cell phone or at her home. That's not like her. Tell me you don't think that's weird."

"No, that is..." Cynthia's voice petered out, but he detected fear before it disappeared.

"What is it?" He was getting another feeling. There was something Cynthia was avoiding telling him. "Cyn?" he prompted.

"I probably shouldn't say anything."

"Even if she could be in danger?" He snapped his mouth shut as the picture filled in for him—and it wasn't a pretty one. "Is she digging into that cold case of hers again?"

"When has she stopped?"

"Unbelievable. The case is eight years old."

"She wants justice." Chelsea tossed that out like it explained Madison's obsession.

Bryan Lexan, a young defense attorney, had repped Dimitre Petrov—head of the Russian Mafia—against a single murder charge and failed to keep him out of prison. Madison was adamant Dimitre had him killed in retaliation. Terry could appreciate that his partner wanted closure, but he was certain there was more to it—a personal vendetta against the mob for reasons he had yet to discover. But surely she hadn't taken things into her own hands and confronted them by herself. He gulped. That sounded just like her.

"Tell me everything you know," he pushed out. "Did you give her an update recently?" His temper was ratcheting, but if something had happened to Madison, he'd be lost.

A pocket of silence, then Cynthia said, "I don't know."

"How can you not—"

"She's got to be okay, right? I mean, she's not stupid."

But she is impulsive! "I need you to focus. What was the most recent thing she had you look into?"

"You're getting me all worked up, and I'm typically a balanced individual."

"Cynthia," he said firmly.

"Well, it was earlier this month. But she had a—"

"Had a *what*?"

"If you would let me finish," she snapped. "She had an envelope she wanted compared to the piece of one found in the attorney's driveway."

"What about it?" he asked. "And where did she get this other envelope for comparison?"

"You should probably talk to Maddy about this."

He gripped the phone tighter and hung up. How much did he want to bet Madison's no-show had to do with her poking her nose into the mob's affairs—again. Only this time she got herself into serious trouble.

There was one other call he could make that would either soothe his mind or make matters worse. He reached out to Canine Country Retreat Boarding—where Madison took her chocolate Lab, Hershey, during the workday—and asked if he was there. They told him Hershey was, but Madison was due to have picked him up last night, and they hadn't heard from her. That sealed it for him. Something was gravely wrong.

Terry stormed into Sergeant Garry Winston's office. "Madison's missing," he blurted out.

Winston slowly peeled his attention from the mountain of paperwork in front of him, as if what he'd been doing was more riveting than his detective's latest drama. "Missing?" Incredulous, as if he thought Terry was insane.

"I believe so, yes. She's not answering her cell phone or home line. Her dog was left at the kennel overnight without her so much as calling them to explain."

"Huh. She usually answers her phone. Though she's never been good at communicating."

Terry had no desire to get into one of the sergeant's gripes about Madison's failure to keep him updated at regular intervals during the course of an investigation. "She lives for this job. That means she'd be by her phone. I've got a bad feeling." Terry didn't want to reveal his suspicions that her vanishing act had something to do with the mob until—or *unless*—it became necessary.

"Go by her apartment. I'll get a BOLO going for her car."

Terry hoped the "be on the lookout" bulletin worked, but he wasn't going to sit around and wait to find out.

Terry tore through the city with the lights flashing on the department car. Whatever worked to clear the road. He was going to her apartment first, and if he still hit a wall, well, he had no clue.

He tried the intercom button for Madison's apartment and imagined her answering—but there was no answer. Maybe if he could go up to her floor and bang on her door, but the building was a lockout.

He pushed random buttons, hoping someone would respond.

"Hello?" An elderly woman based on her fragile voice. Probably someone's loving grandmother.

"Ma'am, this is Detective Grant of the Stiles Police Department. I need access to the building."

"No way, creep. Go away, or I'll call the police."

Terry rolled his eyes, tried another button, and received a more favorable reply. Shortly afterward, the front door buzzed unlocked, and he was in. He took the stairs up to Madison's floor and pounded on her door. Surely it was loud enough to rouse the dead.

The dead... The two words bounced around in his head, torturing him. What if something had happened to Madison, and he was too late?

He stumbled back and leaned against the wall across the hall. Where could she have gone? He could get a trace on her phone, but that would eat up precious time and might not lead him to her. His mind raced with the possibilities and the different business fronts the Russians held. Then it hit.

Homeland Logistics.

It was located at the water's edge but was rather large and isolated.

"Could she be that stupid?" he muttered as he pushed off the wall. "She's going to get herself killed."

CHAPTER THREE

The door opened, then slammed shut. She jolted from the noise, not that she'd been asleep. But she guessed she'd been there overnight, and now it was morning. Her wrist was aching and maintained a steady, thrumming heartbeat. Maybe she had broken it.

"They're going to come looking for me." It was harder to speak than she'd have imagined. Her mouth and throat were dry and raw.

"We'll be ready if they do." The voice came from the shadows, but she recognized it as Anatolli's.

The light came on, and he moved closer.

"Your partner's been calling all morning." He held up her cell phone and tossed it onto her lap. With her hands bound, there was no way for her to catch it, and it fell off and landed on the floor at her feet.

If they left it on, they weren't concerned about it being tracked. Anatolli's claim about being prepared may have been the truth.

"Let me go, and we can work out a deal."

He didn't say anything as he moved closer to her and pulled out a cigarette. He lit it, took a deep drag, and exhaled the smoke in her face.

She coughed.

"You shot my friend." Spoken slowly and almost detached. A person who tried to suppress their rage was a far more dangerous animal than one who lashed out. Wildfire blazed in his eyes, but he stood there perfectly still, staring at her.

She'd always considered Anatolli subservient to Sergey. Maybe she could work this to her advantage by treating him like he was in charge. "Listen, we can…ah…make a deal if you let me go now."

"Deal?" He scoffed. "You, no position to make deal."

His breath was warm on her face and stank of cigarettes. What if she died here? This being one of her last memories? "I am. You and I can work something out."

Her phone rang and vibrated across the floor.

"What will all of your friends think when you're dead, and they were too late to save you?" he asked calmly—too calmly. He'd completely disregarded her attempts to appeal to his ego. *Had Sergey died?* But as the thought passed through, Sergey entered the room, walking with a limp and favoring his right side.

"You look surprised to see me, Detective. But you can't kill the devil." Sergey lifted his shirt and showed her the sutures that sealed up the bullet wound.

"Next time I'll be sure to finish the job." All bravado, no true confidence.

Sergey's teeth clenched tight, and his jaw became sharp, jagged lines. He nodded toward Anatolli, who withdrew a revolver and pushed its barrel to her forehead.

She tried to move to the side, but her motion was limited from the restraint around her neck. Panic stole her breath, but she couldn't let them see her fear. *Stay strong, Maddy. Stay strong!*

"Let's play a little game. You may have heard of it? Only we simply call it 'roulette' when we play. The Russian part would be redundant." Sergey paced the room, and Madison caught the flicker that danced in the man's eyes. He was enjoying the mind games, but she suspected he loved shedding blood at least as much—if not more.

Her breathing hitched, her heart splintered, and her stomach tightened and heaved, tossing bile up the back of her throat.

Sergey continued. "We're going to play it a little differently. Let the fates decide. Anatolli's going to pull the trigger. If you live, we will take our time with you. If you die"—he shrugged—"well, I suppose, game over."

Both men laughed, sending chills coursing through her.

Her entire life didn't flash before her eyes, but moments of it did. Images of kissing Toby Sovereign haunted her, dredging up the feelings she harbored for him, but if she got out of here, could she look beyond the past to a future with him? He had challenged her to say she didn't love him anymore and to look into his eyes while she did so. She hadn't been able to bring herself to reject him. He'd broken her heart years ago by cheating on her when they were engaged. Was what they'd had before even worth trying to resurrect?

A deep breath escaped her lungs.

And Cynthia. Would she understand why Madison had to confront the Russians and try to get more out of them? Her friend knew how much solving the Lexan case meant to her, but would Cynthia understand why she risked her life for its resolution? And, really, look where it had gotten her. Nowhere.

Then her mother. She'd never see Madison happily married with children, which was her strong wish. And there would be no reconciliation between them. Her mother claimed nothing had changed, but their relationship had when Madison's maternal grandmother left most of her earthly possessions to Madison when she died.

And her father. Madison flashed forward and envisioned his grief at losing one of his daughters.

And Madison wouldn't have a chance to say goodbye to her sister, Chelsea, either. Madison wouldn't see her three nieces grow up.

Also Terry. He'd be so disappointed in her, at her impulsiveness. He'd probably be angry with her for a very long time. Madison would never meet his baby—his *son*, as he was so certain it would be.

An ache drilled in her chest with some other realizations too. She'd devoted her life to her badge to the point of isolating herself from other people. She had one best friend, not counting her sister, and a partner who was like a brother. Beyond that was her canine companion—Hershey, her chocolate Lab. She wished she could be caressing the soft velvet of the pup's ears right now, and thinking of Hershey, who would look after him when she was gone? Would Terry adopt him into his household? He already had two beagles and a baby on the way. His hands were probably more than full.

These thoughts occurred to her in fractions of seconds.

If she lived through this, she would do things differently. But would she have that chance?

Tears hit her cheeks, and a part of her soul submitted to the inevitable. She was going to die in this room with no one by her side but the two Russians who would carry out her murder—possibly preceded by torture. Her only hope was that some miracle would intervene before it was too late.

CHAPTER FOUR

Terry had shown up at the waterfront, spotted Madison's Mazda immediately, and called it in. The Strategic Weapons and Tactical Unit had shown up within the hour. Too long as far as Terry was concerned, but there was a lot to consider. One, the approach, and two, the legalities of securing warrants for breach, search, and arrest.

The SWAT team was gathered in a command vehicle on a side street near a park. Troy Matthews was the commander and briefed and directed his men. He'd been in the position for years, but Terry didn't know him too well.

"We're going to come at the building from all corners," Matthews said. "We also have speedboats a half mile out, securing the waterfront in case the perps try to flee. Remember that an officer's life is at risk here, and there's no room for failure."

His officers acknowledged with variations of, "We understand, boss."

Matthews went on, laying out in more detail where he wanted each of them positioned for the takeover. As Terry listened, it was clear that Matthews and his men had the structure covered, but Terry didn't want to sit this one out.

The SWAT officers left the vehicle to get into position, and Terry was face-to-face with Matthews. "I want in on this."

"No way. The best thing you can do is hang back."

"Do nothing?"

"Yeah." Matthews left Terry and went over to a couple of technicians who sat in front of monitors wearing comm pieces in their ears.

"No," Terry snapped. "I can't just—"

Matthews got to within a few inches of Terry's face. "Let us do our jobs!"

Terry wanted to protest, but SWAT was trained for this kind of thing much better than he was, and they had far more effective *toys*. "She's my partner," Terry eventually said, deflated but also angry. How could Madison be so reckless? If she came out of this alive—and she had to—he might kill her himself.

"This must be tough, but trust me. This is the best team of men I've ever led, and I'm crazy about Madison myself. She's a tough one. She'll make it through." Something about the intensity in Matthews's eyes had Terry believing him.

"She *will* make it," Terry said and headed to the vehicle's door. He stopped and spoke over a shoulder, adding, "Keep me updated."

"Absolutely."

Terry emerged into the sunshine, not the same person he'd been when he'd woken up that morning. His first concern then had been his pregnant wife and their baby—and there was reason. Doctors were saying there was a possibility their son could be born with spina bifida. But he'd still be alive. Madison, on the other hand, might not be.

CHAPTER FIVE

Madison studied Sergey, who stood to the left of Anatolli, piercing her with his stare. He'd have no qualms about killing her, and he'd probably relish in the opportunity. For all she knew, they'd emptied the chambers of the revolver to ensure torture rather than a speedy death by bullet.

If she did somehow come out of this alive, there were things that would change.

For one, she wouldn't be so afraid to open herself up and trust people. Two, she'd forgive, forget, and heal much faster than she'd done in the past. Three, she'd love with all her heart and give of herself to those she brought in close. Four, she wouldn't worry about the few extra pounds she carried.

Sergey smirked. "On the count of three."

Anatolli dipped his head and stared at her.

"One."

Madison's stomach lurched.

"Two."

Sweat beaded on her forehead.

Anatolli cocked the hammer, and Madison closed her eyes. *It won't be long now...* She said a silent prayer. Best guess as to whether or not she did it right, but in this predicament it was natural to turn to a Greater Being—even if it was hypocritical. She hadn't prayed or been to church in years.

"Three."

Nothing but silence.

She opened her eyes. Then Anatolli pulled the trigger.

No bullet.

"Bang! You're dead!" Anatolli laughed excitedly.

Sergey's face became dark shadows. "Looks like the fates have decided. Guess we have some fun now, Anatolli."

A bullet to the brain would have been better for her, but now she had nothing to lose. She'd try to get her answers even if she took them to her grave. "Why did you kill Bryan Lexan? Was it because his defense failed to keep Dimitre out of prison?"

Sergey and Anatolli just stared blankly at her as if she hadn't said a word.

She nudged out her chin in defiance. "The jury found him guilty. Why not kill all of them?"

Sergey narrowed his eyes. "You are in no place to ask questions."

"You're not going to kill me, and here's why." *Maybe if I can keep them talking...*

"Not going to kill you? You a crazy bitch. Why wouldn't I? You shot me." Sergey's teeth took on the appearance of fangs, and his eyes were hungry for vengeance. "You are always getting in the way. I sat while they pull your bullet from me. I groan in agony as they fish for it. Then they take long needle and sew me up." He rushed to her chair and placed both his hands on her forearms. "You want mercy? You are looking in wrong place, no?"

"I'm not after mercy. I'm police. You kill me, you'll have heat on your head hotter than the sun."

As if she'd planned the timing, there was gunfire. She could only hope it was her rescue. *Please, Dear God, let it be.* "They know I'm here. You're going to die, not me." A bluff she hoped she made sound convincing.

"Shut up!" Sergey roared. "Go, check it out!" He directed Anatolli with a wave of his hand, and he left the room.

"Stiles PD! Hands up now!"

Anatolli was backed into the room by three members of SWAT armed with automatic assault rifles. One collected the revolver from Anatolli and patted him down. Another frisked Sergey. Both were handcuffed.

The third officer freed her from her restraints, and she could finally breathe. She was going to live another day after all.

CHAPTER SIX

Madison was on a gurney in the back of an ambulance parked in the Homeland Logistics lot, being tended to by a paramedic. The sun was shining brightly when she'd emerged from the building. She asked and was informed it was one thirty. There was a bitter chill to the air for late March, and a breeze occasionally gusted into the vehicle.

Terry hopped into the back of the rig. "It's a good thing you're not dead, but I'm going to kill you myself."

"Sir, I'm going to have to ask that you leave." The paramedic rushed to usher Terry out.

"It's okay," Madison told him. "He's my partner."

The paramedic bobbed his head and proceeded with icing her wrist.

She winced but tried to cover it behind a taunt to Terry. "So you're going to kill *me*? You and what army?"

"Keep your arm elevated," the paramedic instructed her.

Terry pointed at her. "You should be happy you came out of this with nothing but an injured wrist."

"It's just a sprain. Nothing serious," she clarified. "But I also have a cut lip. Quite sure I banged my knee but good too. Prognosis is I'll live though."

Terry grunted. "Cocky and sarcastic, and so soon." He looked away from her then, and she followed the direction of his gaze. Sergey and Anatolli and others from the warehouse were being led out of the building and fed into cruisers.

The paramedic kept fussing with her wrist. He took the ice away, put a splint in place, and wrapped it up. Then he started opening drawers. "Just getting some painkillers."

Terry met her gaze again and said in all seriousness, "You could have been killed."

She didn't need him to tell her that. She'd lived through the ordeal, but still she found herself getting emotional. Terry would have missed her if she'd died. She had made a difference in this life and would have been remembered. But she recalled the vows she'd made to herself; there was work to do and improvements to make. Tears welled in her eyes. "But I wasn't," she pushed out.

His eyes glazed over, and she could tell he was going to get all mushy if she didn't get in front of it. She punched his shoulder with her good hand.

"Hey!" He rubbed his arm where she'd hit him. Same old show that played out between them on repeat. He really was the brother she didn't have.

"Well, enough of this sentimental crap. I'm alive. It's all good."

Officer Higgins's voice, calling out her name, carried in the air and reached her before he popped in front of her. He didn't enter the ambulance but spoke from outside the open doors. "Do you have a death wish? Are you really trying to take on the Mafia on your own? I'm sure I taught you better than that."

Reggie Higgins had been her training officer back in the day, but he'd clung to the rank of officer without interest in advancing, and the department was better for it.

"You know me, Chief." An affectionate nickname she'd graced him with because he could have held the position years ago if he had desired.

"Stubborn, pig-headed, fiercely independent," he listed off.

"Ouch. I was thinking more flattering terminology. Determined, intelligent, courageous."

Terry mumbled something incoherent, crossed his arms, and looked away.

The reflection in Higgins's eyes became serious, and his arms were restless, as if he considered hopping into the vehicle and giving her a hug. But he ended up placing his hands on his hips and tilted out his chin. "Just happy you made it out. But remember"—he gestured to the many officers milling about behind him—"life is better when you're part of a team."

If it hadn't been for the department, for Terry, who had probably tracked her here, she'd either be dead right now or enduring torture. Gratitude squeezed her chest, and she nodded.

"Knight." Sergeant Winston was storming toward her, his large strides chewing up pavement.

"I had better get going." Higgins jacked a thumb over a shoulder and left.

Take me with you. She wished she could disappear into thin air but thought of an option to avoid her superior. She turned to the medic. "Maybe you should take me to the hospital?"

The paramedic smiled at her and kept rooting around in the vehicle's numerous cabinets.

She looked back out the doors. Winston didn't waste time or pleasantries with Higgins, but beelined for her, his gaze intense, and he got into the ambulance. Terry shuffled over to make room.

"What the hell did you think you were doing?" Winston said. "You could have been killed."

He'd miss me. She sat up a little straighter.

"Don't smile at me, Knight. And don't make this into something it isn't." Winston looked at Terry. "That's the problem with women. Emotion factors into—"

"Emotion?" she spat. Her boss was a chauvinistic pig. She was rarely accused of being emotional because she did so well barricaded behind a self-erected wall. "I faced two of the highest-ranking men in the Russian Mafia, and I walked away."

"Only because SWAT saved your ass—and you better be thanking Matthews." Winston's gaze dipped to her bandaged hand. "And don't think this is over. Internal Affairs will be getting involved. You can bet on that. But we'll talk about that later. Tend to this first." He swept a hand to indicate her injury.

She peacocked her posture. "Let's talk now." She'd show him that she had her emotions under control.

"Nope, we'll talk back at the station, once you're finished here." He stalked off.

"Oh, he's pissed," Madison said, turning to look at Terry, but he avoided her gaze.

"You think? SWAT was pulled in to save your ass."

"Well, I happen to think it's an ass worth saving."

He gazed at her now. "Uh-huh. A big—"

"Don't even." She glared at him.

He smirked. "Well…how's the diet going?"

"Come closer so I can hit you again. Much harder this time."

"Hardy-har." He laughed, but it was hollow, and his eyes were shadowed.

"Where is she?" Cynthia rounded the back of the ambulance and stepped inside. She took Madison into a bear hug that had Madison grimacing in pain.

"Oh, sorry." She backed up and looked her over. "Are you all right?" She gingerly touched Madison's bandaged hand.

"It's all right. It will heal. Besides I'm a tough girl." Her statement contrasted the myriad feelings blustering through her. Relief, appreciation, gratitude, sadness, happiness, vulnerability. Facing death and being pulled from the ledge was affecting her more than she cared to admit. And she was touched with people showing up to check on her, but where was Toby Sovereign? If he truly cared about her as he claimed and wanted to resurrect a romance with her, why wasn't he here? She shouldn't have even entertained the thought that he had changed.

"Tough? That's what you like to project any—" Cynthia's mouth gaped open, and she lifted her sunglasses. "Who is that?" Her lips curled in a feral smile.

Madison looked out the doors and saw a SWAT officer approaching—a *gorgeous* SWAT officer—dressed in full gear.

Madison and Cynthia met each other's gazes, and Cynthia said, "Well, if you're going to get rescued, at least you do it in style. Rrr." She pawed at the air. "These SWAT guys have to be the sexiest men on the planet."

"Sure, he's good-looking, but aren't you involved with someone?" Madison countered. Her friend was seeing Lou Stanford, another detective in Major Crimes with the Stiles PD. Interestingly enough, he was also Toby Sovereign's partner.

"I am, but there's no harm in looking. Besides, you're single." Cynthia bobbed her eyebrows at Madison.

Madison rolled her eyes. "I need to get down to the station."

"I don't think that's a good idea," Terry said.

Good idea or not, I'm outta here! She got off the gurney, and the medic turned.

"I'm still working on finding those pills. No idea why everything in this rig is so disorganized."

"I'm just stepping out for some fresh air," she told him. "I won't go far."

The paramedic grumbled something and nodded.

Outside, the SWAT officer was getting closer. Madison went to step off the back of the ambulance. Her head spun, and the next thing she knew, she was lurching forward.

The SWAT guy ran over and caught her in his arms. He was even more gorgeous up close, and he smelled like cedarwood. His face was sharp angles, and his jawline rigid. His nose was prominent, not in an unattractive way, with a faint dusting of freckles sprinkled across the bridge. And maybe it was the drugs—no, she hadn't had any yet—but his green eyes were hypnotic and saw right through her. And his arms and chest were so muscular.

"Ah, thanks," she said awkwardly.

"Not a problem." He put her down, his frame towering above her five-foot-five almost a foot.

She stepped back to put more space between them.

"You've got to watch that first step. It's a big one." He lifted his sunglasses and rested them on his head atop a bed of blond hair. "You probably don't remember me. I'm Troy Matthews."

She searched her brain for that name, for that memorable face of his, then both surfaced. She'd worked with him before. "Yeah, I know who you are."

Cynthia was biting back laughter, and Madison squashed it with a glare. Matthews was just a fellow officer, and so what if he was drop-dead gorgeous? Why should it matter to her? And he was probably only being nice to her because he was doing his job.

"Just glad to see you made it out all right." His tone hinted that a smile might be coming, but one didn't, and she remembered he didn't show the expression often.

"*All right* is debatable. I'll hold my verdict until I get the IA investigation behind me."

"Internal Affairs." Matthews winced. "They've got to have their hand in every little thing." Now he smiled, and though it was sincere, it was small.

"Well, I'm not worried about it." There was a part of her that was, but she didn't need to go broadcasting that.

"I never said you were."

A few seconds of awkward silence, in which Matthews kept his eyes fixed on her with such intensity she swore he was reading her mind.

The paramedic came out of the ambulance with a cup of water in one hand, pills in the other. "Take these, and you'll have some relief in no time."

Madison palmed the pills but wasn't really paying the medic much attention. She was fixated on Matthews, who was now walking away. She wasn't normally so flighty when it came to men. Did it have something to do with her near-death experience, or had she fallen and hit her head and not remembered?

"Detective?" the paramedic prompted her.

"Ah, yeah." She popped the pills into her mouth and took the cup from the paramedic without looking at him. She was still eyeing Matthews's retreating form.

"You'll feel better soon," the paramedic said and slipped a piece of paper in her hand. "It's a prescription." Retreating footsteps told her he was leaving.

She still didn't look at the medic, rather kept her gaze on Matthews. On his solid, athletic frame. He probably had six-pack abs under that shirt. He certainly had bulging biceps. A woman could find solace in those arms…

"Earth to Maddy?"

Matthews went out of sight, and slowly Terry's words sank in. She faced him. She'd forgotten he and Cynthia were even there. "Huh?"

"What is it with you women?" he asked.

She and Cynthia snickered.

"Cynthia, don't you have a crime scene to process?" Terry pushed out.

"I'll get there. Mark's already inside."

Mark Andrews was the newest member of the CSI team, but Madison had faith in him working solo if Cynthia did.

"Whatever." Terry shook his head. "Who is the guy to you…the SWAT guy?"

"Just another cop." And that was all he was. He'd been called in during an investigation related to the Bryan Lexan case actually. But she thought it best to leave Lexan out of the conversation as long as possible.

"Seems like more than that to me," Terry huffed.

"It's nothing. I swear. He's helped me out in the past."

"With the job? That's all? I have a feeling you might have more of a history."

"Let it go. You're married, but are you jealous? You like him?"

Terry's cheeks flamed red.

"Fine," she punched out. "He helped out with the Lexan case."

Terry clenched his jaw. "Is everything about that dead lawyer?"

"You asked," she said firmly.

"Quite sure that lawyer is why we're in this situation now. You risked your life—"

"Maybe, but I didn't die. And now, I really have work to do." She wasn't about to let her moody partner and a sprained wrist stop her. Sergey and Anatolli would be down at the station facing charges of kidnapping and attempted murder. And she had every intention of questioning them.

"Where are you going?" Terry barked.

"The station."

"Oh, no, you're not." Terry rushed in front of her. "You don't know the entire story, but the sarge received a call from the chief. He wasn't too impressed the street was closed down and traffic diverted while SWAT rescued you."

"He's mad because my life was being saved? Seriously, the guy never ceases to amaze me."

"It was *why* you needed to be rescued in the first place," Terry stamped out.

Cynthia interjected, "Terry, maybe it's not the best time to—"

He shook his head to dismiss Cynthia. "I'm just telling you what I heard."

"Whatever. I'm going to the station." She headed toward her car, and Terry and Cynthia followed.

"You're not going to drive," Terry said. "You haven't slept, and you're on drugs."

She waved an arm over her head and kept walking. "You know how many people drive exhausted and doped in this city?"

"No, I'm not allowing it." He shuffled to keep up with her. "Give me your keys."

She ignored him and kept moving.

He jabbed her shoulder. "You know I'm right."

"Madison, for once, don't be so stubborn," Cynthia begged.

Madison stopped walking and looked at both of them, then settled her gaze on Terry. "Fine."

He held out his open palm and wriggled his fingers. She gave him her keys, reluctantly. Her life was slipping out of her control—yet again. *Son of a bitch!*

CHAPTER SEVEN

Terry was relieved that Madison was okay, but he couldn't quite let go of his anger at the entire situation either. She'd gotten herself into the deadly predicament by rushing in like some rogue cop on a solo mission. Her obsession with the Lexan case and the mob had reached new heights.

"Oh, this is just great!" Madison flailed an arm toward her Mazda's windshield and snatched a parking ticket from under her wiper.

"Just have your buddy Winston take care of it." *As if that would happen in a million years.*

"Very funny."

Terry opened the front passenger door for Madison. There was an envelope on the seat—the one that led her here? He went to pick it up, but Madison nudged him out of the way and beat him to it. "Seriously?" he said.

"It's nothing."

"Right. If it's nothing, why did you hip check me?"

"I didn't…" She stopped there, not even bothering to offer up some lame excuse, and got into the car. She looked at him and raised her eyebrows. "It's okay. I've got it from here." She pulled the door shut.

He stood there for a few seconds, fuming, before walking around to the driver's side and getting behind the wheel. He turned the car on but didn't put it into gear. He glanced over at Madison. "Why can't you just leave the Lexan case alone— and the Russians? What is your fixation with all of it?"

"I don't want to talk about it."

"You...*you* don't want to talk about it?" he snapped. "People risked their lives to save yours, or have you already forgotten?"

She stared at him, more like *through* him. He cranked up the vents, but they were still blowing cold air.

"It's something about that envelope." He flailed a hand in its direction.

Something flickered in her eyes, like a flash of betrayal, maybe.

"What could it possibly tell you?" he pushed out when she said nothing.

"It's not just any envelope," she hissed.

"Then, please, help me to understand."

Madison could tell Terry was angry, but he wasn't doing a good job of hiding it. After everything he'd been through in the last several hours, he obviously felt he deserved some answers—and maybe he did. And she had vowed to open herself up more. "Fine, you want to know?"

"That would be nice, yeah." Sarcastic and bitter.

"It's a letter from Dimitre Petrov."

"The head of the Russian Mafia."

She angled her head. "Is there another one?"

"No need to be like that. Go on. Quite sure it's something about envelopes matching—one from Lexan's driveway and the one in your hand, I assume. What's inside it anyway?"

It would seem Cynthia had told him about her latest lead in the cold case. She could be angry at her friend, but if Cynthia hadn't opened up to him, Madison might be dead. But she didn't like the way Terry was watching her, as if no matter what she said next, he'd pounce and stomp on her suspicions until they were pulverized. "I'm not sure you really want to know."

He banged the steering wheel with his palms and took a few deep breaths. "I wouldn't have asked."

She waited a few beats, then pulled the letter from its sleeve and handed it to him. If he could read it for himself, he might see through the lines like she had. *Might*.

He unfolded the note and read.

Seconds ticked away.

"Dimitre says he *didn't* kill the lawyer." He looked over at her, disappointment and possible disgust in his gaze. "He takes the time to write you this, and you still feel he's responsible? I'm not sure what's wrong with you or why you're so obsessed."

Her earlobes heated in anger. "Maybe you don't need to understand. And it's not obsession." The lie sank in her gut. "He did it."

"Explain the note then. How do you read it? Is there invisible ink that shows up under special light that says the opposite of what can been seen to the naked eye?"

With every word from his mouth, her temper ratcheted. He'd never understand. "See, this is why I didn't come to you in the first place. You don't get that all of this is a game to Dimitre. He's playing with my mind. That's what he does. And, of course he can honestly say he didn't kill Lexan. He has men for that. I just have to figure out which one pulled the trigger and find the evidence that Dimitre ordered the hit."

Strained silence stretched between them.

Terry scowled and shook his head. "Why can't you just let the Lexan case go?"

"He was twenty-seven when he was gunned down in his driveway. Sure, he was a defense attorney, he helped some guilty people walk, but he still deserves justice." There was so much more motivating her to find closure with this case, but that was all she was giving him.

"Nah, there's more to it." He studied her face. "This is personal."

"Please just drive me to the station."

"Whatever, Madison." Terry shoved the letter toward her. "You clam up now, but the truth's going to come out." He pulled out of the lot and merged into traffic.

They passed buildings that were nothing more than blurred hues of gray and black, then she glanced down at the envelope in her hand. She was truly alone. No one would understand her side. Certainly not Terry, who was waiting with his ridicule and judgment. But so be it if she had to take on the Russians by herself. She'd do it—even if it killed her.

He held the line and wished there'd be some reason the person he'd called wouldn't be able to make it to the phone.

"What is it?"

No such luck. He gulped and found himself fidgeting. His pinkie ring kept clinking against the receiver, but just talking to this man sent fear scurrying through him—and he feared so few. He laid out what he had to relay.

There was silence, then, "My men are in custody?" the man hissed.

"Yes." He dabbed a tissue to his forehead, swearing he could feel his blood pressure rising.

"You take care of your end, and I'll take care of mine. Do we have an understanding?"

He nodded as if the man could see him. "Yes." The word croaked out.

The line went dead.

Dead... Like he would be if he failed this man. Even if not physically, that man had the power to destroy everything he'd worked for. His career, his wealth, his marriage—all of it would come crashing down like a skyscraper in a high-magnitude earthquake. If only he could find a way to break free from this man's hold, but no one did. Once in, you were in for life.

CHAPTER EIGHT

The station was rather empty, but Madison still got an excited welcome from Ranson, who managed the front desk. She let out a squeal at seeing Madison and got up to hug her.

"So glad you're okay." The phone rang, and her smile faded as she ran back to her post to answer it.

"Thanks," Madison told her and headed down the hall toward the interrogation rooms. Surely someone would be questioning Sergey and Anatolli already. If not, she'd have them hauled in from the holding cells.

"Whoa, what are you doing?" Terry yanked on her arm.

"I'm going to question—"

"Oh no you're not. You're in enough shit for the stunt you pulled."

She stopped cold. Terry rarely—*if ever*—swore. He detested foul language. She met his gaze and crossed her arms but let them drop as she hit her injured wrist. She spoke through the shot of pain. "This is my case. Those men were going to kill me."

"Right. Do you really hear yourself? They were going to kill you. Seems like a mighty conflict of interest to me."

"So, what? I'm supposed to cower in a corner now?"

He let out a puff of air and shook his head. "You just don't get it. Fine, you want to go rushing in there and commit career suicide—that is, if you haven't already—go ahead. Why would I stop you? Why the hell should I care?" He stormed off in the direction of the front doors.

All alone... Just like when she was in that warehouse about to die. She had so few people in her life. The back of her jaw pricked like she could cry, and tears seeped into her eyes. She could recall her ordeal in vivid detail—the sights, smells, and sounds. But life went on...

"Maddy?" It was Toby Sovereign, and judging by his footfalls, he was coming closer.

She stiffened and stood straighter, though a few rogue tears hit her cheeks. She wiped them as discreetly as possible and turned to face Sovereign.

"Thank God you're okay." His gaze fell to her injured arm. "You are okay?"

Was there remorse in his eyes? Sympathy? Worse yet, pity? "Just fine."

He flicked a finger toward her. "Is it broken?"

"What would it matter to you?" She sniffled and blinked back more tears that threatened to escape. It had to be the medication—or the lack of sleep.

"What would it— You're kidding, right?"

"If so, I missed delivering the punchline."

"I love you, and you love me. I saw it in your eyes."

"*Saw*, as in past tense. I almost died today, and you didn't even bother showing on scene to help or to see how I was."

"Oh please, don't do this. I couldn't get away."

"Don't do this? That's rich, Sovereign." She might never forgive him for the past and the deepest betrayal of her life. They'd been engaged when she found him in bed with another woman. She'd held on to that pain for years, and she must have been a fool to think more recently that she could just set it aside like it never happened.

"It seems we're back to surnames." He shoved his hands into his pockets.

"That's how cops refer to other cops. That's all we are. That's all we ever will be." She dared to look at him when she spoke. She swore agony registered in his darkened eyes and that his energy projected a barrier.

"Let's just talk about this. Maybe now's not a good time, but—"

"No." She shook her head. "We're over. Accept it. I have." She choked on the last two words as they came out. It agonized her to say them. She wished she could deny her feelings for him to herself and tamp them down into a dark recess where they would never see the light of day. That way she'd never hurt, she'd never have the urge to cry, tears would never form, so they could never fall.

He rubbed his jaw. "I will. That's if you can look into my eyes and tell me you don't love me."

Her insides were quaking, but she had to be strong. She'd gone years without him in her life and done just fine. "Is that what it's going to take for you to leave me alone?"

His eyes dulled in pain, but he was just getting a taste of how badly he'd hurt her years ago. "I love you, Maddy. I always have. I know that now, and I screwed up. But why can't you forgive me?"

She blinked hard. She was having a hard time swallowing his words. "I can't trust you," she pushed out.

"Oh please, don't go through all of this again."

She held up her good hand. "Let me finish. You know you love me *now*. What does that even mean? That you've had your fill of one-night stands, and now you're ready to make a home for yourself and I'm the safe, comfortable bet? What makes you think I've been sitting around waiting for you to come back? I've got my life together." Stretching the truth a little, but she squared her shoulders.

He glanced down at the floor, then met her gaze. "Just tell me this, do you love me?"

Her heart longed to speak its truth, to come out with how badly he'd hurt her. But to confess such a thing would make her weak, vulnerable—two qualities she detested and refused to show.

"Please, just be honest with me," he prompted.

Her vow to be more open came to mind. She closed her eyes briefly, then met his gaze. "Yes. I do." She thought maybe with the admission, some relief would come. Instead, an ache drilled into her chest. She couldn't get back together with him. They'd had their time as a couple, and it had passed.

He closed the distance between them, but she stepped back, widening it again.

"There's a but, isn't there?" he asked.

She nodded. "It's not enough."

"Love isn't enough?"

"No, it's not." She inserted even more space between them.

His jaw tightened. "Meaning I'm not good for you?"

"We're not good for each other."

He cleared his throat. "All right. I guess we… Well, we had our chance, and I messed it up."

"I'm sorry." And she was—for him and herself.

"Guess that makes two of us." He stood there for a little longer without saying anything and peered into her eyes. "What about friends? Can we at least—"

"Let me think about it." She walked away, her heart hammering.

CHAPTER NINE

Madison had checked in on a couple of the interrogation rooms, and no one was questioning Sergey or Anatolli—which made zero sense. Someone should be grilling them. They'd held a police officer captive, attempted murder, uttered death threats. *A police officer…* As if it hadn't been her that it had happened to. Probably normal to detach given the traumatic situation.

She had Sergey and Anatolli being pulled from holding and waited for their arrival in an observation room that overlooked one used for interrogation.

"What are you doing?" Sergeant Winston joined her, holding a steaming cup, likely filled with brew from the bullpen. He perched his elbow on his ever-growing paunch.

"Why isn't someone already questioning them?"

"In my office, Knight." He ignored her question and blew on his coffee but didn't take a draw. "Now."

She had this feeling he'd interceded, and the Russians were still tucked away in holding. "They need to be grilled, and this is my case."

"You're only going one place, and that's my office. Right now." He held eye contact with her, his gaze driving home the point.

She didn't say a word as she brushed past him and, in the process, bumped his elbow and caused some of his coffee to spill over the rim of his mug.

"Shit!" Winston cussed and stomped toward his office.

Any other time, she'd have received some pleasure in his misfortune, but her mind was fixed on the Russians. She trailed him. "They tried to kill me. What are you not under—"

Winston spun and jabbed a pointed finger in the air toward her. His face was bright red. "And I don't understand what you're not getting. I can't have one of my top detectives running rogue and carrying out vigilante justice." He entered his office first and went behind his desk that was piled with paperwork. "Shut the door."

She slammed it, but he gave no reaction.

"Sit." He gestured to two chairs across from him, then placed the mug on his desk with a *thump*. More coffee sloshed over the edges.

"I'm fine standing."

"Suit yourself." Winston settled back into his chair. "What the hell were you thinking? Rhetorical. There's nothing you can really say to make this better, so don't even think of interrupting me."

She snapped her mouth shut.

He continued. "What would make you think I'd let you within a foot of Sergey Evanoff or Anatolli Belsky? Please. After your stunt."

Her earlobes were heating with anger. The Russians would have killed her given just a little more time.

"Surprised that you have nothing to say."

"Would anything I say even matter?"

Winston seemed to consider and eventually admitted, "Probably not."

She flailed her arms and cussed in agony as fire burned through her left forearm.

"What the hell were you even doing there? Rumor is it had something to do with Bryan Lexan." He regarded her as if he expected confirmation.

She jutted out her chin but didn't respond.

"So that's a yes. You can't go off half-cocked just because you've got something locked in your skull—"

"I wasn't—" *Half-cocked.* Though she wasn't sure what to take offense to first—that or the "locked in your skull" bit.

He held up a hand. "You'll be assigned modified duties for a few days—"

"Modified duty? Is that really necessary? It's just a sprained—"

"Just be happy you're not out the door," he said firmly. "You shot a man, Knight."

"Sergey? I was returning fire." *I was, right?* For some reason, her mind was fuzzy on a lot of what had happened.

"Hmm. I'll need an update from Crime Scene. So far there's nothing to support that there was a shootout."

"What the— How can there not be evidence?" *Why can't I remember?*

"There will be an IA investigation, as I mentioned before. The hearing is scheduled for tomorrow morning at eleven. And before full reinstatement would even be considered, you need to be cleared by a doctor."

She groaned. "I'm fine. As I said, just a little sprained wrist."

"Again, not up for discussion."

"Fine," she mumbled.

"I didn't hear you."

She wouldn't repeat it again. She resorted to firing off a glare instead.

Winston leaned back in his chair. "Give me one good reason I shouldn't suspend you right now."

"If you thought you'd get away with it, you'd have done it." Bold, but true. There was no love lost between the two of them; they barely tolerated each other. If she were a man, they probably wouldn't even be having this discussion.

Winston let out a staggered breath. "You can be exasperating." He paused a few beats. "What? No comment to that?" He sipped his coffee. "I'm also recommending that you go for counseling."

"Counseling as in…" She wasn't going to finish that sentence for him—just in case her assumption was wrong. She wrung her hands—warm and clammy.

"Speaking to a shrink. Your life was in danger. That can change a person."

Needing to see a shrink was what she'd feared he'd say. "I'm fine. I just need to get on with my job and deal with Sergey and Anatolli."

"*Deal* with them?" The way he'd said it and how he was looking at her, she'd wager he knew about her family's link to the mob. But that probably shouldn't be a surprise, as he'd have conducted a full background before she was hired.

"Their crimes against me aside, they know who killed Bryan Lexan—if it wasn't them directly."

Winston sighed and massaged his forehead. "Just back away. You shouldn't have been in their warehouse in the first place."

"They need to answer for their actions. They killed a man and—"

"Did they, Knight? A second ago you said they'd know who did it—*if* they didn't do it themselves. Besides, have they stood trial and been convicted by a jury of their peers—or just you?" He broke eye contact with her and took another draw on his coffee. "I don't have a choice here."

"Boss."

"I should be clear. Seeing a shrink isn't a recommendation, it's mandatory."

"Fine," she seethed.

"Yeah, you bet it is," he huffed. "I'm going to want your written statement of what happened first thing tomorrow morning. Make sure to include how you came to be in the rear of the warehouse in the first place. Before the Russians requested their lawyer, they said they found you back there and you started firing. Did you go back there, gun drawn, or did you react—again assuming any forensic evidence surfaces that supports them even firing on you?"

She froze. Her mind blank. She didn't remember much past entering the warehouse, the vaguest recollection that there had been a gunfight, and her trauma in that chair. Why couldn't she remember the part in between? And if the Russians had fired on her, where was the proof? There had to be casings and bullets. Unless… The Russians cleaned up. Shit.

CHAPTER TEN

Madison opened Winston's door, and Chief Patrick McAlexandar was standing there. *Can this day get any worse?*

He wagged his finger in her face—his signature move. "You better have a damn good reason for doing what you did. But you know what? I'm not even in the mood to hear it."

Maybe she could just slink past him and claim her freedom. She took a step in that endeavor.

"Knight. Sit!" McAlexandar roared, like she was his dog and he her master.

She complied—against her will and better judgment. Facing one of them on their own was bad enough. Now she'd have two obstinate men pitted against her. She had reasons for what she had done, none of which would make it past their ears to any sense of logic or passive humanity they may possess.

"Chief, please." Winston gestured to another vacant chair.

McAlexandar turned to Winston. "You're telling me what to do now?"

"I'm *asking* you."

"Well." McAlexandar clucked his tongue and pulled down on his suit jacket. He undid its button before sitting.

"I've already discussed the matter with her. She's aware of the IA investigation and that, effective immediately, she is assigned desk duty. She needs to pass physical and mental evaluations."

Her...she... Apparently now she was nameless and not even in the room.

"I'm not sure that's punishment enough," McAlexandar spat. "Half of the city was shut down because our resources were tied up getting her out of a situation she shouldn't have been in. Not to mention people could have been hurt."

"You'd rather have a dead detective as the top news story?" she snapped. "And I'm right here. Address me directly."

Winston glared at her, and McAlexandar shook his head.

"Her insubordination and lack of respect for her superiors is appalling. I don't know what kind of ship you're running here, Winston, but it needs fine-tuning."

Her earlobes were sizzling with rage. Again, the chief had referred to her as if she wasn't sitting right beside him. She gave up.

"I have this situation handled, Chief," Winston said.

"Oh yeah? Then you know why she was there?"

"I do."

"I'd like to hear it from the detective." The chief faced her. "So, what is it?" He cocked an eyebrow and pursed his lips. "I doubt you have a good explanation. You always run around doing as you wish. You don't abide by any rules but your—"

"Those men are killers." She clenched her jaw.

"Ah, see." McAlexandar's eyes darkened. "This either has to do with your grandfather or—"

"No. Don't bring him into this."

The chief smirked like a psychopath toying with his prey and twirled the ring on his pinkie finger. "You need to learn to let things go."

She formed her hands into fists, winced as she balled the left one. She wasn't surprised McAlexandar knew about her grandfather, but it was a low blow to bring him up.

McAlexandar went on. "If not your grandfather, then this is about that dead lawyer from many years ago. That case is colder than last night's dinner."

"Do I have to remind you—the police chief—that there's no statute of limitations on murder? Also that when we sign up to be cops, our job is to find justice?" She was heaving for breath but trying to present a calm front regardless.

"Yes, yes, to protect and serve." The chief wasn't even giving her the decency of looking at her. "But there are rules and guidelines we have to play within."

She wasn't touching on the "rules and guidelines," and the chief certainly wasn't one to preach. She didn't have proof, but it wouldn't surprise her if the man was corrupt. He'd shown before he was easily swayed by those with power and money. "I don't like loose ends. I like answers. Sometimes that gets me into—"

"Shit?" The chief spun on her. "It gets you into shit."

She clenched her jaw. As she suspected, there was no point in trying to defend herself to these men.

"Winston, she has a history of disobeying orders, of going about things her own way. Now she's trying to take down members of the Russian Mafia, on her own, I might add. She's carrying out a sort of vigilante justice."

"I take offense to that," she snapped.

"As if I care." McAlexandar tugged on his jacket. "You entered that warehouse without the proper legal authority. No search or arrest warrants were issued."

"I went to *talk*."

"But it didn't exactly work out like that, did it?"

"They were going to kill me." She gulped. That fact wasn't easier to accept with repetition.

"You put yourself in that predicament. You really want us to believe you're the innocent in all this? Pa-lease. You're forgetting that you showed up on private property unannounced," the chief said.

Technically it was commercially owned, but he wouldn't distinguish the shades of gray. "We're done here." She was anyway. She got up and went for the door.

"Knight, you get back here," Winston said. "We're not finished."

"As far as I'm concerned, we are." She stepped toward the door.

"Remember. IA meeting tomorrow morning, eleven AM. Don't be late," Winston called out.

Grr! And so the real circus would begin.

CHAPTER ELEVEN

There was only one place Madison wanted to be right now—well, two, but only one was an option. It was apparent that the chief and the sergeant had tied her hands. She wouldn't be questioning the Russians. And if she couldn't do her job, then she needed sleep. Her eyes were as gritty as sandpaper. But before she headed home, there were some things she needed to take care of.

She reached out to her union rep, Carla Smith, who Madison had never met in person. She filled her in on the situation with Internal Affairs and informed her that the meeting was scheduled for eleven tomorrow morning. Carla wanted some information on what had transpired, and Madison told her everything she could recall, which wasn't much.

Next, Madison grabbed her car keys from her desk, where Terry must have put them, and headed out. She hit a pharmacy to fill her prescription. Then it was off to Canine Country Retreat Boarding.

A young woman of twenty-five, if that, was behind the front counter. Her long, platinum-blond hair was down and worn straight, as always, and her pale-blue eyes housed a pleasant soul.

"Good afternoon, Madison. We were talking about you around here, wondering if you were okay."

"Yeah, I'm fine. Sorry you were left in the lurch."

The girl looked down at Madison's wrapped wrist.

"Just a little sprain," Madison told her. "I appreciate you keeping Hershey overnight. I hope it wasn't too much of an inconvenience."

The truth was in her eyes.

"It was," Madison concluded.

"We made it work. Let me get him for you." She picked up a radio and requested that Hershey be brought to the front.

Minutes later, he came bounding through the doorway, panting with a comical expression that Madison could only term a doggie smile.

She bent down on her haunches to cuddle him and couldn't believe the emotion that overtook her. She remembered being in that warehouse thinking about his soft ears. Now they were beneath her fingertips. She'd been through so much in the last twenty-four hours. She cleared her throat and rose to full height. "Thank you for taking such good care of him. I'd be happy to compensate you extra for the trouble."

The woman waved a hand. "Don't worry about it. It looks like you've been through enough." Her gaze dipped briefly to Madison's arm again.

"You have no idea." Her physical wound was just the beginning. She had two superiors who were against her, two Russians she couldn't touch—even though they'd almost killed her—a looming IA investigation, modified duties, and the prospect of talking to a shrink. Maybe she'd just go home, crawl into bed, and stay there.

As Madison fell asleep, she was briefly haunted by the sergeant's question about who had pulled their gun first—the Russians or her. She hadn't been sure then, and as she started waking up, she still wasn't. Her room was dark when she opened her eyes, and she glanced at her alarm clock. *7:45 PM.*

She looked over at Hershey, who was softly snoring away on the other side of her double bed. She was just reaching out to him when her phone rang. She answered without looking at the caller ID. "Hey." She was hoarse, and her head was groggy. Also, her wrist hurt like a son of a bitch. It was medication time.

"Maddy? Are you okay?"

It was her sister, Chelsea, who was the youngest of the two of them but often came across as the eldest. She had her life together, as their mother would say. Chelsea was happily married with three girls.

"Why wouldn't I be okay?"

"I saw it on the news. Members of the Russian Mafia kidnapped a cop. Was that you?"

The media sure didn't waste any time getting the news out there. It was interesting her sister leaped to the cop being her. "Everything's fine."

"Not exactly an answer to my question."

Chelsea had no idea all that was involved with their grandfather's murder. Neither did their mother. Things had been kept out of the trial. Things Madison had uncovered on her own—maybe with some encouragement from her grandmother. "It's the best you're going to get from me. It's a police matter."

"Why should I be surprised you'd hide behind that? I'm a grown woman, and you don't have to protect me."

Madison figured she always would. "I'm fine, Chels. Please just let it go."

"You could have called me and let me know about this."

I guess she's still running with the assumption I was the unnamed cop. Another detective in the family. "If I called you over everything that came up at work, we'd talk every day."

"Fine by me." A few moments later, Chelsea added, "Maybe you should get away for a while, take a break. And you could call more."

Madison considered it, remembering her vows. "I suppose I could."

"Suppose? Right now it's maybe once every six months or so." Chelsea laughed. "We even live in the same city."

"Work's just—"

"Always busy, right? Well, try raising three girls. It's a zoo around here."

Madison let the line go silent. She needed to go before she let something slip that shouldn't. "Thanks for checking in."

"All right. Well, if you need me, call, okay?" Chelsea's question came out with a serious arc.

"I will." Her attempt at keeping things lighthearted was sabotaged by flashbacks of being tied in that chair with a revolver to her head.

On the count of three…

Her pulse quickened.

"Promise me?" Chelsea said.

Click.

"Maddy?"

"I promise." With that, she also remembered how she wanted to mend the relationship with her mother. But one day at a time.

Sergey's smirking face flashed to mind, the evil intent emanating from him. She squeezed her eyes shut, and images from the warehouse flashed in successive slides. She needed to get off the phone. "I should go. Please hug the girls for me."

"If you came over, you could hug them yourself."

There was no way she'd be doing that right now. "I will. Soon. I'm exhausted, Chels."

"Okay, but be sure to call Mom."

The directive, motivated out of love, clawed at Madison's soul. It would take time—and energy—to repair her relationship with her mother. "Night, sis," Madison said. "Love you."

"Love—" Her sister disconnected. She was always quick at cutting off.

Madison didn't let go of her phone, her thoughts going to her parents. She should call them. It would be nice to hear their voices, but they would likely find it suspicious because she never called. Her mother would start with the questions. Did she have a boyfriend? How serious was the relationship?

Was a wedding in the near future? Babies? Was she finally going to quit being a cop, get herself a safe job or even settle down and let a man provide for her? To heck with that! She could take care of herself.

Take care of herself... Though if it hadn't been for others today, she would probably be dead.

Would her mother understand her hatred for the Russians and her drive to take them down? Madison bet she would if she were armed with the entire truth. Then maybe she'd also understand why Madison had become a cop.

Hershey stirred and crawled over to her. She petted him. "Is somebody hungry?"

She'd feed him, take him out, and then curl right up under the sheets again. But not before popping a couple of pills. Then she hoped to drift away into a dreamless sleep and not wake until the morning.

CHAPTER TWELVE

Terry got the news late yesterday that Sergeant Winston and Chief McAlexandar needed a detective to handle interrogating the Russians. He'd volunteered for the job but was surprised that they'd acquiesced. They must have trusted that he could be objective enough to handle this without compromising the case. That didn't mean Terry relished the idea of informing Madison of this development. But, he supposed, if anyone was going to sit down with them, he was probably the person most in her corner—even if he was still pissed off at her.

And the news that came back from the lab wasn't looking good for Madison. They hadn't uncovered any evidence to indicate a shoot-out between Madison and the Russians. But there were two bullets missing from Madison's gun. It was an assumption that one struck Sergey. Another round had been plucked from a concrete block wall in the rear of the warehouse near a staircase. The right caliber to be from Madison's Glock, but the lab still needed to run ballistics. Casings that matched the ammunition loaded in Madison's gun were also recovered. It would seem Madison had fired on them. Terry found it hard to believe the Russians hadn't retaliated. It was all too…clean. And regardless, even if Madison had gone in trigger-happy, it didn't excuse the Russians of the crimes against her.

Terry was armed with this knowledge for his meeting with Blake Golden, the lawyer representing Sergey and Anatolli, who also happened to be Madison's ex-boyfriend.

Terry was seated across from him now. "I'd say it's hard to believe that you're sitting here prepared to defend Sergey Evanoff and Anatolli Belsky even though they were going to kill Madison." Terry shrugged. "But I don't think much of you."

Blake stiffened and tilted out his jaw. "Don't care what you think of me, nor does it matter. If you're having a hard time keeping this professional, Detective Grant, maybe I should be speaking with another detective."

This wasn't the first time Blake had come across as indifferent to Madison's welfare, so why should Terry be surprised? A man like Blake had lost his moral compass many years ago—assuming he'd been born with one. If he ever had one, he'd probably handed it over when he passed the bar and decided to represent the bad guys for a sweet payday. Speaking of, the Russians would pay well and offer repeat business. But Blake was right—it was time to get down to business. "Your clients are facing charges of kidnapping and endangerment of a police officer's life, as well as attempted homicide."

"The way I understand things, Detective Knight trespassed."

"Even if that was true, that wouldn't excuse your clients' actions. Anatolli was found armed. Sergey present. All while Detective Knight was restrained to a chair in their torture room."

Blake snorted out a laugh. "Torture room? You've got to be kidding me. Where is the hidden camera?" He made a show of looking around. "It must be here somewhere."

Terry clasped his hands calmly, undeterred by Blake's reaction. "Crime Scene investigators are still processing the warehouse in finite detail, but they've already removed trace that ties back to several people." He wouldn't be bringing up the rounds missing from Madison's gun.

"Okay," Blake dragged out. "Other people were there, Detective. So what? It was a place of business."

"The trace came from blood," Terry punched out. "As I said, it came from several people." He paused there and read the attorney's expression, which to his credit remained unchanged.

"As I said, Detective Knight trespassed. She had no right to be on the premises of Homeland Logistics."

"It's a business, not personal property. As such, it would be hard to stay afloat without people entering."

"It's not that type of business. Nor does it explain her presence in the rear of the building."

"There's no proof she went back there." A truth. The ballistics tests hadn't confirmed the bullet in the wall or the casings were from Madison's gun. Technically, that was still speculation.

Blake stiffened. "You know the point I'm driving at. Detective Knight went in there on official police business and had no legal ground to do so. She shot Sergey Evanoff."

Terry shrugged and took a sip of his coffee. "All says you. No bullet was recovered that I'm aware of. But they were caught red-handed holding a police officer against her will."

Blake's lips set in a straight line. "I'll get the charges tossed. Just save yourself the embarrassment of pursuing this. And blood in the room you found her in? You can't prove how it got there. What is this anyway—an Easter egg hunt? I'll tell you what it is: police harassment."

Terry matched Blake's gaze. Terry didn't see it, but Madison had obviously seen something good in the man to have dated him for as long as she had.

Blake added calmly, "She searched the premises."

"Again, proof of that?" Terry smirked. The lawyer was getting desperate, but something in the shadows of Blake's eyes had the hairs rising on the back of Terry's neck.

"Customers come in the front door. They stay there. Detective Knight went into the back of the warehouse, and more than that, she had her gun drawn when she did so. She fired on my clients."

"You must have proof that I don't have. Besides the word of two criminals—"

Blake extended two sheets of paper toward him. When Terry didn't reach for them, Blake let them fall to the table.

"Two signed affidavits from witnesses who saw Detective Knight enter the back room with her gun drawn and saw her fire," Blake said. "Just fair warning before the preliminary hearing."

Terry sank into his chair. "Your clients coerced these men into signing this."

A smile curved the attorney's lips. "Detective Grant, you're grasping. My clients have been in here since yesterday. They would have no means of coercing anyone. And I didn't have to come forward with this. I could have held off until we were in front of the judge."

"So, what? You're the good guy, doing me a favor?"

"I'm giving you a heads-up."

"Right, as if you care about Madison? These men"—he drilled a fingertip to the sheets—"would know what your clients are capable of. They'd do whatever was asked of them."

"Again, Sergey Evanoff and Anatolli Belsky were here. Even if they could communicate with them somehow, that's an assumption, Detective. As you've been so fond of saying: proof?"

"Your clients' reputations should be enough. Money, power, and fear go a long way in buying testimony and ensuring compliance."

"Well, no matter what you think, my men will walk." Blake rose and did up the two buttons on his suit jacket. "I hope you're ready for the shitstorm coming your way." With that, he left.

Terry drew in a deep breath and nearly choked on the lawyer's strong cologne—along with the position he was in. Terry wasn't the type to cause ripples. He usually kept his head down, did his job, and returned home at the end of the day. It was Madison who was always out for the adventure; she was the risk-taker. Maybe it was time for Terry to consider his family and step back from Madison and all the drama that either gravitated toward her on its own or that she created.

CHAPTER THIRTEEN

The tinny aroma of blood teases my nose. My wrists are bound to the arms of the chair, and when I try to move forward, I can't. There's something around my neck. Still, I thrash, bucking with futility against the restraints. Tears stream down my face, and Anatolli moves in closer to me.

"You can't kill the devil." Sergey stands at the doorway, laughing. "We just call it roulette. The Russian part would be redundant. On the count of three. One…"

Anatolli clicks back on the revolver.

"Two."

My eyes squeeze shut, anticipating the bullet.

"Three—"

Madison bolted upright, struggling to break free of the sheets, but sweat had pasted them to her body. She finally managed to rip them off and jumped from bed. Panting, heaving for breath. She closed her eyes, and seconds later opened them and met Hershey's gaze. He was watching her, tail wagging.

She wanted to reach for him but couldn't bring herself to move. Though her legs held steady beneath her, she wasn't sure she could fully trust them.

Hershey wormed closer to the edge of the bed. His little furry face staring at her and the thumping of his tail against the bed made it hard to resist him.

"Just a second, buddy," she said, her voice coming back to her ears almost foreign-sounding. Somehow, she had to put the nightmare behind her, but the fact that it was based in reality made it harder to do so. She wasn't about to let her fears cripple her though. She had to get to work and make sure Sergey and Anatolli paid for all their crimes—the ones against her, likely Bryan Lexan, and countless others.

Hershey's tail stopped wagging, and the silence pierced her.

"Ah, here." She scooped him up into her arms. His fur beneath her fingers soothed her spirit and slowed her breathing. Then came the pain—her wrist. She rushed to put Hershey back onto the bed.

She winced, biting back tears of agony. She reached for the pill bottle on her nightstand, popped one, and downed it with water. Normally, she'd avoid medication, but she needed a clear mind for the day ahead. The pain left untreated would hinder that possibility, and the prescription didn't list drowsiness as a side effect. Today, she'd get her life back even if it meant jumping through some hoops.

The alarm clock told her it was after nine. She'd write up a brief report for Winston on yesterday's events and get the clearance required from her doctor.

"Do you have an appointment with Dr. Talmadge?" Susan, the receptionist at the front desk, wore a white nurse's uniform and a headpiece over an ear. She was smooth and well-experienced at juggling walk-ins and answering incoming calls.

It was going on ten o'clock, and the waiting area was packed.

"I see that the doctor's busy," Madison said.

"He is. He really is." Susan winced. "I can book you in for tomorrow afternoon."

"It's really important that I see him now." Even if she tried to explain the urgency, Susan wouldn't understand the magnitude of the situation. So Madison had the option of standing here trying to state her case or taking matters into her own hands. She opted for the latter and brushed past reception and through the door leading to the patient rooms.

Susan swooped out from behind her desk. "What do you think you're do—"

The two of them bumped heads and stood back, wallowing in their injuries. Ears ringing... No, that was the clinic's phone.

Susan's blue eyes took on a pleading, nervous energy, and she split her gaze between Madison and the front desk. "If you go back there, he'll fire me. Please. Just go have a seat, and I'll get you in next."

"Susan, what's going on?" Dr. Talmadge stepped into the hallway, dressed in slacks and a white doctor's jacket with a stethoscope around his neck. He came up short when he spotted Madison, and his brow furrowed. "Madison Knight?"

"Hi."

The reception phone rang again.

Susan ignored it and looked from the doctor to Madison, back to the doctor. "I'm sorry, Dr. Talmadge. I tried to explain to her that your schedule is full today and that she needs to book an appointment."

"Nonsense. Come on, Ms. Knight." Talmadge gestured to the nearest room and then addressed his receptionist. "Please get back to the front, dear. The phones are ringing off the hook."

Susan stayed put, her mouth agape, before letting out a curt *hmm* and hurrying back to her post.

Talmadge closed the door behind him and came over to Madison, who was already sitting on the examination bed, her legs dangling over the side.

"What can I do for you, Maddy?" His English accent only added to the older man's charisma. She'd been seeing Talmadge since she was a child and he'd practiced in a smaller town, outside of Stiles, where Madison grew up.

His question was a little more loaded, and now face-to-face with the man, she was curious how eager he'd be to clear her for duty. She was grateful she didn't need to see him often, as she was healthy, but she'd forgotten the one thing she'd always respected about the man: his commitment to putting his patients' welfare foremost. That might actually rear up and bite her.

After seconds passed and she hadn't responded, he pointed to her wrist. "What happened there?"

"I fell." It was the truth, just leaving out the nonessential details like the standoff with two members of the Russian Mafia. *There* was *a standoff...*

"I see." He removed the splint and delicately moved his hands over her wrist and forearm. "All right. Well, the good news is that it's likely only a grade one sprain, which means the ligaments were stretched but not torn."

"Sounds like good news."

"Yes. Relatively, a mild injury. Though I'd recommend resting it for forty-eight hours and icing it periodically to reduce the swelling. You should keep it in a bandage to compress it, but keep it out of a splint. They can cause more problems than they help."

Madison soaked up all the advice he was giving her and wished the paramedic had that knowledge. He could have slowed her recovery.

Talmadge went on. "I could prescribe you something for the pain, but over-the-counter medication will work just as effectively. Advil, Aleve, Motrin, pick your poison, but only use it if the pain is too much. Understand? Too much of these nonsteroidal anti-inflammatory drugs can have repercussions long-term. Got it?"

"Yeah." She might as well toss the prescription drugs.

"And ice it for two or three days." He jabbed the end of the pen toward her.

"All right." Something about the man made her submissive, like she didn't want to disappoint him. It must have been the grandfather quality he had to him. "When should it be back to normal?"

"Give it a few days minimum, up to a week, possibly two."

"Two weeks…?"

"That's the doctor's prognosis, but I'm sensing that's not what you wanted to hear?"

"Not exactly."

He angled his head and studied her eyes. "This fall, did it take place while on the job?"

"Sort of. And I've been asked to get cleared by a doctor before I can return to full, active duty."

"Well, no can do. Not yet. Come back and see me in a few days."

All she needed was a signature. Maybe she could bribe him? She would have tried if he had been any other doctor. She should have taken her chances with a walk-in clinic, where she might have found a doctor who didn't care so much. There still wasn't a reason why she couldn't put on a nice smile and give it a go. "So there's no way you'd write a note for me?"

"No can do, sunshine."

She lifted herself off the table, disappointed, but she still thanked him.

"Anytime. And be sure to tell your parents that I said hello."

And just like that her day was off to an even worse start. No clearance, and now there was the overwhelming sense of compulsion that she call her mother sooner rather than later.

CHAPTER FOURTEEN

Dimitre Petrov held a cell phone to his ear. It belonged to a prison guard by the name of Jacob Hall. He'd been married for fourteen years to Robyn, and they had a seven-year-old son named Danny. He knew where Hall and his family lived, where his kid went to school. Hall had been made clearly aware of all of this, and if he failed Dimitre at all—*snap!*—the family was gone. Just like that.

Dimitre stood in the hallway outside his prison cell. The door was open a lot of the time. The institution had become his personal playground over the past eight years. Everyone was either bought or coerced. Fear was a powerful motivator.

That was the case with Jacob. Poor little Jacob, who was too much of a coward to even see his way to a payday. He was cooperative because he wanted to keep his family alive. Really, fear worked better than money. It kept people leery and alert, but eager to please. Jacob brought him cigarettes and gave him free time to smoke in the yard with minimal supervision. He was also why Dimitre had freedoms the other guests of the max facility could only dream about.

Dimitre's caller spoke to him in Russian—the tongue of his homeland—such a beautiful language and one Dimitre didn't hear often enough.

"I was told to call."

"What is being said?"

"They claim the woman detective started all of this. That she went there asking about some dead lawyer."

Dimitre formed his hands into fists and landed his gaze on Jacob, who was standing about eight feet down the hall with his back to him, but the distance didn't matter. Dimitre pictured squeezing the life from him, just because he was there, just because he was convenient. Just because Dimitre was furious. And when he was furious, someone had to die. And he'd had a lot of time to dwell on the people responsible for landing him behind bars. Foremost was an incompetent lawyer—the same one the nosey detective had been asking Sergey and Anatolli about. And she was the other one he'd blamed for his fate. He'd let her live, but she'd been on borrowed time for long enough. It was also time to set other things right.

"What do you want me to do?" his caller asked.

It was time to make the tough choices and cut his losses. "Clean slate."

"Boss?"

"You will be contacted with the time and day." Dimitre clicked off, summoned the guard, and tossed the phone to him when he turned around.

"I want cigarette."

Jacob bowed his head, and Dimitre followed the man into the yard. As he walked behind him, he envisioned killing him many different ways, and his face morphed into that of Detective Madison Knight. He truly had tolerated her for long enough.

Ranson lit up when she saw Madison. "Good morning."

"Hey." Madison wished she was as cheerful as Ranson. After having survived what she'd been through, she should have a new appreciation of life. Right now it was thoughts of Sergey and Anatolli clashing with her inevitable meeting with Internal Affairs that was dampening her spirits. IA wasn't large enough to have their own dedicated department, which meant whoever was going to look into her actions would probably be one of her fellow officers. She'd have to wait to find out who.

Ranson's face soured. "Rough day ahead."

"Modified duty to start." Madison lifted her injured wrist.

"You'll get through it in no time." Ranson flashed a smile, but it was short-lived. Still, if Madison could just soak up a teeny bit of Ranson's positive attitude…

Madison leaned on the counter. "Who's questioning the Russians?" Not much escaped Ranson's notice, so it was worth asking her.

"It's going to be Terry. He's with them and their lawyer now."

She gripped her stomach. He hadn't even bothered to tell her. "Terry?"

"The rumor going around is he volunteered for the chance to handle this."

Volunteered? It told her that Terry still had her back at least. Hopefully at some point he'd stop being mad at her.

"There's something else you might want to know," Ranson began. "Blake Golden is the Russians' lawyer."

"Just great!" She stopped shy of slamming her sprained wrist on the counter. The thought alone sent shivers of pain shooting up her arm. But, seriously, could this day get any worse?

"Yeah, I knew you weren't going to be hap—"

Madison didn't hear the rest of Ranson's words. She was on the move toward the interrogation room.

She hurried by the sergeant's office, pleased that he wasn't there, only to come face-to-face with him inside the observation room. He stood there, one hand in a pocket while the other held a coffee mug.

"You showed up," he said. "There were bets in place."

"Let me guess, you were in favor of my not showing up today."

"I had hoped, in a way, you wouldn't."

What is that supposed to mean? Somehow, she managed the restraint necessary to keep that thought internal.

Sergeant Winston went back to watching events in the interrogation room, and she followed his gaze.

Blake sat beside Sergey and Anatolli, the three of them across from Terry. Blake was put together in his usual manner. Tailored suit, dark hair gelled so heavily that a strong wind wouldn't lift a strand, and a smug expression.

She faced Winston's profile. "Why?" she stamped out, finally not able to refrain from calling him out.

"Why what?" He didn't give her the courtesy of looking at her.

"Why did you hope I wouldn't show?"

Slowly, he turned his gaze from the window and faced her. "We're going to need you back in top form, sooner than later."

She studied his eyes. Something was off. "Since when do you care about my well-being?"

He took a draw on his coffee. "The public is obviously aware of the situation that took place yesterday. Apparently, the press got ahold of your name."

"Wait! My name is out there?"

"Not yet."

"We can't let that happen." She really didn't want the conversation with her family that would result.

"This entire thing has an unfavorable light shining on the Stiles PD. They're saying we went in there without just cause, that we were acting rogue. But it's not *us*, it's you."

A dull ache landed on her chest. It was like the brotherhood of blue was retreating from her. "These Russians murder innocent people without conscience. They kidnapped me—planned to *kill* me. How does that reflect badly on me? On the Stiles PD?"

"Questions have been raised, and frankly, I understand where they are coming from. The public wants to know why you were even there. They somehow found out that you went in there on official business without a legal search warrant."

"I wasn't searching," she snapped.

"Regardless, it's being painted as a personal vendetta, and the entire department is taking the rap for it." He clenched his jaw, and his eyes skimmed her face.

She had nothing to say in defense, and no matter how she tried to twist things, this job was personal to her. This job was her soul, and being a cop made a difference—not just in her life but to everyone's in the community.

"What's worse is I think they're right." He sighed and turned away.

"What is it?"

"The lab never recovered evidence there was an exchange of gunfire." He met her gaze. "What's worse is that two men have come forward with testimony against you."

"What? How?" She laid a hand over her stomach. This couldn't be happening, and why hadn't Cynthia called to give her a heads-up?

"They say you went in past an Employees Only sign, armed."

"Was I armed? Yes. As for the rest, I can't say I did."

"It's the fact you can't say that's bothering me. They also say you fired at Sergey and Anatolli and weren't provoked to do so."

"That's a lie."

"One we can't discredit."

"Even though you're aware of what the Russians are capable of?"

Winston said nothing at first, and it sank in just how alone she truly was. Eventually, he told her, "We need to get in front of this. We've arranged an interview for you with Leland King from the *Stiles Times*. He has agreed to speak with you."

King had praised her last month in an article for closing a case. Just doing her job, but he made it sound like she was some superhero. The investigation had been challenging, and she'd almost lost her badge in the process, but justice won out in the end. It was what she did. She didn't need fanfare or the limelight. Neither was invented for cops—especially her. But if she had to speak with someone in the media, at least it was someone on her side—assuming King still was.

"Are you are hearing me, Knight?"

"Yeah," she mumbled. "I take it I don't have a choice."

"You will be prepped for the interview, on what to say, what not to say. You can't screw this up, Knight. Do you hear me on that?"

"I hear you." She also picked up on what wasn't being said. Winston had to answer to the chief, and he was after her hide again. But when wasn't he? He was probably hungry enough to take a chunk out of her large enough to render fatal. Again, her career, her life, hung in the balance. Dramatic but true.

"You will be prepped for your interview with King by someone in the public information office. And you've been booked in with the department shrink for tomorrow afternoon at four o'clock."

"What about my meeting with IA? That still moving ahead?"

"They'll be coming for you shortly. Eleven, just as scheduled," he said drily.

Isn't he just the bearer of good news?

"You're going to have to explain your actions before this is all over. I hope you'll be able to."

"I emailed you my report."

"Leaving some things out."

For once he was being generous. She still remembered very little.

CHAPTER FIFTEEN

Madison was called to the interview room but was left waiting on her interrogators, and her legal representation was running behind—something to do with a blown-out tire. Madison wasn't fooling herself into thinking the hearing would be a mild inquisition. Especially after the bomb that Winston had dropped about the eyewitness statements.

How did she even get here? Where had she gone so wrong? She shouldn't be preparing to defend herself like a criminal—just as two members of the Russian Mafia would be doing mere rooms away.

Toby Sovereign entered the room with another detective from the division, Erik Brown.

"You've got to be kidding me." She shot to her feet and pointed a finger at Sovereign. "No. There's no way I'm being investigated by you."

"Would you please sit, Detective Knight?" Brown asked. His features were delicate like a woman's, with a narrow beak-like nose.

She stared at him. "Toby Sovereign and I used to be engaged, and recently he wanted to pick things up again, and I turned him down. He's prejudiced." With each word she spoke, her pitch became higher.

"Yes, I'm well aware of your history. But all that is in the past. I trust that Detective Sovereign will carry out his duty honorably."

She bit down on her bottom lip so hard she was expecting the taste of blood. Sovereign was avoiding eye contact with her. He likely didn't want to be in this position any more than she did. Still, he could have refused, but he hadn't.

"And our conversation will be recorded," Brown said, as if that was reassurance.

She narrowed her eyes and dropped into the chair. "I'm not saying one word until—"

"I'm so sorry I'm late." A thirty-something woman entered the room, carrying enough bags that she could be going away for a weekend. She had one large case strapped over a shoulder, one tucked under an arm, and a briefcase in her hand. Once she positioned her luggage between the table and the floor, she sat down and extended her hand to Madison. "Carla Smith." The handshake was short, and Carla set her gaze on the opposing side. "Let's make this quick and stay on point."

Impressive. Madison liked her efficiency.

"As I just mentioned to Detective Knight, everything said here today will be recorded." Brown hit a button on a recording device in the middle of the table, then began, "Please start at the beginning and tell us what happened."

Carla shifted, placing one hand under a thigh and turning her torso toward Madison. Her other arm went to the table, that hand to her face, her long fingers spanning across her cheek. "You can go ahead, Detective."

"I went there to get answers."

"There? Please be more specific," Brown requested.

As if he didn't know! "Homeland Logistics."

"Why did you go there?"

"To get answers."

"Answers about what?"

She took a deep breath and leaned back in her chair. "A cold case. His name was Bryan Lexan, a defense attorney. He represented Dimitre Petrov at his murder trial—the one that saw him put away on a life sentence."

"Please, Detective, stick to the point."

"This is on point," she seethed. "You asked why I went to the warehouse, and I'm telling you."

Brown stiffened.

She continued. "Lexan was murdered after Petrov was found guilty."

"So the two must be connected."

"Absolutely."

"No chance it's a coincidence? The Russian Mafia executed the lawyer."

"How I see it."

"And that's why you went to Homeland Logistics? To get answers about the lawyer's murder?"

There was no way her admission would look good for her—at least from the outside. She was there about an official case, but off the record. "Yes," she admitted.

Carla wiggled again. This time she crossed her arms. Maybe she should lay off caffeine.

"Did you get your answers?" Brown asked.

"Not yet."

"So you broke protocol and entered the warehouse. No warrants. Solo. As a result, there was gunfire, and someone was injured." Brown consulted some papers in a file he had. "Shot in the abdomen. A Sergey Evan—"

"From what I understand, there is no proof that he was shot by Detective Knight—or shot period. There's no bullet, and no doctor has come forward to say he took one from Sergey Evanoff and produced it. What we're left with is the word of a Russian Mafia member against a proven detective. Sound about right?"

Whoa, Carla is good. Still, Madison held her breath. There were the so-called eyewitnesses.

Brown was shuffling through the paperwork in the file.

Carla leaned over the table. "Well?"

"No. The bullet wasn't retrieved from—"

"Very well." Carla eased in her chair again. "Then we'll proceed without the accusations."

"There was a bullet recovered from the brick wall, behind where Sergey says he was standing."

"Okay. What does that mean?" Carla put it out there like Brown was the village idiot.

"We'll prove where the bullet came from."

"Sure. Go ahead. But if—and I say *if*—the bullet in the wall came from Detective Knight's gun, it only proves she was defending herself. Nothing more. And until you have more…" Carla glanced at Madison before rising and collecting her bags.

"She was missing two rounds from her gun. Two .40-caliber casings were recovered, one bullet thus far."

"Sure. Which ballistics hasn't tied to Detective Knight's gun. Am I right?"

"Hasn't been so far. But there isn't any evidence that Sergey and Anatolli fired at Knight—in the warehouse."

"Potato, potahto. They still held her against her will and threatened her life. They were nearly successful too. The records state that SWAT found Detective Knight bound to a chair, the Russian, Anatolli, holding a revolver in his hand." Carla made a demonstration of a finger gun and pressed it against her temple.

On the count of three…

A drop of sweat trickled down Madison's back and tremors surged through her body. She had to focus on something else. On anything else. Deep breaths.

"Did Detective Knight go into that warehouse?" Carla asked. "Yes. She's not denying it, but she went to get answers, not to get into a firefight. The rest is on the Russians."

"Not so quick. Detective Knight's gun was fired."

Carla huffed. "To defend herself."

"Not what eyewitnesses are saying."

Carla rolled her eyes. "Eyewitnesses? They just suddenly manifest? How convenient."

"Their credibility will be considered, but that doesn't change the fact that when members of law enforcement fire their guns, they need to be held accountable. Otherwise cops could run around shooting whoever they felt like, for whatever reason."

"Your statement, again, implies Detective Knight shot someone—unprovoked at that. None of which has been substantiated, as you just admitted." Carla lifted the flap of her satchel and went rooting through the bag. She tossed a business card toward Brown. "You call me if you actually get something on this detective, because right now you don't." With that, Carla left almost as quickly as she'd arrived.

Maybe Madison would see justice after all. She was relieved by that thought, but she still didn't have her answers.

CHAPTER SIXTEEN

Madison headed back to her desk, one crisis averted or at least delayed. Still inevitably on her horizon was talking out her feelings with a shrink. She'd go through the motions, say what they wanted to hear, and get that part signed off at least. One step closer to returning to full duty—and that couldn't come fast enough. Thinking about riding a desk for too long had her going stir crazy.

Terry dropped into his chair across from her. Their desks butted against each other.

"Hey," she said.

"I don't know what you saw in that man," was his counter. His cheeks were flushed, and he clenched his jaw.

That man could only be one person. "Blake Golden? I heard he's representing Sergey and Anatolli." How she ever thought the relationship would work with her and Blake was beyond her understanding now. She was the victim's voice while he defended the guilty.

"It's a nightmare in there." Terry wiped his forehead. "Now I have to face questioning by the rat squad."

Rat squad... "The IA's questioning you?"

"I'm your partner. They figure I knew what you were up to."

"You might not need to speak with them." She wasn't even going to touch on the bitterness in his tone.

"Why's that?"

"The investigation's on hold."

If it weren't for the rise and fall of his chest, she'd wonder if he was breathing. "Why?"

"There's no proof of wrongdoing."

"No proof." He chewed on that, and by the look on his face, it tasted like shit.

"You want me to be in trouble?"

"You should be held accountable for your actions," he snapped.

"Whoa." She leaned back and held up her uninjured arm. "Nice to have you on my side."

"You're like a ticking bomb. You could have gone about it the right way, gone in there on official police business and questioned them. But no. You skulked around by yourself like you were on a special ops mission."

She wasn't even going to waste breath defending herself. What would be the point?

"You don't get it, do you? You could have been—"

"But I wasn't."

"But you weren't." He let out a deep breath and wouldn't look her in the eye. "Things are going downhill fast." He jabbed a pointed finger down the hall, indicating the direction of the interrogation rooms. "They're saying you initiated the attack."

"So I've heard. Not from you." She met his gaze, a chilling betrayal twisting through her.

"Huh. Really? You have some nerve. I'm doing all I can to defend you—and you're accusing me of not communicating with you?"

His question landed with a thud. She grappled for her bearings. "They restrained me to a chair and held a gun to my head. Blake's fighting a lost cause."

Terry angled his head. "You sure about that? I'm at a loss for what to believe."

"Terry." It was all she could squeeze out. She allowed only a limited number of people into her circle, as she trusted very few. She'd have said that Terry was one of her foremost allies. She wasn't so sure anymore.

"All I know is that you're bullheaded." He flailed a hand toward her arm. "You're probably not even taking pain pills. Wanting to tough it out."

"I'm bullheaded? They killed a man. Those men need to pay for that." She wasn't about to let herself get sucked in by his deflection to her injured wrist, as if everything else he was saying didn't cut like a knife.

"*A* man? Those men have likely killed many." He met her eyes. "This isn't just about the lawyer. There's something personal going on here. When you said killed *a* man, were you even talking about Lexan?"

She looked down at her desk. Didn't she owe the full truth to her family before confessing it to her partner?

"This is ridiculous," Terry said. "You expect me to talk to you, but you're tight-lipped. And you go around taking care of things the way you see fit."

She glared at him. "Now you're sounding like Winston."

"The man has a point."

She bristled. She had every right to go into the business, to ask about Lexan. The past didn't matter…even if it did.

"I'll do my job and see this through, but then… I don't know." Terry got to his feet and left.

What did he mean he didn't know—know what? Was he going to stop being her partner, ask for a new one? If so, it just proved how foolish it was to let people in. They stripped her of her power and made her vulnerable, for what? Given time they would only hurt and disappoint her. She really was better off alone, and since she'd gotten herself into the current mess, she'd see it through—with or without Terry.

CHAPTER SEVENTEEN

Madison was introduced to Stephanie Becker, a lawyer, from the public information office. She'd been assigned to guide Madison on her approach with the media. Becker was in her late forties, and with her sleek appearance, one for the other sharks to steer clear of. Her dark hair was pulled back into a low chignon, and she wore a black pantsuit with heels.

They were in a conference room, and Becker coached her on which words not to say and good ones to pepper into the interview. Basically, any that hinted at accountability were to be eradicated from her vocabulary. And she stressed, "No apologies."

No worries there…

Madison would do it all again—if not a tad differently. She hadn't received her answers, just fed her suspicion that Sergey and Anatolli were behind Lexan's murder. On the plus side, there had been Troy Matthews and his bulging muscles— *What is wrong with me?*

"Let's go over this again," Becker said. "What made you go to Homeland Logistics?"

"Ah." Madison shook the SWAT guy out of her head.

Becker was seated across from her, a pen in her left hand and a lined legal pad on the table in front of her. "Whenever you're ready." A pleasant smile, if not revealing some impatience.

"I went there to ask some questions."

"Were you on duty at the time of the visit?"

"No, I was not."

"What questions?"

Was it wrong to admit that she just wanted the Russians to pay for *all* the hurt they inflicted?

"Detective?" Becker gestured with her left hand as she spoke, the tip of her pen making wild arcs in the air. "Was it regarding the death of a young man named Bryan Lexan?"

"His *murder*," Madison corrected.

"Of which you have proof the Russians were involved?"

She considered how little "proof" she had. "I have valid suspicions."

"Ah, see, this is where Leland King may trip you up. You need to drop definitive statements when they can't be backed up by facts. Otherwise, people will start asking what will be next. Does the Stiles PD go into any home or enter the property of any suspect simply because they have their hunches and questions to ask?"

Madison could see that viewpoint, stepping back and thinking ahead. But she wasn't normally the type to sit around imagining outcomes. She jumped in and faced the consequences—kind of like now. Guess she had her answer as to how she'd gotten herself into this mess. "So how am I supposed to answer that question when he asks?"

Becker met Madison's gaze. "You tell King you went there on duty."

"I lie?"

"You lie, or all of this preparation is for naught. The warehouse is a business, open to the public, and you just had some questions. You didn't venture past the front desk until you were under attack."

Madison detested liars and wouldn't be party to a lie herself. "There's got to be another way."

"Your resignation." Becker barely blinked when she dropped that bomb. If there was any confusion over who this woman represented, it was clear now—the department. She didn't care about Madison's welfare. It was all about the reputation of the Stiles PD.

Madison's chest became heavy, and she swallowed hard, her mouth suddenly dry. "I will never—"

"You don't have much of a choice, Detective. This is how the powers that be want things handled. The media doesn't need to know everything we do."

Like mushrooms, kept in the dark and fed shit.. That suited Madison fine as long as she wasn't the one lying in the process. She studied the woman. "What do you think the truth is?"

Becker put her pen down and placed the legal pad in her satchel. "It doesn't matter what I believe."

"It most certainly does."

Becker tugged on the sleeves of her jacket. "I believe you went there to serve a personal purpose."

"Personal? This wasn't personal." Her stomach sank at the hypocrisy, but Lexan had been her dominant motivation. But she'd use whatever she could to get the mob shut down for good. "A young man's life was cut short. He deserves justice."

"Detective, I can tell this case is very…" She paused, obviously searching for another term besides *personal*. "Important to you. But the Lexan investigation is considered a *cold* case, is it not? It's been over eight years since his murder. So why now, after all this time?"

Madison took a few deep inhales, exhaled slowly. The impulse to storm from the room and tell this woman to go to hell was overwhelming. "I've never let the case go," she pushed out. "The people who murdered him walk about freely while he lies six feet under, rotting away."

Becker's eyes fired, not with rage or disgust, but Madison sensed with impatience. "And you're sure you never ventured past reception without provocation?"

Madison averted her gaze, still not exactly sure how everything had played out.

"Hmm. You really need to stick to the script." Becker gathered her things and stood. "I'll see you again in about an hour. King is coming for the interview at two thirty." The woman left without any more comment, and Madison let her go.

Why was it so important to everyone that Madison lie to cover up the truth?

CHAPTER EIGHTEEN

Madison had enough time to savor a Hershey's bar—and that was about all her stomach would handle, for the time being anyhow. She entered the conference room to find Stephanie Becker, Sergeant Winston, and a man she figured was Leland King. Average weight and height with a wide, flat nose and thinning dark hair. A man in his fifties who had played the media game long enough to have several awards to his name. She was surprised the chief hadn't made an appearance. He cherished media attention more than a crowned beauty queen.

Madison took a seat, prepared to tell the truth and test the saying, *the truth will set you free.*

"Good day, everyone." King smiled, transmitting a pleasant charm that he no doubt had fine-tuned over the years. It probably came in handy when prying information from uncooperative interview subjects.

Madison passed a glance at Winston and Becker. Winston met her gaze, but Becker looked away.

King pulled out a tablet and a Bluetooth keyboard. "All right, let's get started." He looked at Madison. "It seems we've had a little excitement in Stiles lately. Two suspected members of the Russian Mafia were taken into custody. Their preliminary hearing has yet to be scheduled from my understanding." He looked at her as if it was a question she had an answer for. Unfortunately, she was out of the loop at the moment.

"When a time and date are scheduled," Winston interjected, "I suspect that due to the profiles of the defendants, it will be withheld from the public."

"Okay," King said slowly and turned his attention to Madison. "An officer was allegedly restrained at Homeland Logistics, and that officer was you, Detective Knight."

There wasn't any question enclosed within that statement. And King was obviously just setting things up. "How did you come to have my name?"

"Now, now, Detective Knight, a good journalist never reveals his sources."

Madison studied the man's eyes and received her answer. "You're not protecting a named source. It came as an anonymous tip."

"I don't see what difference that—"

Winston cleared his throat. "Please, back to the interview."

King sliced a glare at Winston but softened once he reestablished eye contact with Madison. "How did you end up on the property of Homeland Logistics?"

"I drove there."

"More specifically, were you there on official duty?"

"I was there in regard to an investigation." Both Winston's and Becker's eyes were burning into her, but she ignored them.

"So you had a warrant to be on the premises?"

"Nope."

"Yet you searched the property."

"Nope."

"Yet you went into the back."

"Don't answer that," Becker interjected.

King shot out the next question. "What was the investigation pertaining to, Detective Knight?"

"It's ongoing."

"I heard you went regarding a cold case."

"You hear a lot." She hitched her shoulders. "Not everything you hear is the truth, Mr. King." She tossed out his name seeing as he was using hers enough. She was okay with coasting the line between the truth and a lie. Her statement had been avoidance.

"It was a case from over eight years ago. A Bryan Lex—"

"The Stiles PD does not discuss their investigations with the public," Madison said.

"Bryan Lexan, a cold case from eight years ago." King lifted a large briefcase from the floor and opened its double flaps. He pulled out a leather journal and flipped pages until he settled on one. "Here we go. 'Detective Knight accused my clients of murdering a defense attorney by the name of—"

"You were speaking to the defense counsel?" Becker's eyebrows shot up.

"No better way to get a rounded story, Ms. Becker, than to speak with all concerned."

"Mr. King, we ask that anything about Detective Knight's supposed intentions be stricken from any record and that it not be allowed to reach the public. Once out, this could taint the minds of potential jurors when Sergey Evanoff and Anatolli Belsky go to court."

King laughed. "You're assuming this will get to trial."

"Assuming?" she spat, her earlobes heated with indignation. "They were going to kill me." A headache loomed, and her eyes went to the clock on the wall. Only ten minutes had passed. They had allotted thirty minutes with this clown.

"Do you have any relevant questions, Mr. King?" Becker asked, her tone crisp and formal.

"I haven't received satisfactory answers to the ones I've already raised." He passed Madison a mild glare. "Back to the matter of why you were there. I'd like to get clear on whether or not you were on official business. Was it professional or personal?"

She opened her mouth, ready to defend herself, but Winston spoke first.

"Detectives of the Stiles PD do not act on their own accord."

"So she had legal authorization to be there?"

Winston responded. "From my understanding, Homeland Logistics is a business, thereby open to the public."

She wanted to blurt out that asking questions wasn't a crime but didn't imagine it going in her favor. It was like everyone was blind to that basic fact.

"The issue being raised, *Sergeant*"—King attributed a derogatory slant to the attribution of Winston's position—"is whether or not a Stiles PD detective acted rogue. Does the average citizen need to worry about their privacy being violated because a cop has a hunch?"

Becker glanced at her; her gaze said she'd warned Madison about this very thing.

"We're talking about known members of the Russian Mafia," Madison spat and glanced at Becker, who shook her head.

"So they deserved you storming into their business and starting a firefight?"

"That's not what happened. Just cause," Madison pushed out.

"Just cause?" King laughed.

Becker and Winston both looked at her, grimacing. She had gone off script, but she didn't regret it for a moment.

"New evidence came to light, and I had questions for them," she responded matter-of-factly.

"I think you already decided their guilt when you went in there armed."

"I have a valid firearm license. It's my American right to carry."

Becker buried her forehead in her hand.

Madison went on. "As I said, they are known members of the Russian Mafia."

"So you expected a gunfight, seeing as they were convicted as killers by you?"

She stayed silent. This conversation was veering far off the preferred track.

King continued. "You went in there with a mission in mind—"

"I don't like the direction of this interview, Mr. King. If the tone and implications don't change, I'll need to ask that you leave," Becker said stiffly. "After all, the reason this interview was even granted was because you were going to tell the story from the side of the Stiles PD."

"Something I'm trying to do, but I keep getting spun in circles."

"You sound more like you're eager to accuse the department of wrongdoing," Becker countered.

King put down his pen and clasped his hands. His lips, which naturally rested in a frown, settled there. "Why have me ask questions then? There is obviously something that the Stiles PD has prepared that they just want me to print."

Becker slid a sheet across the table.

Seriously? Her earlobes heated. Why all the time prepping her for this meeting? Why arrange it at all if they were going to take her words, the truth, and twist them the way they saw fit? Maybe this had been a contingency plan in case she went off course or the direction of the interview took an unfavorable turn.

King left the sheet where it came to rest and sat back. "I'm a taxpayer in this city, and I deserve answers to my questions. And so does everyone else." His eyes skipped between Becker and Winston. "Yet you are taking that basic human right away."

Becker laughed. "This is not the first time you've been handed a prepared statement, Mr. King, nor will it be the last."

Madison swallowed deeply and looked at Winston. He shot her a brief side-glance.

"You want your questions answered," she began, "then you should appreciate why I also wanted mine answered."

King lifted the paper hesitantly. His eyes looked into Madison's. "Just cause? But I understand that one of the Russians was shot in the standoff."

"Mr. King," Becker cautioned.

"There was a standoff," Madison said.

Becker gasped. "Detective Knight."

Madison held up her hand to silence the woman. "I went into Homeland Logistics to ask questions about an investigation and was met by Sergey and Anatolli." She couldn't recall this, but it had to have taken place like that. She wouldn't have fired without provocation.

King leaned back in his chair. "So they fired first? Made the first aggressive move?"

"They were going to kill me." One certainty. Images flashed back.

I arrived. Asked to see Sergey. The receptionist flipped the sign on the door to CLOSED *and left. I should have left too, but I didn't.*

But then what?

Anatolli's gun was against my skull. "On the count of three..."

Her heart began racing and a clammy sweat blanketed her brow. She failed to remember the segment of time between the front door and being in that horrible chair.

"Detective? Did they fire at you? Raise their guns first?"

She came around to the inquisitive eyes of the reporter. She looked about the room. Winston was facing her, his head lowered and shaking back and forth. Becker looked mortified, her face pale, her jaw tight, her lips pursed.

"Mr. King, we're finished here." Becker gestured for the man to pack up his belongings.

He didn't move. His eyes were on Madison.

Despite the glares of her superior, she said, "I did go there about a cold case. Do you know what usually happens to them? Nothing. The victims are forgotten. But I don't forget."

"Knight, stop right there," Winston snarled, his eyes ablaze.

But she couldn't back down and had to tell the truth. "I needed answers."

"So you went to get them?" King asked.

"Yes."

"Who made the first aggressive move?" he repeated his earlier question.

Becker rose. "That will be all. Mr. King, please ensure that Detective Knight's name and what was said during this interview are not used in your article at all, or you'll have legal issues to deal with."

"It's called the First Amendment. I have the freedom and right to publish without restraint or censorship." King said this as he got his things in order and prepared to leave.

As Madison watched him, she racked her mind for the missing pieces. Surely they were lurking in her head somewhere.

CHAPTER NINETEEN

"That was an effed-up disaster! What the hell was that?" Sergeant Winston was parked behind his desk, and Madison was in a chair across from him. "What the hell were you thinking?"

Apparently, that was the question of the week. "I only spoke the truth."

"The truth? You never cease to amaze me. I'm not sure how long—"

"You're not sure how long what, Sergeant?" She further challenged him with eye contact. He had no right to fire her, and it would be a legal mess if he attempted to do so at this point. But that didn't mean wrongful dismissal never happened. "Should I secure a lawyer?"

Winston let out a long, steady exhale. "It might be a good idea."

She'd hoped that wouldn't be his response. She nodded, trying to hold herself together. Winston was being manipulated by the chief—had to be. Her mind went back to King and his anonymous source—could that be Chief McAlexandar? She shook the notion aside. He was a dick, but was he actually corrupt?

Winston continued. "You've got to start following the rules, Knight. If you don't, I won't have much choice other than to…" He never finished the sentence, but it was easy enough to piece together. Her job was on the line if she didn't start following orders. "We can't even use you to work this case against the Russians. You need to be as far from it as possible."

"But—"

He held up a hand. "I don't want to hear about it. I just want to get through the rest of this day, preferably the week even, without another upset or smudge on the department. The charges against Sergey and Anatolli are being heard by a judge Thursday morning at nine AM. The closest you get to any of this is you'll need to testify."

She smiled. He'd made it sound to King like the hearing hadn't been scheduled yet. "Let me reopen the Lexan case," she blurted out. It might not be the best timing for such a request, but no one could accuse her of waiting for the "ideal" moment to broach a topic. Besides, was there any such thing?

"You can't be serious."

"I most certainly am. Besides it's not a conflict of interest."

"How can you think it's not? You want to pin Lexan's murder on the Russians."

"All I want is justice. It's all I've ever wanted. Let me reopen the Lexan case," she petitioned again. When he didn't say anything, she went ahead. "Listen, boss, the Lexan case is important to me, but it's not because the Russians almost killed me." Saying those words caused her to take a pause. *Almost killed me.* She cleared her throat. "My purpose in all of this now, as it was before I entered that warehouse, is to see justice for—"

"Lexan. Yes, Knight, you've made that clear."

"Do I have your permission to pursue the Lexan investigation? I will stay away from Sergey and Anatolli as they pertain to charges related to me." It was a long shot and she was asking for a lot—as far as Winston would be concerned—but she had to try.

Winston met her eyes now, as if he were giving her proposal honest consideration. "Fine. But tread discreetly… if you're capable. Also, the reach of the investigation will be from behind a desk while taking care of your modified duties. They are your priority for the time being."

On the count of three, pull the trigger.

The flashback hit her unprepared. She'd been propelled right back to that warehouse. She gripped the arms of the chair.

"Knight?" Winston prompted.

She heard him say her name. She saw him watching her. She could only part her lips—nothing was coming out.

"See. Whatever is going on in here"—he tapped his head—"you need to take care of it. You're blanking out. You've been through a lot."

She'd almost mistake his words for concern about her well-being, if it wasn't for his tone that projected judgment. He really meant she'd been through a lot—because she'd brought it upon herself. Probably because she was a woman too. "No need to worry about me." Her statement was drenched with sarcasm. "I'll handle the investigation of the cold case and get resolution once and for all."

"Save the speech, Maddy."

With him addressing her by her first name, his eyes held the warmth of a father—a rare sight. Maybe she'd been too quick to judge him, but it also made her uneasy. For him to flip-flop like this only added credence to her suspicion that someone behind the scenes was pulling his strings, and he was nothing but the puppet.

CHAPTER TWENTY

Wednesday afternoon. Madison's first day officially on desk duty, and the hours were dragging by. She put a man's hand on the fingerprint scanner.

"I need to get my club's doors open," he said. "I need this background check to go through as quickly as possible so I can get that liquor license."

Ken Russet came up from Indiana with dreams of opening a bar. Why he chose to settle in Stiles was beyond Madison. He had thick, bushy eyebrows that could have been salvaged and used in a treatment for the top of his head, which hardly had any hair. His eyes were sincere, but a dull brown, matching his personality—quiet and withdrawn. Odd for a would-be club owner—but to each their own.

"There's a process, and it takes the time it takes." That was true about a lot of things. For one, her being able to return to full duty—clearance from a GP and a shrink. She let out a deep breath and surveyed the room for signs of life. It went on all around her.

Terry had stopped by his desk, then headed off to the lab. How nice for him to have freedom while she was tethered to her chair doing rookie work. The Russian bastards really needed to pay for what they did—

On the count of three, pull the trigger.
I almost died. I would have if—

She shook her head, willing the recollections to shift and lodge back into the darkness from which they kept slithering.

"Officer?"

She blinked, realizing that Russet was addressing her. The title he assigned her was enough to sober her to her current reality. "Detective," she corrected.

"Well, you mind easing up there?" He pointed to where she held his other hand against the scanner. "It's not like it's ink anymore."

"Oh." She let go of his hand, which he pulled back and cradled.

"What happened to your wrist anyway?" he asked.

"Injured in the line of duty."

Russet studied her with skepticism. He was probably curious how that applied to desk work.

"I'm not usually cooped up in here."

"Ah. Right. Detective." Russet smiled, revealing his genetic asset. "Very cool."

You can't kill the devil. Sergey's words stabbed her consciousness, and her skin went clammy.

"You all right? Your face—"

"I'm fine." She reached for his other hand. Her cell phone rang, and she held an index finger up at Russet.

"Oh, I'm in a hurry," he mumbled, his foot tapping.

She silenced him with a look and answered her phone.

"Maddy, you've got to get to the lab." It was Cynthia.

"Can you tell me over the phone? I'm a little busy at the moment." She was also a little miffed her friend hadn't filled her in about the round and two casings.

"Rather talk in person."

Cynthia's tone and apparent need to see her right away had Madison's stomach churning. "I'll be right there." Madison hung up and finished with Russet's other hand in a couple of seconds. "All right, you're good to go."

He looked from one hand to the other, likely curious why the second one went so fast.

She stood.

"Where are you going?"

"Work to do, Mr. Russet. Good day." She hurried down the hall.

"What about my license?"

"We'll be in touch." She turned and waved a hand at him. When she faced forward again, she slammed right against Troy Matthews. His hands went to her arms to steady her, and hers went flat to his chest.

Definitely six-pack abs. She peeled herself back. "Ah, sorry about—" She looked up at him, his height towering inches above her. And there were those green eyes again…

"Where are you off to in such a hurry?"

"I just… I have… The lab." She could have punched herself. Could she be any more obvious about her attraction to the man? She had to get herself together. She slipped out of his arms, albeit reluctantly.

His eyes were still welded to hers.

Either the air was thin or her head light. One or the other? Both? "Sorry, I didn't mean to—"

"Run me over? If you wanted to be in my arms, Madison, all you'd have to do is—"

"Listen, I really have to get going." She couldn't let him finish what he was going to say. She stepped away, hoping he wouldn't notice her heated cheeks.

"Oh, I wanted to say congratulations on the stayed IA investigation, Bulldog."

"I'm a…what now?" She stopped walking and turned to face him.

"Bulldog. Hardheaded, determined. You're going to get the answers you seek no matter what."

Just yesterday, Terry had called her bullheaded. She hadn't liked it then and didn't care for the implication now. She crossed her arms. "You make it sound like it's a bad thing to go after what you want."

He didn't waver under her glare. In fact, he didn't give any indication that her response affected him at all. "I never said that. Don't read any more into it."

She swore the glint in his eyes challenged her. She wasn't sure if she liked it or took insult to it.

"Well, you better get going," he said. "It seems I've slowed your stride. You go get 'em, Bulldog."

Inside, she was screaming. What was it with this man? He took it upon himself to read her mind, assign her a nickname? Did he think all of this was endearing? And if so, why was he trying to be? God, she really didn't have time for men and all the associated drama.

CHAPTER TWENTY-ONE

Madison found Cynthia at her desk in the corner of the lab.

Cynthia swiveled in her chair. "There you are."

"What have you found out?"

Seconds passed with steady eye contact, neither woman looking away until Cynthia broke the silence. "Are you upset with me?"

"It would have been nice to find out about the bullet in the wall and the two casings from you instead of Winston."

"I'm sorry. I'm not technically supposed to loop you in at all."

Madison staggered back at that, but why should she be surprised that would be Cynthia's orders? At least, Cynthia was coming forward with something now. "There's bad news?" Call it a hunch.

Cynthia paled. "The round that was embedded in the wall has been processed, and it came from your gun. Same with the casings."

"Why do I have a feeling there's more?" She was finding it hard to breathe.

"Where the round was in the wall disclosed the location you were in when you fired."

"Cyn." Madison took a few steps forward.

"And based on that, you had intended to shoot Sergey."

"I'm sure I did."

"Shh." Cynthia held her finger to her lips. "I'll pretend I didn't hear that."

"It was either shoot or be shot." Madison was going to run with that, even if she couldn't remember and "eyewitnesses" were speaking against her.

"Well, I'm very happy you came out the other end, but some other people…" Cynthia didn't need to finish her statement.

"No surprise. The chief for one. He's certainly hungry for my badge, and I think I might have served it up."

Cynthia caressed Madison's arm.

"No, I'm not giving up. I refuse. It's not in my DNA. If that man wants my badge, he won't get it without a fight."

Cynthia smiled. "There's my girl."

"Dang straight. If he wants to play hardball, I'm more than willing."

"You've got this look in your eyes. What aren't you telling me?" Cynthia had a way of reading Madison's thoughts sometimes.

Madison had just been thinking about the chief's loyalties and where they lay. "Don't worry about it."

"Are you sure?"

"Yes. Was there anything else? Feel free to keep me here a while longer. I've been printing people and pulling backgrounds for liquor license requests all day. If I have to deal with one more walk-in—"

Cynthia cringed. "I can't even picture you—"

"Please don't."

Cynthia laughed. "For how long?"

"Until I get cleared by a doctor *and* a shrink."

Her friend's laughter got deeper.

"Is something funny?"

Cynthia covered her mouth to stifle her amusement, but tears were beading in the corners of her eyes.

Madison crossed her arms and played the power of silence.

"It's just…" A snort.

"Cynthia!"

"Sorry... Sorry. It's just the thought of you talking out your feelings—" Another guffaw. She held up her hand. "I'm sorry." She sniffled and took a deep breath. "All right, I'm all better now."

Why was Cynthia finding it so hilarious that she had to see a shrink? Madison didn't think it was funny at all. "Anything else?" she prompted.

"Ah, yes." Cynthia cleared her throat. "You're off the case when it comes the Russians, but I couldn't shut you out of this."

Madison was curious what her friend meant by "this," but said, "The sergeant actually cleared me to investigate the Lexan murder." She didn't need to point out she was limited to doing so from the confines of a desk for now. And given the steady flow of tasks, she wasn't sure how she was supposed to fit it in anyway. Maybe that was why Winston had consented.

"Really?"

"Trust me, I was surprised too."

"He must feel guilty about something."

Guilt could very well explain Winston's mood swings.

"We're still working on analyzing everything we pulled from the room you were in at Homeland Logistics, but you're not going to believe what we've already found."

More flashbacks threatened to move in, but this time Madison was able to keep them suppressed to the edge of her consciousness. No doubt when she saw the department shrink this afternoon, he'd try to convince her that she had mild PTSD. But that was something other people got, not her. And having some control over the memories had to be a good indicator that she hadn't lost it altogether. The fact that other recollections were completely lost she'd keep to herself.

"Maddy, are you still with me?"

"I'm waiting. I thought you hated it when I interrupt you." She offered the excuse, hoping her friend bought it.

"Uh-huh."

"Are you going to tell me or what?"

"There she is. My impatient Maddy. I'm feeling a little more at ease now." Cynthia walked over to the table and picked up a watch in a plastic evidence bag. "This watch has the initials *JC* on it."

Madison shook her head. "Not following."

"*JC* are the initials for James Calin." Cynthia paused for a second. "Are you still not following?"

"No, I am." In an effort to cheat death, Bryan Lexan had staged his death. He had the family money to make that happen, and that was where James Calin came into play. He made a call to Bryan Lexan's fiancée, Jessica, claiming he was dead, or as good as, and made it sound like it had come from a Russian. Obviously, the ruse hadn't worked in the end because he ended up murdered for real. It was believed that James Calin had also met a similar fate, though his body was never found—just blood in his apartment indicative of a violent struggle, possible murder. "And you found this in the room?"

"Well, under a cabinet in the office outside of the torture room. Possibly there had been a scuffle, and it came off and slid across the floor. But who knows?"

"So Calin was there at one point, but why? We've never found Calin's body or uncovered any connection between him and the Russians."

"Looks like you have one now."

Madison's mind was whirling with possible scenarios. "So was Calin somehow working for the Russians, and when his usefulness was up, they killed him? Or had Calin become a victim because the Russians thought he could help them get to Lexan?"

"Or did the Russians exact revenge on Calin because he helped Lexan stage his death?" Cynthia tossed out.

"Interesting, but maybe JC on the watch stands for someone or *something* else?" Not that she believed that for a second.

"Really? Well, okay... I expected you to be all over this."

Normally, Madison would be. Maybe the events at Homeland Logistics had screwed her mind up more than she realized. "How did you tie the initials back to him?"

"I might have taken a leap of faith and just went straight to your notes on the Lexan case. I found that you had mentioned Calin's name there and surmised JC stood for James Calin."

"You're brilliant." Any recollections, or throbbing pain, were muted.

"Not so sure about that, but thank you anyway."

"Did you tell Terry all this when he was here?"

"I wanted to tell you first. Besides, his job is to hold the Russians responsible for what they did to you. The watch is really more related to the Lexan case, which you told me you're on, so…"

Madison smiled at her friend. "I like the way you think."

"Figured you would."

"And it's probably best not to throw too much at Terry. He could get overwhelmed." She was teasing—partially anyway.

Cynthia laughed and shook her head. "He's not that bad, and you know it."

"Do I?" Madison let some silence drag out, then laughed. "Were you able to find anything else that could put Calin at the warehouse besides his watch? His watch could have made it there without him—and that's assuming it's his. Blood maybe—either in the office or the torture room?"

Cynthia nodded. "There was. Several donors, none can tie specifically to Calin. All we can get from the stains on the floor are some blood types, no DNA." Cynthia kept talking, but Madison's thoughts shuttled her back in time.

The door is opened. I am shoved in. They turn on the light, and I see it. The chair, its restraints, the neck latch…

Her legs buckled.

"Maddy?" Cynthia rushed to help her regain her balance. She held on to Madison with one hand and reached for the wheeled task chair with the other. "Here, take a seat." She helped Madison into it.

Madison's vision pinpricked, and her chest tightened.

"You're going to have to—"

"Start taking care of myself? So everyone tells me." Madison massaged her forehead and went to get up. She met with Cynthia's hands on her shoulders, holding her down.

"Stay right where you are."

"I'm not an invalid."

Cynthia crossed her arms. "You almost fainted."

"I didn't almost—"

Cynthia cocked her head.

"Fine." She hated feeling like this, helpless and unable to perform her job. All she wanted to do was confront the Russians—adding questions about James Calin to the list. "Any blood type a match for what was left in Calin's apartment?"

"Sure. Type O, but that's incredibly common."

"Damn. Well, Calin pretty much disappeared. He's probably dead, and he had no living relatives to even talk to."

Cynthia was looking at her with concern, and if there was one person Madison could open up to, it was Cynthia. "Between us, Cyn, I am a little off my game." She pointed at her friend. "But you tell anyone, and I'll—"

"Kill me. Yada, yada. Maybe we should go out and get drunk." A listless smile lifted Cynthia's mouth.

Madison wasn't a huge drinker, but it might not be a bad idea.

CHAPTER TWENTY-TWO

Madison reached her desk just as her phone started to ring.

"I have someone here to see you about a liquor license." It was Officer Ranson from the front.

"Knight, in my office now." Sergeant Winston came up behind her, snapping his fingers and disregarding the fact that she held a phone to her ear.

"I've gotta go."

"I heard. Don't worry about it. I'll get someone else."

Madison hung up actually thankful to be saved from another mundane background check—even if it meant dealing with the brass.

"What's up?" she asked before she cleared the doorway and saw Chief McAlexandar sitting across from Winston. *Is it too late to turn around and leave?*

"Close the door," Winston directed her.

She jacked a thumb over her shoulder. "There's someone here needing to get a background and prints done for a liquor license."

"Someone else will handle it," Winston stated firmly. "Sit."

She shut the door and sat beside the chief, but not before moving the chair a few extra inches away from him.

McAlexandar slapped the *Stiles Times* on Winston's desk. "Do you have anything to say for yourself?"

She wasn't inclined to answer or explain herself to this man—not when she had a strong suspicion that she couldn't trust him.

"Have you seen the article yet?" McAlexandar raised his voice with this question.

She gave him a shake of her head, but that was all.

"Well, it seems King made you out to be a hero," Winston interjected.

She looked from her sergeant to a flushed McAlexandar. "A hero?"

"Yeah, Knight, the city has a savior, and that's you." McAlexandar scoffed. "Ridiculous. What the hell is this city coming to?"

"Read the article." Winston extended the paper across the desk to her.

She picked it up, almost afraid it would scorch her, and read the title: "Stiles PD Detective Out for Justice." She looked at Winston, not wanting to continue.

"Go on," he urged. "It gets much better."

Okay... She scanned the article, plucking out random words and phrases.

> *... for her own purpose... to bring resolution to a forgotten case... she needed to find justice... she was willing to sacrifice her own life in exchange.*

She read the last paragraph in full.

> *It can be concluded that the city has a gem in Detective Knight, who isn't a stranger to the pages of the* Stiles Times. *Her courage and determination have her pursuing justice, even when most would have turned their back on it. The events that led her into Homeland Logistics can be summed up in two words: Just Cause.*

She swallowed heavily as she put the paper back on Winston's desk. McAlexandar was glaring at her, but she refused to let on she'd even noticed.

"How does that feel?" Winston asked.

It left her speechless, except for one concern that was sinking in. "He mentioned me by name." She blanched, ill.

"That he did," Winston said, "and it's too late to retract it. Though that's hardly the point."

To Madison it was. If her family saw her name, there'd be more questions. As if on cue, her cell phone rang. The caller ID showed it was her sister, Chelsea. She routed the call to voicemail.

"We're pleased that King has spun things in the favor of the department," Winston continued. "It was pretty risky in that interview room, wasn't it? But we're not going to beat a dead horse. Listen, we need your help."

She sensed McAlexandar growl beside her. "You need *my* help?" she croaked.

"Don't make us beg for it, because it won't happen," Winston said stiffly. "You're still going to have to see a shrink, but we want you actively pursuing this case."

"This case being?"

"Do you believe you can fire a gun?" Winston gestured to her left sprained wrist. "You can fire a gun?"

Her dominant hand was her right, though she steadied her Glock with her left. "Yes."

"The murdered lawyer case," Winston said, finally answering her question. "That's if you're still interested."

"Bryan Lexan," she pushed out, not sure why Winston avoided his name. "And I will have full clearance to pursue this? Reinstated to full duty?"

"Don't make us say it twice," McAlexandar hissed.

"What about clearance from a doctor?"

"No longer required." Winston's eyes shifted briefly to McAlexandar. "Along with the IA investigation that has been closed. Permanently."

Madison followed his line of sight. The chief sat with his hands clasped in his lap. He didn't acknowledge either one of them.

She was loving the irony of having a man who hated her being forced by circumstances to give her the green light. If the chief had a choice, he would rather fast-track her to the unemployment line. And if her suspicions were correct about the chief being tied to the Russians somehow, this situation would really upset him—especially if Lexan's blood was on their hands. "So the shrink… Can I avoid that too?"

"Not seeing one isn't an option."

At least she'd tried. "Fine."

"Fine? We're rushing you to full duty and we get *fine*? Unbelievable." McAlexandar shook his head, disgusted.

"Don't make it sound like this was your choosing," she said, calling him out.

The chief wagged his finger at her. "You have no respect."

She had a lot she'd like to say in response to that but bit her tongue. *Respect has to be earned*, for one.

Winston leaned back in his chair. "There is one condition, though, seeing as you'll be participating in the active investigation."

Active used in reference to the Lexan case filled her with excitement. Lexan was finally going to get the justice he deserved, and she was going to be the one to bring it to him. She'd been so distracted by the good news, she almost missed the bad. "One condition?"

"You are to clear every step by me," Winston said. "Do you understand? You've never been any good at communication."

The urge to come to her own defense bottled up in her chest, but she mentally forced it aside. "I can do that."

"You *will* do that if you want to keep the case."

She nodded.

"Detective Grant will accompany you wherever you go. He doesn't go, neither do you. Something isn't cleared by me, you don't go."

The chains that restricted her had only been replaced by rope. But still, the pressure eased up. She could breathe.

"Do you understand, Knight?"

She smiled. "Absolutely."

"Now get your ass out of my office, and get some real work done."

"Yes, sir."

She bumped McAlexandar's shoulder on her way out and held up her hands in apology as if it were an accident. Though she was pretty sure he saw through her. And while this meeting would have been a hit to his pride, it had bolstered hers. She would finally see resolution for the dead lawyer, and possibly even set the past right when it came to her family's history with the Russians and take the mob down once and for all.

Madison came up behind Terry at his desk. "I'm back," she announced.

"So I hear." He kept his eyes on his monitor.

She stood beside him and looked at his profile. "Terry, aren't you happy?"

"Of course."

"You don't seem—"

He matched eyes with her. His gaze was bitter. "You almost died. You need to take the time to rest and heal. Deal with what you've been through."

Now he was telling her what she needed? "You're pissing me off."

He ignored her.

"Terry, did you—"

"Yes, I heard you." He pushed back from the desk.

"What is your problem anyway?" she asked.

"You. Plain and simple."

There was a spark of animosity in his eyes, and it stabbed her heart. "Terry?"

"Well, you run off to God knows where. You don't call me for backup. Hell, I would have gone with you."

She laughed.

His lips set in a flat line.

"You would have gone with me?" she pushed out. "You've been wanting me to let go of the Lexan case for a long time. You say that sometimes we don't get all the answers. You say—"

"Listen, if I'm such a bad partner, maybe you should get a new one." He walked off.

Wow. She clenched her chest. Her eyes misted, and she had to swallow the lump that formed in her throat. She wasn't used to being so emotional, and she didn't like it. She'd gotten along just fine hardening herself and tamping down all her feelings. Facing her own death had made her weak. After all, history taught her men especially would turn their backs on her when she needed them the most. Look at her love life—first Sovereign, then Blake. And yet people wondered why she had an issue with men. Not one but her father gave her reason to trust them.

Her phone rang. Chelsea again. Might as well get this conversation over with.

"Maddy, Mom is flipping out."

"I don't have time for this." *Or Mom's flipping out.* And for being so upset, it wasn't like their mother had reached out to her directly.

"Make time. She called me this morning all upset. Has she called you?"

"No."

"Guess you know how she can be sometimes."

Stubborn, single-minded, judgmental…

"She saw that article."

Which Madison assumed was the cause of the *flipping out*. Not that she knew why her mother was even reading the *Stiles Times*. Didn't the papers in Florida offer enough bad news?

Madison glanced at the clock. *3:33 PM.* She had to be at the shrink's office in half an hour. "I really need to go," she said.

"Stop right there. Don't you hang up—" Chelsea paused as if trying to ascertain whether Madison remained on the line. "Why, Madison? Why would you do something so stupid?"

"It's all right. I'm okay. Everything is fine."

"Everything is *fine*? You're patronizing me, and you think you're a superhero? Those movies are quite popular. Jim and the girls love 'em, but trust me when I say you do not possess special powers. You *are* mortal." The last word cracked as it came out.

On the count of three, pull the trigger…

Madison could hardly breathe. "I am fine."

"So you keep saying, but what about us? What if we lost you? Did you think about that? The paper made it sound like you went in there on a solo mission. Why?"

Only her sister—and mother—would twist the article to make Madison out as the bad guy. How was it that at thirty-five, her family could still guilt-trip her? Madison had taken action. Everything had worked out. The end.

Chelsea went on. "You don't want to talk about it, but I need you to. They said it was about a cold case, but surely you wouldn't have risked your life just for that?"

"Come on, Chelsea, I'm fine." The word *fine*—again. She had to get off the line before she said that word one more time. "I'll call you later."

"If you don't, I'll be call—"

"Love you." Madison cut her sister off and ended the call. She couldn't afford to let emotions run the show. She had to be in control—now more than ever.

CHAPTER TWENTY-THREE

The psychiatrist's office was located downtown on the fifth floor of a multi-use building. As Madison took the elevator, she had to shake aside concerns about her family and Terry's attitude. If she didn't, the shrink could think Madison actually needed help. All she needed was for the doctor to sign her form and give her a pass. The sooner, the better.

She'd likely have to face an egotistical male who would tell her she had anger management issues and a problem with authority figures. He would pin the blame on her upbringing and her parents—after all, isn't that how those in this industry worked? Dredge up the past and create issues you don't actually have? And by the time you talked out your feelings, your relationships were destroyed and you had more questions coming out than going in?

Madison opened the door and entered a reception area that had ten chairs set around the perimeter of the room. The color palette consisted of soothing shades of greens, yellows, and oranges. Somehow the designer had managed to combine them and make it esthetically pleasing. Like a meadow speckled with wildflowers.

Madison reported in at the reception desk.

The woman there said, "She'll be with you in a moment."

She? Did she just say— Madison grabbed a business card from the holder and found a chair. Three doctors worked out of this office. It didn't take her long to find Connor—*Tabitha* Connor, PhD.

The thought of talking to a woman doctor was even worse. Women had the natural ability to see beyond words and *feel* what wasn't being said.

"Madison Knight," the receptionist called out.

One deep breath. It was go time.

Connor's office followed the theme of the reception area and utilized a soft color scheme. Her walls were taupe, but artwork, throw pillows, and furniture were used to inject pastels. There were walls of bookshelves filled with journals and bric-a-brac—various sculptures and statues. There was a chaise lounge, a couch, and a plush, egg-shaped sofa chair, which swiveled around to face the door when Madison entered.

"Detective Madison Knight, welcome. Please have a seat." She gestured toward the couch.

Tabitha Connor was a woman in her midsixties and had a maternal appearance. Panic set in. Madison didn't do well with her own mother. She hesitantly slipped onto the couch.

Connor leaned forward and smiled, the genuine expression lighting her bright-green eyes. "Nice to meet you."

"You too." Madison had never felt so awkward in her life. She forced her gaze to settle on the woman.

"Why don't we start with getting to know each other?"

Which means she wants to drill into my brain…

Connor angled her head, softened her facial language. No doubt a skill she employed often. Madison would need to guard herself, or before she knew it, she'd be crying like some lunatic while making claims that she had "mommy issues." Maybe it wasn't too late to make a run for it. "I really don't need to be here," she eventually said. "I'm fine. Best not to waste your valuable time on me. If you could sign off on the paper saying that I came and I'm good, my boss would be happy, and then you and I will be able to go our separate ways." Madison was pleased with her insertion of flattery; it usually worked.

Connor remained silent, though, and looked at Madison's hurt wrist.

"Oh this?" Madison held up her arm. "No big deal. Yes, I had an ordeal. I consider this a little memento, but I'll be good as new. Actually"—she rushed to add—"it's feeling better already." A slight deviation from the truth.

Connor's eyes steadied on her, and Madison's level of discomfort ratcheted up a few notches. The woman pried into her mind, and Madison didn't care for it—that space was reserved for her and no one else. Troy Matthews possessed a similar ability, the way his eyes pierced through her. She thought back to his fit chest, and his words. *If you wanted to be in my arms, Madison, all you'd have to do is...* Do what? Maybe she shouldn't have cut him off. She shook the thought aside. She was getting carried away. "Listen, the truth of the matter is, I don't need therapy. Your time would be better spent with someone who actually needs help."

"I have this piece of paper." Connor extended a sheet to her, and Madison made out the department letterhead before it reached her hand.

"Like I said, that's why I'm here in the first place."

"Hmm."

Madison shifted on the sofa and placed her good hand beneath her thigh. "I just don't see the point in all this."

"Well then, if you're as good as you say, this should be easy. Let's start with why they think you need to see me."

"Protocol."

"You feel that's the only reason?"

Feel. Such a taboo word. And this woman was good, Madison would give her that, but it would take more than direct prodding to get her to spill her feelings. She would stick to the meat of things and not divert course. She could handle her own emotions. She didn't need someone justifying the way she felt, telling her it was completely normal "under the circumstances." She didn't need their permission or absolution.

Connor's gaze was unrelenting. It was obvious she wasn't going to retreat.

"All right, here goes. I made a decision that put me in a bad spot," Madison stated simply.

"You did? Do you regret that decision?" The woman was at it already—twisting her words.

"It wasn't my fault. I mean, what happened wasn't…"

"Are we talking about the lawyer?"

Madison's eyes locked with Connor's. How much did she know? She supposed Connor could read the newspaper.

"You seem surprised. I do get full backgrounds on new patients, especially when they're sent from the Stiles PD." She offered a placating smile. "You went into Homeland Logistics to speak with Sergey Evanoff and Anatolli Belsky of the Russian Mafia, for which you had your reasons."

Madison stood and paced behind the couch. She was relieved Connor never tapped further into the past, but it made her uncomfortable that Connor aligned herself as an ally with her statement. "Guess they tell you everything."

Connor wrote in her notepad. "So you said it wasn't your fault. *It* is what exactly?"

The question threw Madison for a second, but that had been her initial defense. Madison wasn't even sure now what she'd meant by that claim. She'd only been here a matter of minutes and her mind was already messed up. She stood. "I've got to go."

"Please, just sit." The doctor glanced at her watch. "Just give me ten more minutes."

Madison looked at the clock on the wall. *4:35 PM.* As she turned to face Connor again, the stark truth sank in. She needed this woman to sign off so the brass would be happy, but it was Connor's gaze that had her consenting. She wouldn't be going anywhere until she opened up a bit, and there was that piece of paper that hung over her head like a thundercloud. "I'll give you six more. I've been here four already."

"Fair enough."

Madison took a seat again with another glimpse at the clock. She wouldn't let the minute hand go past forty-one.

"Please continue," Connor encouraged her.

"With the cold case, I just needed to get it taken care of—once and for all. I wanted answers."

"There's nothing like getting answers."

This woman's tactics were clear. Relate and become friends so that Madison would drop her guard, but she didn't need understanding. Madison knew what she did, and she knew *why* she did it. The fact that the rest of the world didn't comprehend the purpose wasn't her issue.

"Why did you become a cop?" Connor asked.

"I wanted to make a difference and have a purpose in life."

"Very commendable. Many people just like to get through life."

There was something lurking in Connor's eyes. How much of a background did she get? *Does she know why I need to be a cop?* "I'm not like everyone else," Madison began. "I also don't need to take it easy. Have no desire to either. I don't need people to relate to me. If they have a problem with something I've done or a choice I've made, that's their issue to deal with."

"I take it that not everyone understands where you're coming from."

Madison's inclination was to resist Connor's efforts at relating and encouraging communication, but she still found that she elaborated. "My boss, for one. He doesn't understand why I do half the things I do. My partner, well, I'm not exactly sure what his problem is."

"He doesn't get you either?"

"No, he gets me. He just doesn't agree with me. He thinks I'm careless and jump into things too fast."

"Do you?"

Madison's eyes diverted to the clock for a second, back to Connor. "At least you're not trying to relate to me with this one."

"It's an honest question."

Madison let out a rush of air. "I go by my feelings a lot."

"And this gets you into trouble."

"It can, I guess."

"There have been other occurrences?"

"Terry, that's my partner, he's— How do you say it? He doesn't want to upset things at work and jeopardize his job. He's going to be a father."

"Oh."

Madison would use Connor's obvious interest as a welcome detour to keep the focus off her. "He doesn't know if it's a boy or girl, although Terry is certain it's going to be a boy. Terry and his wife were supposed to find out, but the baby's position didn't afford a clear view." Madison let out a small laugh, but it faded quickly. "I have a feeling there might be more going on with the baby that he hasn't told me."

"Sounds like a scary place for your partner and his wife."

"For sure. Family is everything to him, as is commitment."

Connor uncrossed her legs and recrossed them in the other direction. "You talk about your job with passion. You talk about your partner, and I sense sadness. You mention commitment, and I sense fear."

Madison ran her good hand down her thigh, inwardly wishing she could spring from the couch and run out the door. She looked at the clock. Three minutes left. "I love my job. I love my partner. And you're right about the commitment thing. I'm working on that."

"Why are you sad when it comes to your partner?"

"Well, it's his baby and whether or not it will be born healthy."

Connor pressed her lips in a grandmotherly, all-knowing sort of way. "There's more, Madison. I've been doing this a long time."

The conversation with Terry replayed in Madison's head.

What is your problem anyway?

You. Plain and simple.

She swallowed. "There were some words spoken before I came here."

"Between you and Terry?"

"Yes."

Connor remained silent.

"He's mad at me," Madison found herself offering. "I'm not sure why." Maybe that wasn't entirely the truth.

"He could be worried about you. Pain and hurt can manifest themselves as anger."

"I haven't seen him quite like this before."

"You almost lost your life. He's expecting a baby with his wife, and there may be possible complications. He's facing numerous uncertainties."

"You're trying to tell me that he's mad at me for being okay?"

"Not at all, but he could feel that you put yourself at risk when it wasn't necessary. It could have made him face feelings he didn't want to have."

"So it's his job to control my life choices?" Madison consulted with the clock and was relieved. She stood. "As I promised you, ten minutes total. Time is up. I assume you'll sign the form saying I was here, and we can put this behind us."

"I believe we're just getting started, Madison. There are issues here you need to talk out before you can move forward. We hardly even touched on your experience at the hands of the Russians. How that made you feel, and how it's affected—"

"Let me make it simple for you. I was scared. I got through it. I got over it. End of story."

"Oh, nothing in life is that simplistic, Detective, and you of all people should know that."

There were a few seconds of resulting silence. Madison suspected Connor knew her family's history, but she was letting it rest for this session. Madison jutted out her chin. "So you won't sign my release form." It wasn't a question so much as a dire observation.

"I would like to see you again on Monday." Connor scribbled something on a small card and extended it to Madison.

An appointment card, telling her to return Monday at three PM. It was confirmed: this venture with a shrink wasn't over yet.

Son of a bitch.

On the drive from Connor's office, Madison's mind was whirling. Not so much with what had just transpired, but her thoughts were on the Lexan case. James Calin, someone who had been tied to Lexan, had likely been at Homeland Logistics—and was possibly murdered there. But how to prove it after all this time? And no one needed a supposed dead person coming back to life after the fact.

Another thing weighing on her was Terry. He could be moody at times, but it typically was never directed her way—at least not to this extent. Connor had said, *It could have made him face feelings he didn't want to have.* Could it simply be like Chelsea had suggested, that he was thinking about where he'd be if something happened to her? But that didn't excuse him turning his back on her and walking away when she needed him more than ever. She had to just let her mental wanderings about Terry go. He didn't have the right to control her life. He had a family he could hold power over, but not her. All she wanted to do was get going on the Lexan case in earnest, but two things were stopping her from doing so today. One, she was drained from the day with all its emotional ups and downs. The terms of her approval to investigate were clear too—she was to run every step past Winston *and* take Terry along. She couldn't face him right now. Nope. It was best she call it a day, head home, get some rest, and manage her emotions. Tomorrow was going to be another big day. She'd be testifying against Sergey and Anatolli. She could demonstrate no weakness.

CHAPTER TWENTY-FOUR

The courthouse was a mammoth building located in the middle of downtown. Its ostentatious white staircase led to marble columns that presented themselves as guardians in front of the doors. Inside, more marble, and on the ceiling, decorative artwork cast color into the large space.

Today Judge Keller would determine the legitimacy of the charges being levied against Sergey and Anatolli in regards to Madison's capture, imprisonment, and threat to her life. Madison would be called upon to testify under oath to all that she had undergone. Most wouldn't dare cross men of their reputation. In that, Madison stood alone. But it was all black and white to her—for Better or Worse too.

Madison took a seat in the front row of the public benches next to Terry without saying a word to him. He didn't speak to her either. She put her attention on the defense. Blake Golden wasn't paying her any attention, but she was quite sure he was aware of her presence. Sergey and Anatolli were seated beside him. Sergey cast her an arrogant gaze.

On the count of three, pull the trigger...

She squeezed her eyes shut. *Not now!*

She fought to establish control, to return to the courtroom, but she was standing on the edge of a precipice eyeing jagged rocks below.

The smell of blood... feet shuffling around me. I can't move. Chains are secured to my wrists and metal cuffs are around my ankles. A collar is clasped tightly around my neck.

When she opened her eyes, Blake was standing in front of her. She blinked and forced herself to focus and make eye contact. To refuse him that, he would sense her weakness as if it were blood, and just like a shark that hunts in the seas after a plane crash, he would come after her. "What do you want?" she hissed.

"I hope you're ready to see me in action." He tugged on his suit jacket.

"I'm not sure why you waited so long. Maybe things would have turned out differently between us." She held his gaze, nailing home the personal insult.

His tongue flicked out and wet his lips. He said nothing but gave the separating wall in front of her a tap of his hand before he returned to his side of the courtroom.

The potshot wasn't really justified. He was a good lover, not that she'd ever admit to that out loud, especially now. He did have *some* human compassion. It had been responsible for drawing her to him in the first place, but it was just too bad that it lay so deeply buried.

She scanned the room. SWAT officers from *that* day. They'd testify to how they'd rescued her and state the condition they'd found her in. Troy Matthews was also there. When she met his gaze, he offered reassurance just with a look. She turned away, not sure how to handle his attention.

Why would he care so much about her well-being? It must have been because he'd orchestrated her rescue. Did he view her as weak, a delicate flower petal? That idea chafed. Or did he fall for all the women he rescued? Though she didn't see him as the type to give his heart over easily. Not that she knew him well. And even if he was suffering from some inexplicable effect, it didn't justify her reaction to him. She'd long ago learned that she didn't need a man to complete her life. So why couldn't she just brush him aside?

The proceedings started, and it wasn't long before her name was called.

"You can do this," Terry whispered to her by way of encouragement. It was the first thing he'd said to her since she sat down.

She made her way to the stand on legs that possessed barely enough strength to hold her upright. Her mind slipped into the past, to the moments when she feared she may have taken her last breath. To the hatred that filled the eyes of Sergey and Anatolli. To their fiery intent to torture and kill her.

Clay Simon, the prosecuting district attorney, was a well-seasoned match for Blake. He came over and stood in front of her. "Please tell the court what transpired at Homeland Logistics that evening, starting from the beginning."

She had the beginning and the end. It was the bits in between that were fuzzy. Definitely not clear enough to form a definitive picture. She would stick to what she knew. "I went to Homeland Logistics to speak with Sergey Evanoff and Anatolli Belsky about an old case."

"And they were willing to see you?"

"No idea. The woman at the front desk closed the storefront and left when I told her I wanted to talk to them. I sensed she was scared for some reason."

Blake jumped to standing position. "Speculation, Your Honor."

"Agreed. Detective, please answer the questions without assuming how other people were feeling."

"The next thing I remember was being held at gunpoint." She offered another truth.

"And who held the gun on you? Would you be able to point them out in this courtroom?" Simon asked.

"Yes." She raised her finger toward the defense table. "Anatolli held the gun, with Sergey's encouragement."

"Now, you were also armed, correct?" Simon asked.

"Yes, I was."

"What happened next?"

The gun barrel is slammed into my jaw. Blood coats my tongue. I'm pushed into a dark room where I imagine shadows dancing as waking nightmares and where the whispers of the dead call out to me.

The click of the revolver. The pounding of my heart beating as I anticipate the bullet.

You can't kill the devil…

The memories slammed into her with the force of a tsunami. She took a few steadying breaths and went on to lay it out as she remembered. She did so from a detached perspective, her voice sounding to her ears as if it belonged to a stranger.

"Thank you, Detective."

"Would the defense like to question the witness?" Judge Keller asked.

Madison went cold, holding her breath.

"We would, Your Honor," Blake answered.

"Very well then. Proceed."

Blake came in front of the stand and wasted no time getting to his point. "Did you go into the employee-only section of the warehouse with your gun drawn?"

She couldn't bring herself to form any words.

"Detective," he prompted.

She blinked, breathed out slowly. For a second, she met Terry's gaze. "I don't remember."

Blake smiled and addressed the judge. "Your Honor, the defense would like to submit signed affidavits from two eyewitnesses that testify to seeing Detective Knight not only enter a restricted area of the warehouse but that she did so gun drawn. She also fired upon my clients without provocation."

Judge Keller appeared somber as he held out a hand to receive the paperwork from Blake.

Minutes passed as the judge read. "These are from employees with Homeland Logistics?" the judge asked Blake.

"That they are, Your Honor."

"From my understanding, Homeland Logistics is operated by Sergey Evanoff and Anatolli Belsky—known in this courtroom as the defendants. Is that right?"

"It is, Your Honor."

"The same men who have connections to the Russian Mafia."

Blake stiffened. "Allegedly."

"That wasn't a question, Mr. Golden." The judge dropped the reports on the bench. "Do you have any further questions for Detective Knight?"

"Not at this time, Your Honor."

"Good." The judge nodded toward Madison, and she returned to the prosecution's table. Next, SWAT Officer Dunn was called on to state the condition in which he'd found her.

As he spoke, she put herself out of mind, as if he discussed finding someone other than her. If only it weren't for the tactile recollections—the scent of blood, the taste of it on her tongue, the pressure of the gun barrel against her skull, the tight restraints on her arms and neck.

"Does defense have any final words?" Keller asked.

Blake stood, pressing a flattened hand against his suit jacket. "Defense would like to move that the charges against my clients be dismissed."

Simon remained seated but projected his voice. "Ludicrous, Your Honor. We have heard convincing evidence that they held one of the Stiles PD's own hostage with the intent to torture and kill her."

On the count of three, pull the trigger. On the count of three, pull the trigger. On the count of three, pull the trigger.

The phrase repeated on a reel in her head.

"Defense, despite your appeal and the affidavits, this doesn't change the fact that the prosecution has provided enough evidence to prove that a crime did occur, and that the defendants probably committed the crime. The request for the charges to be dismissed is hereby declined. All charges will be handed over to the next level. Bail is set at one million each." Judge Keller passed a glance at Madison. His eyes didn't communicate empathy for her but held a deep sense of camaraderie. The Russians hadn't gotten to him—yet anyway. The judge banged his gavel. "Hearing dismissed."

Terry turned to her. "Are you okay?"

"Yeah. Just fine." Apparently *fine* was her new word. She was quaking, not because of fear but rather anger. The bail was high, but they'd be free men within the hour. She certainly didn't have any preconceived ideas that they would continue their stay behind bars—even if that was where they belonged, caged like the animals they were. But life went according to its own code of divvying out retribution and often fell short of the bar she set.

CHAPTER TWENTY-FIVE

The media was congregated outside the courthouse and clamoring around every person coming out. But that didn't make sense. Winston had made it clear the time of the hearing was being withheld from the public.

Madison pushed through but was stopped by a male reporter with a cameraman behind him. The reporter thrust a mike in her face.

"Are they going to walk for their crimes?"

"Direct your questions to the public information office," she pushed out.

"You don't have anything to say as the Stiles PD officer they are accused of holding hostage?"

The words from his mouth might as well have been filtered through a megaphone. A rush of reporters headed over.

"Is it true that you are the one the Russians held hostage?"
"You're Detective Knight?"
"Why did you go into Homeland Logistics?"
"Were you on duty at the time?"
"Do you think they killed that lawyer?"

"No comment," Madison stated firmly.

Just when Madison didn't believe it possible that any more reporters could swarm around her, another one placed a microphone in front of her. She was about to tell the man off when a hand grabbed her upper arm from behind and tugged her backward. She spun, ready to deck the person, but it was Terry. "Thank God for you," she told him.

He smiled. "Remember that the next time you're pissed off at me."

They worked away from the crowd, walking backward, and then turned to watch their next step. When they made it to a small clearing, she came face-to-face with Sergey. Anatolli stood to his left, and Blake to his right. It hadn't taken any time to post bail.

"You didn't think you'd keep us behind bars forever, did you?" Sergey snickered.

She stood her ground, held eye contact, and was determined not to allow her composure to falter. "I'm not finished with you yet."

"Oh, I think you are, sweetheart."

Anatolli and Blake were already on the move, heading toward a waiting limousine.

Sergey was in the middle of blowing her a kiss when a spray of pink mist filled the air. A black hole in the middle of his forehead seeped blood as he fell to the ground.

People screamed, scurried, and crouched.

Terry wrapped his arm around Madison and tugged her down just as another shot rang out.

Several feet away, Anatolli dropped.

Madison saw it all through blood-soaked lashes. Her stomach lurched; the urge to vomit was strong. Sergey's blood was all over her, and its stench wormed into her sinuses.

"Maddy, are you okay?"

It was Terry asking, and she became aware of his hand encased around hers, squeezing it tightly. "I'm okay," she assured him. "You?"

Terry nodded, and her thoughts went to Blake. Had he— She swallowed roughly. Her eyes took in the area, surveying the damage, expecting to see him dead too. Her gaze landed on Sergey. His eyes were vacant, yet even in death, he appeared arrogant and untouchable, as if he had the ability to haunt from beyond the grave.

"Blake!" She yelled his name. Tears, blood, and adrenaline all hindered her vision. "Blake!" she repeated.

Hunched over, he walked to her. "I'm right here."

At that moment, she accepted that they were connected by their past even if the thread was thin.

"I'm all right." He leaned in and put an arm around her.

She was speechless and numb. She had to place herself out of body. Focus. Being a cop, she was made for this type of situation. Yet the smell of blood burrowed more into her sinuses with each breath, inundating her and threatening to sap her strength.

Seconds had passed—or had it been minutes?—since the last round fired.

She looked over her shoulder to the right, trying to spot the ideal sniper perch, but the sun was right there, shining in her eyes.

Sirens wailed, increasing in volume as they approached. The noise impaired her ability to form solid thoughts.

She went to stand, but both Terry and Blake held her in place.

"Just stay down," Terry said.

"No. Please. Let me go."

Terry was the first to do so, then Blake. She rose to full height and shielded her eyes with a hand and searched the roofline across the street. Did she really expect to spot sunlight reflecting off a rifle barrel? A man standing on top of the building or on a balcony? An open window with a gun sticking out? Of course she saw none of these things; their shooter was a professional, and he was probably long gone. He'd gotten the targets he'd come for.

"We have to get across the street," she barked at Terry. "Now!" She took three steps before Terry hauled her back to him.

"You stay here. Wait for backup. Stay with the bodies."

"Terry—"

"I'll check on this. Not an option."

They locked eyes. He wasn't going to let her win this one. She wouldn't be going anywhere.

CHAPTER TWENTY-SIX

Blake paced in a circle near Madison, as if needing to relieve himself. His face was flushed, and his hair, which was usually perfectly set, was disheveled.

"They weren't after you," Madison said, attempting to provide some comfort. "If they were, you'd be on the concrete with your clients."

He blinked slowly. His jaw shifted slightly askew, then he nodded.

"Now, I need you to get it together." Speaking those words reminded her of the blood that soaked her face and, looking down, stained her shirt. For a brief moment she had left the present, her mind compiling everything and analyzing what the next step should be. First, she needed something to wipe her face. She couldn't carry on in this state. Her attention went to the limousine. "Do you have any tissues or wipes in there?" She nudged her head toward the vehicle.

"Ah, yeah, probably." Blake set out in a slow jog toward the car, but his steps stopped when he reached Anatolli's body. He stared down at it like he'd never seen a dead person.

She went to him without thought, but as she neared the blood pooling around Anatolli, she gagged. *Get it together, Knight,* she coached herself. *Focus somewhere other than here.* But the smell and sight of the blood was overpowering and— She emptied her stomach on the sidewalk just inches from the blood.

She straightened, wanting to sink into the concrete and disappear.

"Madison?"

A hand touched her shoulder, and she turned around. Troy Matthews. His eyes were piercing through hers again, and for a second or two, everything had gone quiet and time had stopped.

Dear God, I just puked in front of the guy.

She held up her hands to brush him off. "I'm fine." She couldn't bring herself to meet his eyes again. He was probably looking at her with a boatload of empathy, and she didn't have the luxury of getting weighed down with feelings. As if to spite her, tears fell. She probably looked like a ghoulish clown, the blood on her cheeks streaked by tears. "Just because I..." She gestured to the mess she'd made on the ground, trying to defend the waterworks, and just stopped short of wiping them away. "Cloth, Blake?" she pressed.

On the count of three, pull the trigger.

Sergey's voice, back from the grave. It was so clear, she spun around expecting him to be standing there—only to see him lying dead on the ground. Her legs buckled. Matthews reached out to her and stopped just shy of making contact. It must have been the glare she shot him. What did he take himself for? Her guardian angel?

"Here." Blake extended a white towel toward her.

She took it and wiped her face. The blood had already become tacky, and it clung to the fibers of the towel, like Velcro being pulled apart. Her stomach swirled again.

Focus.

She stared through Blake to a point beyond him, to the car at the curb. People were scurrying all around her as if they were scattered marbles seeking a hole to sink into.

A woman reporter hurried toward her and lost her footing, only avoiding full impact with the concrete due to a balancing act worthy of a circus performer. She was facing Madison when she resumed full height and made no steps to close the distance. She went to direct her cameraman to find that he was nowhere in sight.

"You need to go into the courthouse." Madison gestured with the bloody towel to the building that, due to the traumatic events, didn't seem quite so daunting anymore.

"In there?" the reporter said. "Why?"

Where the hell is backup? She pulled her badge. "We have to question everyone here." Thankfully her voice came out authoritative, despite her internal struggle for emotional equilibrium.

"But I didn't see anything." The reporter's chin quivered, ever so slightly, her dam of cool reserve about to break.

"Please, ma'am," Matthews said, his voice calm and reassuring. "You probably want nothing more than to get out of here, to go home and have a drink—am I right? But we need you to stay. Two men are dead."

The woman's eyes filled with tears.

"They were evil men," Madison was quick to add, hoping somehow that would tone down the tragedy and ease the reporter's discomfort.

Somewhere between the eye contact and words spoken, the woman had touched Madison emotionally. No longer fighting against each other, they were both in this unfortunate—and surreal—experience together.

"All right. I will go inside." The reporter touched the back of Madison's hand and left.

The intimate contact at the scene of such turmoil, in which the world had been flipped on its head, righted things again and cleared her mind. Madison and Matthews went around and directed everyone into the courthouse.

Cruisers screeched to a halt, their tires likely leaving black skid marks on the road. She breathed a little lighter. Help had finally arrived.

Higgins came running over to her.

She held up her hand. "I'm fine. Everything is okay." She gestured toward Sergey and Anatolli. "Two casualties."

"Glad to see you're okay." Higgins stood there watching her as if she were a china doll that had fallen off a shelf from a great height. His energy questioned how she had survived without a mark.

But had she? She didn't have time to consider the repercussions. Right now, she had a job to do.

"There are a bunch of people inside the building. Terry has gone across the street looking for the sniper."

Higgins's eyes went to Matthews for the first time, and the men nodded in greeting.

Madison gestured to the courthouse. "We've got to get in there and start taking statements."

Higgins directed a couple of uniformed officers to guard the bodies and sent others inside the building. As he did that, she was on the move. She couldn't remain static, or everything came in on her—the way the red bloomed from Sergey's forehead, her fear for Blake's safety, a man she thought she had zero feelings left for, yet that wasn't what was eating at her at the most. As much as Madison figured the world to be a better place without these Russians in it, their deaths needed to be accounted for. And she'd been cheated by their murders. She wasn't sure their paying the ultimate price for their sins was going to be enough for her.

She panted, trying to derive a full breath. *It would have to be...*

Somehow, she'd have to find a way to at least accept that they were no longer within her grasp. She would still confirm, without a doubt, who killed Lexan and find out what happened to Calin. And if they could find Sergey and Anatolli's shooter, she might be that much closer to resolving everything.

She glanced over a shoulder, but Matthews wasn't following her. He was headed across the street, and she already missed his presence.

Madison spent hours with uniformed officers collecting statements from everyone and came away with nothing more than a lot of excited stories and proclamations about needing a stiff drink. Some people hugged themselves and shook, their eyes blank and distant. They were the ones who'd never seen a dead body before today. They were the ones who had let the media desensitize them to violence. As a result, they were ill-prepared for reality and the blunt, unforgiving truth of mortality.

Terry came into the courthouse. His blond hair stood straight up at his brow, resulting in one-inch spikes. His face was flushed, but his features sharp. "Nothing. Not a damn thing up there." He was slightly out of breath. "Crime Scene is over there now, crawling over every nook and cranny. If, and I say *if* lightly, there is something to find, they'll get it. But right now, if it weren't for the two dead bodies, a shooter could be explained away as imagination."

Madison's gaze instinctively went to the front door of the courthouse, thinking of across the street. If the shooter left anything behind, Cynthia and her team would find it. Madison had to believe that.

CHAPTER TWENTY-SEVEN

Madison had a shower at the station and changed into an extra set of clothes she kept in a department locker. Her bloodstained clothing was taken for evidence, and she and Terry had given their statements. Now they were in the sergeant's office with him and the chief, both of whom appeared to be in the mood to execute someone. She was the first unwitting victim to stumble up the steps to the guillotine.

McAlexandar kept his gaze unwavering on her. "If you hadn't taken things into your own hands and rushed into Homeland Logistics, we wouldn't even be talking right now. Those men were in that spot because of you."

Now she was being blamed for their murders, but then, why should she be surprised?

The sergeant ran a hand on top of his head and passed a glance to the chief before he spoke. "I don't have anything else to add. You've left me speechless."

She'd always considered herself a strong person, one who never backed down from a confrontation—though not one to seek them out—and would persevere until all wrongs were righted. But right now, standing in this room, with two men who obviously had it out for her, her badge as their goal, it was too much. Maybe it was the turmoil of the day with this on top of it. She expected this absurd line of reasoning from the chief, but the fact that the sarge was in agreement hit hard. Her heart heaved, its rhythm bumping offbeat and bringing with it an overwhelming sadness. Her eyes filled with tears, and she cursed this reaction as a weakness, an evident display of vulnerability. She feared speaking, believing her voice would crack if she dared.

"I think you're being a little hard on Madison." This came from Terry, and she looked over at him. He continued, and the sergeant and chief were paying him earnest attention. It had her briefly cursing her gender, but really it was their outdated mentality that deserved cursing. Terry added, "Today had nothing to do with Madison, and the longer you keep us in this room, the further behind we get in the investigation."

"Well, it seems you two are intent on sticking together." The chief crossed his arms, and he took a few steps forward. He solidified eye contact with Terry and said, "Duly noted."

"Don't be like that." The words rushed from her mouth without thought.

It garnered a single raised eyebrow from the chief.

"You're both being unreasonable," she snapped. "Let us do our jobs. You do yours." *Whatever the hell that is…*

"What do you suppose we're doing right now, Knight?" Winston leaned back in his chair.

"Your job is to berate your detectives?" The tension in the air electrified, but she didn't apologize. "Make sure that everything from this shooting gets top priority in the lab, let anything else fall down the list. It's a foregone conclusion that the Russian Mafia has things to hide, and they were terrified we were getting too close. That's all this is."

"Ludicrous," McAlexandar barked. "You can't just go on a wild fishing expedition and hope you catch something."

Madison leveled a glare at him. "Why wouldn't you want your city to be a safer place?" She wasn't going to put her suspicions out there, but the only way Sergey and Anatolli ended up dead was if Dimitre Petrov himself ordered the hit. And there was the matter of how the media and the shooter knew about the time of the hearing.

McAlexandar met her gaze but was the first to look away, only leaving her with a deepening sense that the chief had things to hide.

Winston glanced at McAlexandar, back to her and Terry. "Consider your requests approved, Detective." Winston's voice had lowered from his previous register. "But if King contacts you about your response to any of this, direct him to the public information office."

"Not a problem at all." She left the room, grateful for a partner who had stepped in when she needed him. Maybe the tension that had been there with Terry had finally blown over.

CHAPTER TWENTY-EIGHT

Madison and Terry returned to their desks, him with a coffee, her empty-handed. She was still in shock that the Russians had been assassinated, let alone in broad daylight. Their murders weren't just about getting rid of them, it was a message. Whatever that was. Had it been her seeking closure on the Lexan case that netted this response? "Why kill his own men?" she asked, looking over at Terry.

"You're assuming Dimitre's behind this."

"I have no doubt of it. No one else would dare take out two of his men. I also feel their deaths tie back to Lexan somehow. We solve his murder once and for all and move forward. Might even find the sniper who took out Sergey and Anatolli."

"So you suggest we start by focusing on Lexan? A dead end." There was the hint of a partial smirk on his lips at the play on words.

"It's past time to resurrect the case. Besides the Russians, let's look at who else was around Bryan Lexan at the time."

"Wasn't everyone else cleared?"

"Yes, at the time, but—"

Terry rolled his eyes.

"Don't get like that on me. The letter left in Lexan's driveway had an infinity symbol woven into the fiber. My research led me in a couple of directions."

"Yet you still chose to go into Homeland Logistics and confront the mob?" He tapped his head. "Not sure what you were thinking there."

She stiffened. "Something you've made abundantly clear."

"And you're still relying on a stationery match to lead you to a killer?"

"I'll use whatever I can. Anyhow, Knockturnl uses the same envelopes."

"Knockturnl...Knockturnl," he repeated as if trying to jar a memory loose. Then his eyes lit. "Ah, the company owned by Lexan's ex-fiancée."

Apparently, he listened to her prattle on about the case more in the past than she gave him credit for. "Technically, it's owned by Jessica's husband, Mason Freeman. They got married a year after Lexan's death."

"But he was cleared, right?"

"To be thorough, we need to talk to him again."

"Sure, if you say so."

"I do. We also can't ignore the evidence at the warehouse of several victims."

"And this connects to Lexan how?"

"Cynthia found a watch with the initials *JC* at Homeland Logistics."

Terry let out a jagged breath. "A watch with the initials *JC*? Obviously I'm missing something."

"James Calin. He was the man we tracked the phone call to." Terry still looked confused, so she elaborated. "The day Lexan went missing, his fiancée received a call that his life was pretty much over. That call traced back to James Calin. At the time, we searched his apartment and found his blood, but his body has never turned up. Not to this day."

"Let me guess. You think the Russians killed him too."

"Seems quite possible. Blood samples were found at the warehouse too, but they're not useful beyond blood type. Calin's type was there, though his is a common one."

"Okay, so you also want us to look into a murder for which we don't have a body? I'm hearing that right?"

"Why are you being so difficult?"

"One of us needs to remain grounded."

She'd pretend he never said that. "I say we keep focused on Lexan. As you so crassly put it—a murder for which we do have a body. I say we go talk to Mason Freeman now."

"I'm not going anywhere right now." He nudged out his chin. "Not after today."

So, he still had an issue with her. "What's really bugging you? Can we at least talk about it?" She slapped her mouth shut. Now she was encouraging a conversation about feelings? After only one visit to a shrink. She shook her head. He got up with his coffee, and she followed him to a conference room.

She closed the door behind them. "Do you want a new partner?" The question hurt to verbalize. "Listen, what I did—"

"Was stupid." He took a seat.

She sat beside him. "I did it for a reason."

"It was still stupid. You could have been killed. I know we've hashed it to death. Ha." He put his cup to his lips.

Was he hiding his emotions behind his mug? Dr. Connor may have been right. What Madison had done may have been a lot for him to process, and he could have faced feelings he wasn't comfortable with.

Madison glanced around the room, her eyes taking in the side table, the framed print on the wall, the clock. "How is the baby doing?" she asked, showing personal concern.

He eyed the door as if he was debating whether to get up and leave. He'd become good at walking away lately. It was like he didn't want to confront any issues but would rather skirt around them.

He put his cup on the table and swiveled his chair to fully face her. "We don't know yet."

"So there is something you're concerned about?"

"Spina bifida."

"Oh." She wanted to tell him everything would be all right, but she wouldn't dare. She couldn't secure the future for his baby any more than she could her own. With the thought came a revelation. Nothing was worth gambling one's life on—even justice, and especially pride. "I hope things work out." She smiled, hoping he would accept the gesture at reconciling the friendship.

"Thank you." He studied her. "So my turn to ask. What's really going on with you?" The spark in his eyes disclosed that his question probed so much deeper than she was willing to go. He was after what fueled her against the mob. "You say it's just about Lexan…the reason you went to Homeland in the first place, but there's something else that has you obsessed with the mob."

"I just want them to pay for the things they've done, for the people they've murdered."

"Huh. Sticking to that, I see, and you're willing to die for this." He didn't pose it as a question.

Madison swore his eyes were wet. "Like I've said, I came out of it alive."

"Just because you're here doesn't mean you're all right. You're going to a shrink, for crying out loud, Maddy. Your wrist is sprained. You're on medication for it. Maybe it's affecting your judgment?"

"It's only Aleve, over-the-counter, now." She rose and took a few steps, pacing the perimeter of the conference table. "There are still questions that need answers."

"I just wish you weren't willing to sacrifice yourself to get them." He wasn't looking at her now.

Connor had been right. There was no way around it. She needed to apologize. "I'm sorry I hurt you, Terry." The words fell from her lips, and she hoped he would accept them for their sincerity and that they could get back to the way things were before.

He didn't respond. It was time to come clean about her past—why she hated the Russians, and the true reason she'd become a cop in the first place. But she still couldn't bring herself to verbalize it to him—not yet.

CHAPTER TWENTY-NINE

He toyed with the ring on his pinkie finger, the Scotch having successfully lulled him into complacency, where right and wrong didn't exist, only instinct for survival. He was starting to lose count of the times he revisited the same thoughts, the same fears.

He lifted the crystal tumbler for another sip, his hand shaking as he did so. There would be no need to make a confirmation phone call saying the job was completed. The story was the top headline for every news station in a hundred-mile radius—if not farther.

He looked at his TV, to the evening report playing out on the screen. The volume was muted, but the story was obvious as the cameraman panned the chaos that had unfolded at the courthouse that morning.

With each replay of the assassinations, it sank in that he had essentially pulled the trigger. The lives of those two Russians were taken by his hand—even if he was only one link in the chain.

While he wagered on the results of sharing the information he had, the reality was harder to accept. He had started out with his ideals and morals—but money, it had the magic spell necessary to thwart all his good intentions. He quickly came to realize with money came power. With power came authority. With authority came control.

In fact, the highest price was paid to those willing to sell their soul, and this statement could define him. Its premise had lined his pocketbook well.

He gulped the last of the Scotch, the amber liquid burning all the way down his throat.

He was growing impatient. A good friend of his had assured him his time in the limelight was coming very soon, but as was the case with those in control, could he be trusted?

Madison and Terry benched a visit to Mason Freeman until tomorrow. She remembered Cynthia's offer to get drunk and it held appeal, but Cyn would be tied up in the lab all night processing evidence. Madison had only two options—go home and drink with Hershey for company or go out. The thought of staying in after today sounded horrible. At least with the second choice, she would be surrounded by people, so it wouldn't be quite as lonely. She popped home for Hershey, though, and spent some time with him and tended to his needs before loading into a taxi.

It was eight o'clock when she was dropped off in front of the Cracker Jack, a popular watering hole on the edge of downtown. They played good music, and the lighting was always dim. The crowd they drew was in their thirties and up, and people here typically stayed to themselves or within their pack of friends. And being a weeknight, it probably wouldn't be too busy. People around, but she'd have some privacy.

She slipped into a corner booth and ordered a large red wine. She tapped a foot to the music playing over the speakers. It had a good beat.

"Here you go." Her server, a thin rail of a woman, delivered the wine and walked away.

Madison took a long draw on the cabernet sauvignon. A couple at the bar were flirting with each other. The man's arm was wrapped around the woman, his fingers caressing the top of her arm. She was leaned against his side, her fingers pointing at him as she broke into laughter at something he must have said.

Madison took another swallow of her wine. Maybe she had been too hard on Sovereign. She had loved him at one time, and a part of her still did, but was it enough to overlook all the pain he'd caused her?

Another sip of wine.

There was no way she could find it within herself to forgive him to the point she would become vulnerable again. Why would she be so stupid as to risk heartbreak a second time? She certainly wouldn't be able to turn to her mother for comfort. She'd just be prepared with the cliche "leopards don't change their spots."

As Madison's drink soothed her, she could imagine forgiving Sovereign and even forgetting—to an extent. But she wasn't prepared to hook up with him again.

At the bar, the man nestled his face in the woman's neck, and she turned to him. Their mouths were on each other's in a hot second.

Madison took a deep breath. Her glass was nearly empty. She needed more wine, but the way the alcohol was hitting her head due to her empty stomach, maybe she should order something to eat too. She signaled her server, asked for a refill, and ordered an appetizer sample platter; she was too hungry to decide on one thing.

She pinched the stem of the glass, and despite trying to keep her eyes off the couple, she was gawking at them.

In the moment in which she thought she might die, she'd promised herself many things, including letting people in and loving them with all her heart. Easy to vow when she didn't think she'd have to follow through.

It's said that time heals all wounds, but that hadn't been true in her case so far. Or was it that she hadn't given it a fair chance? She had let the pain Sovereign inflicted make her bitter and hold her back from opening up to new relationships. If she was going to stand a chance of having a true, meaningful romance, she had to release Toby Sovereign completely. Forgive, forget, and release.

She drained the rest of her glass, and when she lowered it, two people were headed to her table.

"Here you go." The server set down a full wineglass in front of her as Troy Matthews slid into the booth across from Madison. The server smiled from Madison to Matthews. "What can I get you?" she asked him.

"I'll have a couple shots of Jameson. Neat."

He's staying?

"You got it." The server flashed a smile, hinting at seduction, and snatched Madison's empty glass before leaving.

Madison supposed Matthews was used to this treatment, but she wasn't willing to sacrifice her intelligence and start batting her eyelashes at him. And if it were anyone other than Matthews who'd just invited himself to sit with her, she would have told him where to go. But he had saved her life. She took a long draw on her wine.

"Rough day, wasn't it, Bulldog?" Troy said, his eyes penetrating hers again.

She wanted to be sarcastic, as *rough day* went without saying, but she was also assaulted by that dreaded nickname again. She grimaced.

"Oh, the nickname. You don't exactly like it."

"Someone's a detective." She smirked and took a small sip of wine.

Just barely the hint of a smile graced his lips. "Well, I think it suits you."

"Hmm." She took another sip of wine, then lowered her glass and pushed it away. She needed to slow down.

The server returned with his double shot in a rocks glass and left.

"So you're a Scotch man." Madison pointed to the amber liquid.

"Oh, this isn't Scotch. It's Irish whiskey."

"Same thing."

"Oh, no, it is not." He reacted quickly, almost like he took offense to her conclusion. "They have different base ingredients, and Scotch is distilled twice, while Irish whiskey is distilled thrice."

"*Thrice.* Now there's a word." It sounded like something her partner, Terry, might say or like it belonged in a Shakespearian play.

"Well, three times then. It results in the Irish whiskey having a smoother finish."

"I'll take your word for it."

"As you should."

There was something in the way he looked at her, his eyes tracing her face and studying her eyes. She let her gaze drift to the couple at the bar. They were getting up to leave. The man was helping the woman with her coat. Madison's attention went back to Matthews. He was perfect to look at, in every way a man should be. He had the sharp jawline, the athletic build that likely came from hours spent in a gym, a toned chest, strong arms… She couldn't forget the ripped abs.

"Toast?" Matthews held up his glass.

She lifted hers. "To…?"

"How about the beginning of a new friendship?"

"Ah, yeah, sure." She clinked her glass to his and downed a swallow. Maybe it was time she left and took a taxi home. In the least she should stop drinking until she ate, before she made a stupid mistake. Then she remembered her food order. She couldn't leave just yet. Maybe if she focused on what she knew best—work—her mind would get off his stunning green eyes. "Today's events came as quite a shock."

"That's for sure. Guessing it's what drove you here tonight?"

She nodded. She debated whether she should admit she didn't want to go home and be alone, for fear it would make her look like a loser, or he'd take it to mean more than it did—that she'd love his company.

"Yeah, me too," he admitted. "Plus, I didn't want to go home and drink alone. It's nice to at least have people around."

She couldn't imagine he'd ever be alone. She also admired his fearless honesty.

"You did well today," he said, saving her from the need to cultivate the previous topic of conversation.

"You think so?"

"Well, your testimony was enough to support that a crime had been committed, so I'd say, yeah, you did well."

Her mind went straight to the aftermath. It was hard to believe it was the same day that she'd pointed at Sergey and Anatolli from the stand, identifying them as her captors, and now they were dead.

"How are you feeling?" His question struck her like he'd read her mind.

At first, she wasn't sure why he'd asked, but then the horrid details came back to her. "Just so you know, I don't normally vomit at a crime scene." *Not even at a really bloody one despite the inclination.* She pushed out her chin.

Amusement touched his features, but he didn't laugh or smile. "That's probably a good thing."

"You could say that." She took another sip of wine. "I got good news today."

He took a draw on his whiskey, and she felt a stirring of envy watching his mouth on the glass. She pulled her thoughts back to work.

"I've been reinstated to full duty."

"Great. Well, congrats."

"Thanks." She locked gazes with him, self-conscious. She had to be delusional to think Troy would be interested in her. She sucked in her gut and sat up taller and hated herself the moment she did. Maybe she should just leave and cut her losses. "I should probably get a cab home. Food's coming. Enjoy. This should cover it and my wine." She slapped thirty dollars on the table and got up.

"Why are you leaving now? Something I said?"

"No, not at all. It's getting late. Maybe another time?" There would be no other time. And it was far from late. She'd gotten there at eight. She just needed to guard herself from Troy Matthews.

The server came with the appetizer platter and two plates. She glanced at Madison but let her gaze linger on Matthews. He was busy watching Madison, and the server left.

"You can't go now," he said to Madison. "The food just got here."

The smell of jalapeno poppers, sour cream, potato skins with bacon, mozzarella sticks— Her stomach growled, and she sat back down. She was just eating with a coworker. There was nothing going on. She took a mozzarella stick and dipped it in the marinara.

"This stuff will kill you given time." Matthews waved a hand over the assortment of finger foods.

"So will our jobs."

"I'll drink to that." He toasted again, and they clinked glasses.

Troy downed the rest of his whiskey, summoned the server for a refill, and held up two fingers, gesturing toward Madison.

Madison glanced at the waitress, back to Troy. "Oh, I don't think I—"

"Nonsense. Just have one."

"Okay. A single shot." She smiled at the server, and she walked off.

His face became dark and serious. "You were so lucky."

It was clear he was referring to her time at the warehouse. "I was," she admitted.

"It must have been terrifying."

She didn't really want to talk about it, desiring to keep the conversation light.

He continued. "I found myself in a mess years ago, but it's clear in my mind. Everything went wrong from the start. I was working under— Oh, I won't tarnish anyone's rep, but let's just say he shouldn't have been the boss. He wouldn't listen when I told him we were breaching a property all wrong."

"What happened?"

"So now I have your attention." He took a drink.

He had no idea how much he had her attention. Why was she just noticing him after all these years? Why would he even be interested in her? Then she came to a conclusion. He was probably like every other man and looking to take advantage of her recent misfortune by being the shoulder to lean on. Nope.

"Actually, I'll leave it there for now. I have a lot of stories, Maddy, and all of them are true. Give us some time, and you'll hear all of them."

Give us some time? She stuffed a jalapeno popper in her mouth, chewed, swallowed, and redirected to safe territory, though not light. "So I've been trying to figure out why the Russians were knocked off, and why now? Am I getting close to finding the truth about something Dimitre Petrov doesn't want exposed?"

"I think that's a good possibility. The one thing troubling me is how did they know when and where to strike? The sniper would have had to receive advanced notice so he that could get set up, be there at the right time."

"Here you go." Two glasses of whiskey were set on the table. "How is everything?" The server pointed to the food.

"Good. Thank you." Matthews dismissed her and lifted his glass toward Madison. "We'll toast again."

"You're big into toasting."

"I love new beginnings."

Beginnings. There was that word again. It was like she had a life before entering the warehouse and one after. She'd been thinking brave thoughts before he arrived, about opening her heart and moving on, but faced with that real possibility—she was terrified. She'd get up to leave, but the food was delicious and she was pleasantly buzzed.

"Now, it's not as strong as regular whiskey, flavor wise, and it has an almost creamy texture to it." They clinked their glasses, and he said, "Cheers."

They both took a draw. Madison's eyes widened.

"A little strong?" Matthews asked.

"Actually, it's pretty tasty." Madison licked her lips.

Matthews smiled, a treat that didn't present itself often.

She took another sip, and it was like her mind cleared. Matthews had mentioned the sniper would have needed the time and place in order to strike. She'd considered McAlexandar before, and that suspicion was only growing stronger. "There's a leak in the department," she blurted out.

"The time of the hearing wasn't publicized, but it obviously got out somehow—as you said. I'd also thought the same thing," she rushed to add.

Matthews swallowed his mouthful. "Suppose that's possible. Do you have someone in mind?" The way his eyes scanned her face, he thought she did.

"I do." She reached for her whiskey.

"Are you going to tell me who?"

She shook her head. "Not until I'm certain, but I know what my first step is going to be tomorrow morning."

"What is that?"

"If I told you, you wouldn't like it."

"Try me."

"I'm going to see Dimitre Petrov, feel him out about Sergey's and Anatolli's murders." She expected an adverse reaction, him choking on his food, followed by protestations about how stupid that was. Behind bars or not, the Russian Mafia don was lethal.

"Brave, but I think that's a good idea." He pointed a fry at her. "And it sounds like a job for Bulldog."

"Would you cut it out?" Madison laughed, despite herself.

"See, you say you don't like the reference, but I think you do." He popped the fry into his mouth.

Not really, but she liked that he cared enough to assign her a pet name. That had to mean something, right?

CHAPTER THIRTY

Hershey slept at the bottom of Madison's bed, which had become a regular occurrence—all because she had forgotten to latch the kennel a few times. He figured out that her soft spot was him pawing at her comforter, begging for refuge in the "cloud."

Madison beat the alarm and, between squinted eyelids, made out a six on the clock. She listened to Hershey's light snores and stared at the ceiling, thinking about the assassinations. The same questions circulated—why, why *now*, and who killed them?

If Dimitre had ordered the hit on Lexan years ago, he'd gotten away with it so far. *So far*. She wasn't letting the case go, especially after recent events. She had met Sergey and Anatolli on their turf and essentially came out the victor. Was that too unsavory for the Mafia boss? Still, it seemed so drastic to wipe out his right-hand men—and risky. Surely, he'd have to see that the evidence would lead the police straight to him. It wasn't like people made a habit of taking out Mafia affiliates—not unless they, too, had a death wish.

But the one thing that had kept her tossing and turning until the early hours was Mason Freeman and his company's envelopes. Was it simply a coincidence that Knockturnl had also chosen stationery with the infinity symbol? Was Freeman caught up in all this with the mob?

But Freeman had been questioned in depth and cleared of suspicion in Lexan's death. The strongest motive was winning Jessica's love, but as Freeman had pointed out, he already had it by the time of Lexan's murder. On the surface it was a good defense, but if Lexan hadn't been murdered, would Freeman still be with Jessica? She could have forgiven Bryan and ran off with him. As for Jessica, she hadn't benefited from Lexan's death, so she had no discernable motive in that.

It was time to have a nice, long conversation with Mason and Jessica Freeman. Maybe after all these years, motive, means, and opportunity would reveal themselves. She definitely wanted to talk to the Freemans today. Something she'd happily do with Terry. But first there was something she wanted to take care of herself—regardless of what she'd promised Sergeant Winston. But just as she was going to rush out on her own, she was bombarded with guilt. She'd at least loop Terry in on what she had planned, but she wouldn't let him talk her out of it.

The yearning for retribution had been replaced by vindication, but it was still one step at a time. There were ways to go about things, and sometimes that meant biding one's time.

"You have a visitor, Dimitre." Jacob unlocked the door.

Dimitre looked up from the cot where he was reading a dark crime thriller. "Who is it?"

The guard's Adam's apple heaved and lowered. "She told me to tell you to…"

"To what? Speak." While he had patience when required, he possessed very little to none when it came to timidity. He stood and walked to the open door.

"She said to get your ass into the visitor's room." Jacob's eyes begged for mercy at the directness of his statement, but pity and compassion were not part of Dimitre's genetic makeup.

"Who the fuck does this woman think she is? I will not see anyone without a name."

Another heaving swallow. "She thought you'd say that."

"Spit it out, Jacob, or you will bury your family."

"She says her name is Detective Knight."

Rage surged through his system, and he clenched his fists. The last time he saw her, she was doing her best to hammer the last nail into his proverbial coffin, and that didn't account for her latest transgression that had cost him two good men. But her time was coming.

Usually one ages in prison. Isolation wears on the human soul. This stark truth is in the eyes, but Dimitre's told the story of someone living the high life.

He walked in, secured by cuffs, but the guards didn't follow him and latch him to the table. Despite being imprisoned, he'd been granted free rein and, Madison would wager, more yard time than the other inmates. His skin was tanned, and if his complexion wasn't enough proof, his bulging biceps were. She could tell that he ran this place like he did people on the outside—not that this fact should come as a surprise. He was basically living in a resort of his making.

When Dimitre's eyes connected with hers, they widened with what Madison concluded was delight. All an act. An uneasy energy filled the room.

"Detective Knight. Surprised to see you."

Alive was probably what he meant. She slapped the photographs of Sergey and Anatolli on the table—both pictures taken at the crime scene outside the courthouse.

Dimitre never reached for them and barely looked at them, yet Madison swore she witnessed gratification touch his features.

"Oh, what a pity," he lamented with zero sincerity.

"You seem really heartbroken over it."

"No sense wasting tears. Accomplishes nothing." He looked into her eyes. His cold soul on display.

"You had them killed," she accused.

He leaned back, casual, unaffected. "Now why would I do that?"

"You tell me."

"Why would I? That's assuming I had them killed," he backpedaled quickly.

Madison studied his face. There was no doubt in her mind that he had ordered the hit on his own men.

He went on. "I must say, you come in here with all this drama, and I thought you just came for me. Make small talk. Chitchat."

"Hardly."

"And you're not here to free me?"

That question wasn't worth a reply. "Who works for you on the outside?" Obviously, he had his puppets.

Dimitre's face went stoic.

"Who besides Sergey and Anatolli?" she pressed.

Sergey's and Anatolli's laughter pierce my ears.

On the count of three…

I can't move. Then the click of the revolver…

She wiped her forehead of sweat. The men were dead, yet they haunted her from the grave. She had to pull herself together. Terry had insisted on tagging along, and he was in the next room watching behind a one-way mirror. "Answer me this at least," she began. "Why did you kill Bryan Lexan?"

He looked through her.

"You had him killed," she said, not relenting.

His eyes snapped to hers. "I have been behind bars."

"There was a letter…" Madison switched the topic of discussion to see if he'd keep up or *slip* up. "It was from you, about the lawyer."

Dimitre slammed the sides of his fists into the table. "Like I said, I did not kill the lawyer."

"Oh, I believe you." Madison leaned back in her chair, playing along.

"You believe me? Ha, that is joke, da?"

"I mean it. You didn't kill him, but you *had* him killed. Who did it?"

"After all these years you're back again? You came here before. We have what you call déjà vu moment."

She remained silent.

"I take care of my own business," he volunteered.

The sliver of evil that flashed through his eyes rushed Madison's mind back to the torture room.

On the count of three, pull the trigger...

She took a deep breath. "Let me help you."

"You are funny woman. I am in prison. What can you do for me?"

"Guess you haven't heard. We have evidence that your business, Homeland Logistics, was used as a location for serial murder." It was no wonder Sergey and Anatolli were executed, though killing them had been a bold move. Cops were crawling all over the warehouse, and that spotlight would extend to Dimitre. "You would be lucky to see life on the outside again. Unless—"

He laughed. "You cannot tie anything back to me. And I have been in here. Thanks to you."

"Thanks to me, you'll rot in here if I have a say. You work with me, then maybe we can cut a deal." Saying the words pained her, but she would feed him any line if it made him talk.

"What deal?"

She suppressed a satisfied smirk. It was probably as close as she'd get to an admission of his involvement. "We'll discuss it after I get some information."

Dimitre looked up at the ceiling, and then lowered his head. "You want information from me? In exchange for what? Nothing?"

"Let's start with the lawyer. Who killed Bryan Lexan?"

"There was a man who used to come to see me."

"We don't have time for games."

"He wore a strange hat. Round top with flat edge. Bowler hat, I think they call it."

Can this be a fresh lead? She had searched Dimitre's visitor log in extensive detail years ago, but it was a trail that led to a dead end. And it wasn't like the list noted wardrobe preferences. "Why did this man come to see you?"

"He used to be an acquaintance."

"Used to be? As in he's dead?"

Dimitre shrugged.

"What was his name?"

Dimitre leaned back. Silent.

"When did he come see you?" she asked unswayed by his lack of cooperation.

"Nah, you get everything while I get no deal. Not stupid." He tapped a finger to his head.

Madison suspected it must have been around the time of Lexan's murder, but she acted as if he bored her and stood.

"I will give you one more thing because I like you," he said, stopping her from leaving. "I don't think he went by his real name."

She slipped back into the chair. "What was the name he—"

"I said one more thing, not two."

She dared to continue holding eye contact with him. While most would back down from a man with such an evil reputation, she had proved she held no fear—hadn't she? She had stormed into a mob business front and confronted Petrov's two right-hand men. She didn't back down. Even a threat from the head of the Mafia wouldn't stop her from pursuing answers. Only her cold body on a slab in the morgue had that stopping power.

She swallowed roughly.

We simply call it roulette when we play. The Russian part would be redundant.

Her eye contact faltered for a fraction of a second. "I will be back."

"I count on it, love."

The term of endearment slipping from his tongue made her stomach churn. He was trying to gain control over her. She refused to let that happen.

CHAPTER THIRTY-ONE

Madison brushed past Terry en route to the prison warden's office.

"If you're after Dimitre's visitor log, I thought you went over that in detail many times," Terry said.

"I did. Years ago. But it's not so much what's on record that I'm curious about." She stopped walking and waited for Terry to catch up.

"You think Dimitre runs this prison."

"There's no doubt in my mind, just as he's behind Sergey's and Anatolli's deaths."

"But why, and why now?"

"The questions of the day, and I'm going to figure it out."

"I heard everything he said in there. Are you sure you're all right?"

"Fine, Terry." She resumed walking.

She knocked on the warden's door, and she and Terry were summoned with, "Come on in."

A man in his midforties sat behind the desk. A nameplate announced him as Howard Buckley. He straightened when he caught sight of their badges.

"We have questions about one of your prisoners," Madison said.

"Dimitre Petrov?"

"Good guess." Not that she believed that's what it was for one hot second.

"Heard you were here to see him." He laced his fingers on the desk and directed Terry to close the door.

Terry did so and took a seat in one of the two chairs across from the man. Madison remained standing but passed a glance at her partner.

"We need a list of his visitors," Madison pushed out.

"Whoever's on the books, I guess."

"Not exactly what I'm looking for here," she said. "More interested in off-the-record visitors."

"He doesn't get any."

"None? I find that hard to believe. Let me guess, and no phone calls."

"Yeah, that's right."

"Uh-uh. Did he buy you too?"

"Excuse me."

Terry looked over his shoulder at her as if she was being too direct and brash. She ignored him.

"We'd like to get this over with, nice and quick." Madison paced a few steps, her fingers grazing the edge of the paperwork that sat on his desk. "Honesty is a good way to get there. You tell us what we want to know, and we won't dig into your life." She made eye contact with him and held the silence. This was what some might consider a strategic chess move, not that she'd ever played the game.

"I can't tell you anything," he said, his voice fluctuating.

"The man has power in here. It's obvious. How much power? Well, we dig a little further and find out." Her gaze slipped to a framed photograph on a filing cabinet. It was the warden on a beach with a beautiful woman. She picked up the picture. "Your wife?"

"Listen." The warden got up from his chair and took the photo from her. "He is a powerful man, but I run this prison."

Madison gave him a look and sat down. "Are you sure you do?"

He cleared his throat, reset the frame, and took his seat again. His eyes shifted around the room.

"Those must be your kids." Madison pointed to another photo.

"Get your focus off my family, Detective. What is it you want?"

Madison glanced at Terry. "Tell us about Dimitre's visitors, the ones off the record."

"There aren't any, I told you. If it's not in the book—"

"You run this prison. That is what you just said, isn't it?"

The silence was a live entity in the room, and it crackled with energy.

"That man has blood on his hands," Madison began. "I'm not going to lie to you and say those murdered by him were all innocent, but some of them were." Madison gestured to Terry. He pulled out his phone and showed a photograph of Lexan's dead body to the warden.

Buckley's eyes fixed on the image. "Who is that?"

It was probably too great a wish to hope that the visitor Dimitre had mentioned was the assassin they were after, but she said, "First, you tell us about Dimitre's more recent contacts."

Buckley refused to look at her.

Madison snapped her fingers.

Slowly, his eyes lifted from the phone. He took a deep breath and let it out on a long, steady exhale. "These days only one man comes to see him."

"One man?"

He nodded and eventually met her gaze. Fear was buried deep within his eyes. Dimitre had guaranteed loyalty with this man.

"What you tell us doesn't go beyond this room. He will never know."

"How do you expect to keep it from him?" The warden scoffed. "He has eyes and ears everywhere. He knows where I live, where my wife works, that her dream vacation is to go to the Australian outback for a month. If he finds out that I told—"

Madison signaled Terry, and he brought up photographs of Sergey's and Anatolli's lifeless bodies.

Satisfied Buckley's eyes were on the picture, Madison continued. "You likely saw the news? Well, those were Dimitre's men—his *right-hand* men. Where do you figure you fit in? Don't ever think you're out of his reach. When you have satisfied your usefulness, *poof*, you will be finished too."

"And this is to encourage me to talk?"

"This is to help you make the right decision, to make a difference."

"What can I do?"

"If you help us out, you may be able to point us in the direction of a killer."

The warden rose, his fingertips pressed against the top of his desk. "I can point you in the direction of a killer. He resides in cell three seventeen, D block. His name is Dimitre Petrov." He shook his head rapidly. "I'm not talking."

Madison studied his face, absorbed his body language, and tried to read his thoughts. He wasn't simply fearful of Dimitre Petrov, he was terrified.

"If you could please go." Buckley gestured toward the door.

"All right, but if you think of—"

"I won't."

Madison slipped her card onto his desk and left the room.

"Since when do you back down so easily?" Terry hustled to keep up with her as she hurried down the hallway.

"I didn't back down."

He jacked a thumb over his shoulder. "It looked like you did."

She stopped walking and spun around. "That man is terrified. There is nothing that could make him talk, short of suspending him over the Hoover Dam or waterboarding him. Unless he believes his entire world is going to come to an end, we'll get nothing. We have to go about this another way."

"You're giving up."

"I've never given up a day in my life, and I'm not starting now."

"Then what is this?"

"Time to move on." She resumed her steps toward the exit.

"Where are you going now?"

"We're going to see Mason Freeman."

"Mason Freeman?"

"Yes, the man who married Jessica, less than a year after Bryan's murder. We did talk about him and Jessica before. You do remember?"

"Ah, yeah, but do you really think you're going to get something there after all these years?"

"It's worth a try." She was also curious about the man in the bowler hat that Dimitre had mentioned. Maybe Mason or Jessica would know who he was.

CHAPTER THIRTY-TWO

Knockturnl was nestled in a single-story warehouse on the outskirts of Stiles. It had ample parking for at least a hundred vehicles. When Madison did a quick background, she found that the business employed seventy-three people, with Mason Freeman as the CEO. He'd inherited the company when his father passed a couple of years ago.

The receptionist was in her early twenties, with lively brown eyes and bleached-blond hair. Her physical features and perky attitude reminded Madison of a young Britney Spears. "Welcome to Knockturnl."

Madison flashed her badge, and so did Terry.

"We're here to speak with Mason Freeman," Madison said.

The receptionist's lips formed a pronounced pout. "I'm sorry, but he's not in. He's in Jamaica."

"Jamaica?"

"Uh-huh."

"When is he expected back?"

There was a flash in Britney's eyes. "He went to a business conference there for those in the beverage industry."

Not exactly the answer to Madison's question. "When is he due back?" she repeated.

"Oh, well, he should be back tomorrow. That is unless he prolongs the trip. He has done that before."

"Did his wife go with him?"

"Not this time."

"We'll be back."

"Sure. We'll be here."

Madison slid behind the wheel, pulled the car door shut, and looked up Freeman's residential address. Maybe they'd get lucky and find the missus at home.

Freeman's house was a beige-sided, two-story detached. A covered porch stretched the width of the house, and the supporting columns sat atop a river-rock foundation. There was an attached three-car garage, which was more dominant than the house.

Madison parked, and her phone chimed with a text message. She read it and shared the gist with Terry. "Sergey's and Anatolli's autopsies are scheduled for this afternoon at three PM."

"You good to attend?"

"Yeah." She got out of the car before he had a chance to push for an elaboration.

Madison rang the doorbell, and it chimed some fancy tune.

Not long after, a woman answered.

Madison had no doubt it was Jessica. She was simply an older version with some notable lines around her eyes. She was tall and still slender, with blond hair that cascaded over her shoulders. Her hands gripped the door, showing off her French-manicured fingernails and a large diamond wedding ring. She wore a white pantsuit made of flowing fabric that draped on her frame. She opened her mouth like she was going to speak, but she didn't because a little boy of about six wrapped his arms around her legs.

"Mommy!" He stared at them, his blue eyes enlarging when they settled on Terry's gun holster.

"What can I do for you?" Jessica asked.

"Detective Knight, and this is Detective Grant."

Jessica's painted eyelids lowered as she analyzed them, but she settled her gaze on Madison. "Yes, I remember you. You told me Bryan was dead. Twice. I asked why you're here."

Unfortunately, Jessica had gotten pulled into Lexan's ruse—a body in a burned-out car ID'd by dental records as Bryan Lexan had Madison serving notice. "We have a few questions for you."

Jessica placed a hand on her son's head. "Is this about Bryan again?"

"Yes, it is." Madison held eye contact with her.

"I put this behind me a long time ago, Detective. I've moved on with my life. I'm happy now. If you would please excuse me." She inched the door shut.

"Are you police?" The boy let go of Jessica's legs and stepped onto the front porch.

"Come on, Michael, in the house." Jessica almost had a grip on the boy's arm, but he got out of her reach and shuffled over to Terry. The boy bent his head back as if he were looking up at a giant. Madison supposed, to the kid, that's what Terry was.

"I could be a cop one day," Michael said with delight.

Terry smiled at him. "You can be anything you want to be."

"Yeah. Yeah. I can be a cop." Michael circled Terry, who was beaming. He was going to make a terrific father.

"Michael, get in this house. Now." Jessica stared at her son.

He responded with a pout and stomped a foot.

"In the house," Jessica repeated.

Michael huffed and ran past his mother inside.

Jessica went to close the door, but Madison pushed her foot in there.

Jessica crossed her arms and sneered. "Detective?"

"No one was ever charged with Bryan's murder." Madison studied her eyes for a reaction. They didn't disclose anything but irritation.

"I told you, I had to let it go."

"He was a man you loved most of your life." She pulled phrasing she remembered Jessica using years ago to describe her feelings for Bryan Lexan.

"I thought his case went cold. Maybe it's best that way."

"Let's just say it's warmed back up again."

Jessica placed her right hand on her hip. "I can't think of anything I could possibly offer the investigation."

"That day, when Bryan first went missing, you received a phone call," Madison said, plowing ahead.

"Yes." She looked between Madison and Terry.

"You said he had a Russian accent?"

"Yes, we've been through all of this, years ago." Pain flickered across Jessica's eyes.

"We even discussed how, in thinking back, it sounded like a fake accent. Sometimes, when we're too close to a situation, we can miss things." Madison had to approach this delicately. Mason Freeman, now her husband, could have a connection to the mob, possibly even be linked to Lexan's murder. If Madison came anywhere close to exposing that suspicion, the door would slam in her face.

"I did see something." Her eyes lifted to Madison's. "It was in Bryan's den. I haven't told anyone about it all these years."

Terry's face registered surprise, and Madison was sure hers did.

"What did you see?" Terry was the one to ask.

"I really don't think it factors into finding out who, uh, killed him."

"Please, just tell us what you saw and let us be the judge of how important it may be," Madison said impatiently.

"One morning, I woke up and went to Bryan's den. He was always in there. He didn't see me right away, and I watched him reading a letter. He looked fearful. When he noticed me, he stuffed it into a drawer and slammed it shut. He tried to brush it aside by whisking me away for the weekend." Jessica took a jagged inhale. "He proposed to me that weekend."

"Did you go back to see what he put in the drawer?" Madison asked.

"The first opportunity I had."

"What did you find?" Her patience level was running low.

"There was a letter. I'll never forget what it said. It was printed in a bold red font and said, 'I pay with my life, you pay with yours and with those of whom you love.' No signature."

Dimitre Petrov. He had to be the sender of the note. Lexan had represented him in a murder trial. For it to read "I pay with my life," that probably referred to losing the case and going to prison for life.

"You remember exactly what it said after all these years?" Terry asked, sounding skeptical.

"I do…to this day."

It would have been best if Jessica had come forward with this information years ago, but at least it was coming out now. "What happened to the letter?" It was probably too much to wish that it was still kicking around.

"I put it back in his drawer. After that…?" She shrugged.

"And you never questioned him about it?"

"Never got a chance."

"Why didn't you bring up this letter at the start of the investigation?" Indignation whirled through her. The Lexan case could have long been closed.

Jessica bit her bottom lip. "I was scared, I guess. I knew it came from the Russians, and it didn't seem important."

"You *knew* it was from the Russians?" Madison pressed.

"It made sense to me, and you were already focusing the investigation on them. I didn't see the point in risking my life speaking out against them. And it's not like I had the letter to hand over to you. I did consider doing that, by the way, but when I went back for the letter, it was gone. I figured Bryan had destroyed it. I mean… maybe that was part of Bryan's ruse too?"

"You remember what the letter said clearly," Madison started. "Was there anything special about the stationery?"

"The paper? I don't think so."

"So no watermarks?" she pushed.

"Actually," Jessica began, "come to think of it, the sheet had a pattern…"

Madison's heart ticked up a few beats faster. "Did it look like a sideways number eight?"

"The infinity symbol? Yes, I think so. Oh."

"Jessica?" Madison said.

"It's the same pattern we use at Knockturnl for our stationery. Coincidence, I'm sure."

Madison wasn't ready to completely release the Mafia from her sights for Lexan's murder, but it was curious how the stationery Knockturnl used had also been a match to what was found next to Lexan's body. It was obvious back then Mason wanted Jessica for himself. Had he made that happen by getting his hands dirty? Further, was Mason Freeman somehow connected to the mob? Not her first time considering this recently, but it was carrying more weight. "Why did you withhold this?" Madison asked.

"Like I said…" There was a catch in her throat. She paused, then added, "I didn't think it—"

"You didn't think," Madison spat. "Did you see a man hanging around with a bowler hat?" She was grasping to put a name to the man Dimitre had described—assuming the man wasn't fictional.

"No. I just feel horrible." Jessica's gaze fell to the porch.

Madison was beyond the point of offering any sympathy or compassion for this woman. A man she had claimed to love for most of her life was six feet under, and she'd withheld a potentially vital link all this time. It was unsettling to say the least. She was certain her eyes were steel when they matched with Jessica's. "Don't leave town."

"Part of Lexan's elaborate scheme to fake his death involved using a cadaver from the university," Madison said to Terry. After the conversation with Jessica, her mind was back on the stunt Lexan had tried to pull.

"So he had a connection there."

"It would seem. But with Lexan murdered for real, that aspect faded into the background. It became irrelevant. But I'm thinking we should go back to the university and see what we can find out. Maybe the passing years have loosened tongues there, too, and we can find who might have slipped a cadaver out. On a different track, there was another name that came up during the investigation. It was one noted on Dimitre's visitor log at the time, a Mitch Hanover." She remembered this without needing to dig out the files again. "We never found him. No record on him. I'm just thinking, what if that wasn't his real name? What if he's the man with the bowler hat that Dimitre mentioned? Although, if he was involved, I bet he's dead, along with James Calin. Call it a feeling."

"I love it when you go by your gut."

She glared at him. "Cut it out."

He shrugged. "I'm just being honest."

"What if this Mitch fella is the guy who got the cadaver? Was he playing both sides—working for Dimitre *and* Lexan?"

"If so, he must have some huge cojones."

"Dimitre never would have told us about bowler hat guy if he was happy with him."

"Or he could want to waste our time," Terry countered.

"Maybe." The purpose Dimitre had for doing so was on the edge of her consciousness, but she couldn't quite grip it. "But we don't have a choice but to retrace the early steps in the investigation. We'll go to the university. Maybe this time, we'll have some luck unravelling this mess from where it started—the staged death." She was peeling out of the lot before Terry replied.

CHAPTER THIRTY-THREE

Stiles University took up acres of land and had a campus that rivaled those in larger cities. Madison had called ahead, and she and Terry were set to meet with Luke Sullivan, head of the sciences department staff. He was who Madison had spoken to years ago about the cadaver. Hopefully mentioning a bowler hat paired with someone who may have had access to the morgue, a name would present itself.

His secretary, a petite woman who wore her blond hair pulled back into a loose ponytail, escorted them into his lavish office.

Sullivan sat behind a mahogany desk that had a lamp on the corner with an emerald-green shade. Between this and the ornate touches of original wood trim, Sullivan suited the setting as if he were staged for a magazine shoot. He had a wild mane of white, and the corners of his mouth curved upward, even in a relaxed state. He wore a conservative gray suit paired with a white-collared shirt, but showed a splash of personality with an orange necktie.

"Good day, Detectives." He gestured to the chairs across from him.

Madison and Terry both took a seat.

"We want to ask about the staff that worked here eight, nine years ago and who would have had access to the cadavers," Madison said.

"Oh, have we spoken before? You look familiar, come to think of it."

"We did."

"You were asking after a Mitch Hanover if I remember correctly. And I told you then that no person by that name worked here."

"Great memory, and you did." Mitch's name had been one she'd tossed out.

Sullivan scanned her eyes and smacked his lips. "Not sure what I can do for you then. Well, assuming this is about him?"

"Do you have, or did you have, a staff member who wore a bowler hat?" she asked.

"Ah…no."

Madison remained silent and studied the man. "That was a quick response. Eight or nine years is a long time ago. Take your time to consider."

Seconds passed, then Sullivan's eyes sparked. "Ah, oh, yes. Darrell Kinton. He was in charge of the morgue."

"The name doesn't sound familiar. Was he on the employment records you provided at the time?" Even though she didn't fully press the matter of the cadaver, she had questioned the university staff. Everyone had checked out at the time.

Sullivan averted eye contact. "I believe you requested current employees, but Darrell was gone by the time you came around. We thought he went to take care of his mother."

"So you withheld information from an investigation?"

Sullivan adjusted the lay of his tie. "You came in claiming that one of our cadavers was used to stage a death. The accusation being that one of the staff was involved. Bad publicity."

"When did Darrell leave?" she asked, not impressed—at all.

"Not long before you came around."

"So the timing of his leave never struck you as odd?" Anger boiled within her.

Sullivan's cheeks flushed. "I had the university's reputation to consider. A board to answer to."

Madison studied his eyes, and Sullivan pulled on his shirt collar. "What aren't you saying, Mr. Sullivan?" Madison pressed.

"Er, rumor going around at that time was that he'd killed himself."

"Killed himself?"

"He, er, blew his brains out." Sullivan paled.

CHAPTER THIRTY-FOUR

Madison hurried toward the department car. "There's no way he killed himself. Not buying it. This Darrell Kinton, aka Mitch Hanover, got in over his head." She was trying to figure out why Dimitre had, in effect, sent her looking for this guy.

Terry performed a slow jog to catch up. "You sure can move when you want to."

"I'm driven, Terry. That's all."

"But you're not driven in a running pursuit?"

"Running? Never."

Inside the car, she typed the name Darrell Kinton into the onboard laptop, and sure enough, his body was found in his apartment eight years ago. A bullet to the brain had proved to be the cause of death, and the case was closed as a suicide with a notation of "no evidence of foul play."

"According to this, we're chasing a ghost." She slammed her hand on the steering wheel. "How are we supposed to fill in his story? Why did Dimitre bring him up? Maybe there's someone close to this Kinton guy who could provide answers." She scrolled down Kinton's background information and found next of kin. She clicked some keys and waited for the screen to fill in. "Kinton's mother is still alive. Melanie Kinton. She lives at Pleasantview Retirement Community."

"And what's she supposed to do for us?"

"Kinton is dead, but I never got anywhere with James Calin. Now I wonder if that's his real name. Nah." She shook her head. "I'm getting carried away. His identification was confirmed."

"You're thinking that Kinton and Calin were not only working with Lexan but knew each other?"

"Why not?"

"Guess so. Maybe Calin killed Kinton for some reason and took off? Not sure where that leaves us with Calin's watch being found in the warehouse though."

"Let's just go with Kinton committing suicide." She'd questioned Cole Richards, the medical examiner, and his findings more recently. Best not to go down that road again.

"Whoa. You're trusting the report? Impressive."

"Stop it." She gave him a warning glare.

"Were you ever able to track down any friends or family of Calin's?" Terry asked.

"Nope. Calin was orphaned at a young age, and his landlord described him as sticking to himself. No phone recovered or a bill to subpoena records and contacts. If he had a phone, it was a burner." She started the car and pulled out of the parking lot. "It's time to get some answers. Let's hope Mrs. Kinton can give them to us."

CHAPTER THIRTY-FIVE

Pleasantview Retirement Community was nestled on a few acres of land that backed onto a wooded area. Concrete paths snaked through the property, allowing easy access for those in wheelchairs.

Nina Priest managed the center and greeted them with an extended hand.

They shook hands, and Madison introduced herself and Terry and said, "We'd like to speak with Melanie Kinton."

"But of course," Priest said with her attention on Terry. "This way."

She led them down a hall and past a common area, where several senior citizens played chess, watched TV, or stared off into space. Madison shook off the sadness that threatened to capsize her. She'd lost her sweet grandmother, but at least she'd never had to live a single day in one of these homes—waiting rooms for death.

Priest entered room 132, and Madison and Terry followed. "Mrs. Kinton, you have company."

Melanie Kinton's bed was inclined, and she was watching a popular daytime talk show on the mounted television across from her. The topic of discussion was eating healthy.

"Mrs. Kinton?" Priest repeated.

"Yes, I heard you," Kinton barked, raising her voice and talking over the program. She glanced at them, her eyes a dull brown. "Who are you?"

"These two are from the Stiles PD, Mrs. Kinton." Priest lowered the volume on the TV.

"Please, stop calling me Mrs. It makes me feel old. And don't you be touchin' my remote." Kinton snatched it from Priest. As she spoke, her voice wavered, and combined with her long white hair, it belied all claims to youth. She flicked her gaze over Madison and Terry. "What do you want?"

"We want to talk about your son, Darrell," Madison replied.

"Bah. That there is a good-for-nothing nobody. 'Shamed he came from my womb." Kinton waved a dismissive hand and went back to her program.

Priest passed Madison a brief look, her eyes saying, *good luck*, before she left the room.

Madison had faced much worse. "Mrs. Kinton—" The older woman glared at her, and Madison corrected her address to a less formal one. "*Melanie*, we're here to talk about your son and—"

"My boy is dead and buried. Nothing left to say."

With her mouth shut, it would be possible to deceive one into believing Melanie Kinton was a sweet older woman. But once she spoke, the contortion of her face, the arch of her brow, and the darkness in her eyes made it apparent she had seen a lot in her life, and it had made her bitter. "All right," Madison said. "Have you heard of a man named James Calin?"

"Ha." Melanie waved two arms in the air, and then turned the television volume up a couple of notches.

Madison raised her voice. "James Calin?"

Melanie's eyes snapped to Madison. "Never heard of him."

Madison pulled up the dated DMV photo of Calin from eight years ago—the fact that it was never renewed was just another aspect that made his death all the more likely. Then again, he could be living under forged documentation. She held her phone in front of Melanie. "Does he look familiar?"

"No, and if he was a friend of Darrell's, I wouldn't know."

"You weren't close," Terry said, stepping a few feet toward the bed.

"Your name Sherlock, boy? 'Cause you're one hell of a detective."

Wow, what a peach! One more question, and then they'd go. "Have you heard of the name Mitch Hanover?"

"Have I…?" Melanie laughed.

"Mrs.— Melanie?" Madison wasn't sure what to make of the woman's reaction.

"That was one of Darrell's favorite aliases. He probably made good on that name over and over. The kid was such a screwball, he probably believed Mitch was his real name."

Mitch Hanover and Darrell Kinton *were* one and the same. He wore a bowler hat, so he was most likely who visited Dimitre. But for what purpose? Dimitre had described this man as an acquaintance too. What did that mean in the grand picture? As much as it felt like they were getting close to seeing what that was, there were several missing pieces still.

"Last question," Madison said. "Did he like to wear a bowler hat?" She just wanted to verify what Luke Sullivan had told them.

"I think that boy came out with one on his head."

"Thank you, Melanie." Madison extended a card, which Melanie ignored and looked back at the TV.

"Don't interrupt my program again over him."

Madison dropped the card on the corner of the bed. "Just in case you remember James Calin."

The older woman mumbled something indiscernible, but Madison suspected it contained profanity.

CHAPTER THIRTY-SIX

For now, looking into James Calin was a dead end, and Mitch Hanover, aka Darrell Kinton, was *dead*. Madison and Terry were back at the station to determine their next best step. Sergey's and Anatolli's autopsies were still almost two hours out.

"Let's just go with the theory that Dimitre ordered Lexan's murder because he failed him at the trial," Madison said to Terry. "Were there other lawyers who worked for Dimitre in the past?"

"Who parted ways amicably? Probably not."

"He can't kill everyone, can he?" It was sort of a rhetorical question, because a man like Dimitre probably could. But then again, he had to use some common sense in who he had taken out. It was possible there was someone out there who had dirt on him and who wasn't afraid to talk to them.

"So far Blake Golden's still on this side of the grass," Terry said.

"Yeah, he's not going to talk to us."

"Okay, but how would we find out who Dimitre employed in the past as his lawyer?"

She went on the internet and googled *Dimitre Petrov allegations* as a search term and found some articles. Although Dimitre had been accused of several crimes, only the one murder charge stuck. That was why she was on the internet and not pulling a background. She clicked on the first link. "We start with him." She pointed to her monitor. "Emanuel Douglas. Looks like he repped Dimitre against the IRS after he was already sentenced."

"So he followed Bryan Lexan?"

"Looks like."

"And the result of the trial?"

Madison scrolled down, picked another related article. "He was found two hundred grand in tax arrears."

"Yikes. Maybe this lawyer's long dead and that's why Dimitre has Golden now."

"Or Dimitre keeps different types of lawyers on his payroll."

"Still… Look at what happened to the last lawyer who failed him."

She smiled at Terry. His words might as well be him conceding that Dimitre was behind Lexan's murder.

"I never said it wasn't likely. It's always been about getting the evidence for me."

"Uh-huh. Well, even if this Emanuel Douglas is mostly a tax lawyer, it doesn't mean he won't have dirt on Dimitre." At least she was hoping he would—and that he was still alive and willing to talk.

Madison and Terry grabbed something to eat from a drive-thru and headed downtown. According to the records, Emanuel Douglas was alive and doing quite well for himself. He owned a medium-sized law firm in central Stiles, and his company specialized in both tax and criminal defense.

The receptionist was a woman in her early thirties with bright-red hair and a beaming smile. "Mr. Douglas has not come in yet today."

Madison glanced at the clock behind her. It read two. "It's the middle of the afternoon. Are you still expecting him?"

"He was scheduled to be in today."

Madison glanced at Terry, back at the receptionist. "Is it normal for him to not show up?"

"I'm not paid to pry into his personal business, but he has been different lately," she tagged on.

"Different how?" Madison asked.

"Well, he's been really quiet and jumpy…anxious? Yes, that would be the right word."

"Why is that?"

"I don't know." Her response came a little too fast to be credible.

"You can tell us," Madison said.

"Not certain this is the reason, but there's been this guy." Her gaze flicked behind them briefly. "He's been calling for Mr. Douglas a lot in the last few days."

"His name?"

"He never leaves it."

The skin tightened on the back of Madison's neck. "Have you seen this man?"

"No, he just calls."

"Anything stand out about his voice?"

"I think he's got a Russian accent."

"I need the number he called from."

"I'm sorry, but I can't do that."

"You want a warrant? We don't have time to—"

"No, not that. I don't have it. He never left it, and before you ask, we don't have caller ID—not that I could tell you precisely when he called either."

Madison and Terry saw themselves out. In the car, she got behind the wheel, Terry in the passenger seat.

"No name, no number, Russian." Her eyes enlarged as she looked over at Terry. "Do you think it's the sniper who took out Sergey and Anatolli?"

"Why the calls though? Why not just show up and whack him?"

She raised her brows.

"What? That's the term."

"The calls could have been to scare Douglas and toy with him. But you might not be far off with what you said. Douglas could be in real danger of being *whacked*." She put the car into gear and floored it to Douglas's residence.

CHAPTER THIRTY-SEVEN

Douglas lived in a palatial estate, and the front lawn was landscaped with more money in stone than the median selling price for residential property in the Stiles housing market. Douglas's BMW was in the driveway.

"His vehicle is here," she said and got out of the department car. She huffed it up the slight incline of the drive, chastising herself for her lack of discipline when it came to exercise. She thought of Troy Matthews's toned body. One could be certain he worked out. She was losing it. She shook away thoughts of the SWAT guy and rang the doorbell.

"Stiles PD!" she yelled. She gave it two seconds before pressing the button again and looking through the sidelights. Nothing within sight. "Stiles PD! Is anyone in there? Mr. Douglas?" She let a little time pass, then glanced at Terry. "It's too quiet. A man like Douglas would have help. Where are they?" She peered through the sidelights again. Nothing to justify entry. Still, she twisted the handle. "It's unlocked."

"We still don't have the right to enter." Terry's voice was near a screech.

He was right but something was *off*. She cracked the door—

"What are you doing?"

She held up a hand and inhaled deeply. Then gagged. "Yep…ah…as I thought."

"Decomp?"

"Yeah." *And blood.* She wasn't about to advertise her aversion to the smell and sight of blood. Given her line of work, she'd never live it down. "I'm going in. Let's see what we're dealing with first." She stepped inside.

The door opened to a grand foyer with a grandiose chandelier hanging overhead, and there was a wide staircase that swept up the right wall to the second floor.

"Stiles PD," she yelled as she withdrew her weapon. Terry did the same.

They spread out and cleared the first floor, then headed up.

The master suite was the size of a luxury hotel room. It even had a large chandelier to mimic the one in the entry.

"This guy lives like a king," Terry said.

"Guess that's what blood money buys."

Terry gave her a look that accused her of drawing conclusions based on a stereotype again.

"Hey, I dated one, remember? I should—" She stopped talking. Running water. "You hear that?"

"Yep."

The sound was coming from the en suite bathroom. Her instinct had her barging ahead, but Terry pulled back on her arm.

She slowed her stride. "Stiles PD. We're coming in."

He butted ahead of her, and not long after, he was holstering his gun.

She couldn't see past him. "What is—"

Terry opened the door all the way and moved to the side.

The sink was running, but it didn't have her attention as much as the woman on the floor. She wore a black-and-white maid's uniform, and near her feet was a cleaning caddy stuffed with chemicals and brushes. Her head was at an unnatural angle and braced against the toilet, her chin touching her chest. It wasn't a fall that killed her though. There was a bullet hole in the middle of her forehead. Blood had seeped down from it and marred her face.

"Looks like we found the maid." Terry gloved up and reached over to turn off the sink.

"And the source of the stench."

Madison fought the urge to cover her mouth and turn away. The blood was pungent. But equally disturbing was that the woman appeared to be in her midthirties; Madison was thirty-five. Guilt washed over her. "We should have gotten here sooner." Sorrow burrowed into her bones the way it always did at a crime scene. Her heart ached for the victims, tugging at her humanity while the violent acts simultaneously repulsed her from humankind.

Madison studied the room. There was a double-sink vanity with a built-in makeup table and wing-back chair. It was the cosmetic bag and powder brush that stood out because Douglas wasn't married.

Marble paved the floor and surrounded the Jacuzzi tub, which was big enough for four. On the far side of the tub, burned candles were in a large sconce. A romantic bath for two?

"It seems Douglas had a woman in his life." She gestured toward everything, and Terry nodded and turned to look out a picture window. "Time to get Crime Scene here."

"Say that again. I think I also just found Douglas." He pointed outside.

She stepped next to him and followed the direction he indicated. There was a man's body in an outdoor hot tub.

CHAPTER THIRTY-EIGHT

Madison couldn't get to the backyard fast enough, and Terry's footfalls hit the steps behind her. He caught up and edged past her. He had his gun drawn and ready.

"I don't think you're going to need that for Douglas."

"I'm not taking chances with our lives, Maddy." He gestured for her to hold back, and he went ahead of her into the backyard. She was briefly taken aback at his unusual behavior. Normally he had no qualms about her leading the way. It must have to do with wanting to protect her after her ordeal with the Russians.

The hot tub was sunken into the deck. Douglas sat inside, wearing bathing trunks, his back against the edge of the tub, his hands dangling down into the water. His head was slouched forward on his chest. There was no sign of a bullet hole, and clear water bubbled from the jets.

Terry rushed toward him and, still gloved, took his pulse. He shook his head.

"So he shoots the maid and finds Douglas here and kills him another way? What kind of a killer are we looking for?" Madison asked.

"Well, whatever the answers, the lawyer's in hot water now."

She raised her brows at his silly and tactless humor. "Seriously?"

He grinned and made the call to Crime Scene and Cole Richards. It looked like the autopsies on Sergey and Anatolli would have to wait.

Richards and his assistant took Douglas out of the water. While the cause of death was apparent with the maid, who came to be ID'd as Sonia Pike, it wasn't as clear with the lawyer.

Richards worked over the body in the meticulous fashion that defined the man. "Petechial hemorrhaging in the eyes, lips, and mouth. He was deprived of oxygen. From the look of the bruising starting to rise on his neck, he was likely strangled."

Madison imagined Douglas soaking before going into the office when the killer came up behind him. "Strangled from be—"

"Thank you, Milo," Richards interrupted her to speak to his assistant, who had motioned that he was going in the house.

He never would have cut her off before, but he was obviously still miffed about the recent past. Not only had she called some of his previous findings into question, but she'd also done some digging into his personal history. Prior to those transgressions, they had been good friends and allies. Now, that seemed like another lifetime ago.

"I will join you upstairs shortly," Richards added.

Milo sauntered off without a look in her direction. Maybe Richards's animosity toward her had rubbed off on him.

Richards looked at Madison. "He was strangled from behind." His voice softened along with his eyes.

That brief dent in his hard demeanor took her to the past when they had a level of camaraderie. A time when they would joke around and she was even somewhat attracted to him in a "very harmless, not going anywhere" way. Besides, he was a married man. He also had the brightest white teeth that stood in contrast to his dark skin.

"We'll wrap him up, take him back to the lab, and run the full autopsy. Preliminarily, I'd place time of death for both victims between seven and nine hours ago. I'll know with more certainty once I run some more tests."

Terry looked at the time on his phone. "Four fifteen now, so between seven and eight this morning."

Madison considered. Either hour was early for a maid, but… "I'd think closer to seven so he could get in a soak before work. Ah, speaking of autopsies, when are the ones scheduled for Sergey and Anatolli now?" She was surprised they hadn't already been conducted in all honesty.

"Monday morning. Eight AM." Richards proceeded to zip up the body of Emanuel Douglas into a black cocoon and take him away on a stretcher.

He might not want to talk anymore, but too bad. "Why not over the weekend?"

He stopped all movement. "I'm one person most of the time, Detective. And most of us need some time off."

Apparently, that was to excuse the delay? She shook her head. Two more bodies. One connection to all the victims thus far: Dimitre Petrov. And while several methods were used, she had a hunch they'd all died at the hands of one person. She hadn't forgotten the Russian caller the receptionist at the law firm had mentioned. She doubted it was Dimitre, but rather someone who wanted to toy with Emanuel Douglas's sanity before moving in for the kill. They were looking for a Mafia hit man. Had to be. "Dimitre's cleaning house."

Terry turned to her. "You believe he's behind all of this?"

"Why you wouldn't escapes me. Dimitre figured we'd hunt Douglas down, and if that's the case—which I'm confident it is—that means Douglas knew something we could use against Dimitre and his organization."

"Guess we're out of luck there then. Douglas is no longer talking."

"Unless…" She trudged past him, into the house, and up to the second floor. They'd never made it back there after finding Douglas. She now went into an office, the door of which had been shut. Papers were strewn all over the floor. The closet was open, its contents vomited into the room.

"Our killer was looking for something," Terry concluded. "Maybe you were right? Douglas didn't just know something; he had something on them."

She narrowed her eyes at him. "Forget *maybe*."

"All right, but why did they not come back for it before now?"

She didn't want to answer him because guilt was burrowing in her soul. It was all due to her poking her nose into the Mafia's business. Now they were doing their best to clean house as quickly as possible. "We have to find Douglas's girlfriend," she said, sidestepping his question. "If our killer didn't find what they came for, they'll go after her."

"How do we know they didn't get what they came for?"

"Not taking any chances. Just trust my gut."

"Your gut?" Terry laughed, but it ended abruptly when she glared at him.

She said, "Think of it this way, you have important information you don't want anyone to get their hands on. Where would you put it?"

"Somewhere people would least expect to find it."

"That's right, and in this case, it just may be with the woman who goes with that makeup table." Madison didn't remember anyone mentioning Douglas's phone or seeing one herself. They could subpoena for his call records from his provider, but that would take precious time. She considered the hour and another possibility. "We have just enough time to get back to the law firm to see if our nice receptionist can point us in the right direction."

CHAPTER THIRTY-NINE

Madison pulled into the law firm's lot just after five. Employees were filing out of the building and getting into their cars. Any later, and she and Terry would have had to hunt down the receptionist at her home. They still might need to get Douglas's phone records if she didn't know the girlfriend's identity.

"There she is," Madison said to Terry, pointing out the receptionist walking toward her car, her hand extended with a key fob.

Madison parked and jumped out to catch up with her, then asked if she knew the name of Douglas's girlfriend.

"I'm sorry, but I don't feel right giving you that information." Her bright smile from earlier was gone, and she threw her purse into her car.

On the way over, they'd looked for Douglas's next of kin and came up empty. He had no siblings, and his parents were dead. Typically, immediate family should be notified before anyone else, but since he didn't have any, Madison could tell the receptionist. She softened the delivery. "We found your boss at his home, and it seems he was murdered."

"He was...?" She covered her mouth and leaned against the car. Definite shock. "How? When? Oh my—" She looked at them, her eyes wide but dry.

"I'm sorry, but we can't answer all those questions right now," Madison said.

The receptionist pushed off the car and crossed her arms. "Does any of this have to do with that Russian guy who kept calling for him? Mr. Douglas was a good man. He always let me have time off when I asked. He gave out good bonuses at Christmastime. He—"

"This must be hard for you to accept." Madison did her best to convey sincerity—she did empathize—but the urgency of the situation trumped delicacy. Another life could be at stake. "We need to know all you do about his girlfriend."

She nodded. Tears beaded in the corners of her eyes now that the initial shock was wearing off.

"Where can we find her?" Madison asked.

"Yeah. Sorry, this is just—" She blinked away tears, but a few fell. "Her name is Lillian Norton. She's a really nice lady. I don't recall her address off hand, but I have it in the office. Emanuel sent her flowers for her birthday last month. Well, he had me send them to her."

"Can we please get that information?"

She palmed her damp cheeks. "Of course."

Lillian Norton lived in the north end of the city, a more affluent area of Stiles. Her address took Madison and Terry to a redbrick home. The windows were large and framed with white shutters that were purely cosmetic.

The doorbell chimed a fancy tune, and the door was opened by a handsome woman in her early fifties. Her eyes were warm and sincere, a pale green, but they held a wildfire.

"Can I help you?" She held one hand braced on the door, but it wasn't rigid, and her energy communicated openness.

"Lillian Norton?"

"Yes."

"We're detectives with the Stiles PD. Can we come in for a moment?"

Lillian led them into a sitting area that held two sofas, a loveseat, and two chairs. There was an oak coffee table in the center of the arrangement and a couple of matching end tables. Artwork lined the walls. Madison wasn't educated in the art world but swore she recognized some as priceless masterpieces.

Lillian sat on one of the chairs. Madison and Terry each took an end of the couch. Lillian looked between them, and Madison passed a glance to Terry. They had discussed this on the way over. It was his turn to provide notification, and with all Madison had recently been through, she was thankful for the reprieve.

Terry cleared his throat. "We understand you are a close friend of Emanuel Douglas."

She bit her bottom lip, and her eyes watered. "Ah, yes. What is this about?" Leery, tentative. She must have good intuition.

"We have bad news," Terry said gingerly. "Mr. Douglas was found murdered at his home this afternoon."

"What? No. No, it can't be. That's why I couldn't reach him." Lillian's facial features fractured, giving way to tears and a look of puzzlement. "Are you sure it's him?" A heaving sob racked her body. Lillian rocked back and forth. "I guess you said you found him at home… Oh, I just saw him yesterday."

"What was your relationship?" Madison asked, wanting to hear it from Norton.

"We were—" She pulled her hands from her face and placed them palms down on her thighs. She took a deep breath and looked at Madison. Her cheeks were now damp, red, and blotchy. "We were pretty much married—without the license or living together. But I spent a lot of time at his place, and him at mine. In my heart, I liked to believe we were married. Oh God! What am I going to do without him?" She flexed her fingers, and her eyes drifted to the floor but lifted up quickly. "You said he was murdered?" She sniffled.

Terry leaned forward. "Yes. Do you know of anyone who had a problem with him?"

"Yes, I do," she pushed out stiffly. "He told me he'd be safe, that he took precautions, but these people, they have a way of finding things out."

"Who, Ms. Norton?" Madison prompted, fending off the urge to come out with her suspicion.

Lillian leveled her gaze at her like she was obtuse. "The Russian Mafia."

Madison trembled as adrenaline infused her system. "The Mafia? Why?" Madison chose to play stupid.

"He had information on them. They didn't trust him. I tried to tell him they'd come for him one day."

Madison's insides were jumping. "What information?"

"I've been with Manny—that's what I call him—for nine years. I was with him when he first took over as Dimitre Petrov's lawyer about eight ago, and I told him I didn't like it one bit, but he was a stubborn man. He said he could handle it, that nothing would happen to him. All I could think about was the lawyer before him. That young man. Can't remember his name, but the mob killed him, I'm sure of it." She latched gazes with Madison, and she was tempted to offer her agreement, but she resisted the urge to speak. Lillian went on. "Actually you're that detective, aren't you? The one who was holed up in the Russians' warehouse earlier this week. You're also the one from before, the one who originally investigated that young lawyer's death. In fact, you're why that mob boss was on trial in the first place, aren't you?" Lillian shot to her feet. "You are probably why my Manny is dead. Get out! Get out of my house!"

Madison's body shook at the accusation, at the fierceness of it, at the accuracy. "Please, Ms. Norton, we need your help."

"Oh, you need my help? Now that the only man I've ever loved has been taken away from me?" Lillian doubled over with heaving sobs.

Madison went to her and debated whether to touch her. She didn't. "Please trust me when I say we will find him justice."

Lillian straightened out and stared at her coolly. "Like you did for that other lawyer?"

Again, the verbal attack may as well have been a physical blow. It stole the air from Madison's lungs, and it took a few seconds to find the strength to speak. "You said he had things on the Russians?"

"Yes."

"Help us help you," Madison petitioned.

Lillian let out an arrogant laugh. "Help me? Is that really your concern, or is it more to save face for yourself, for your career, for the Stiles PD? You can't bring my Manny back."

"No, but we can find justice for his murder."

Lillian's shoulders dropped, and her face softened—appearing like a damp rag.

"I can't even imagine what you're going through," Madison offered gently. "What does he have on them?"

"You mean *did*, Detective." Fresh tears streamed down Lillian's face.

Madison gave it a few minutes and then asked, "Was Mr. Douglas still working for them?"

She shook her head. "He cut ties about a year ago because of me. At least that's what he told me, but I suspect he still helped them out from time to time. The mob doesn't just let you go. You're in for life." Lillian excused herself from the room.

Terry leaned in toward Madison and whispered, "What are you thinking?"

"I feel for this woman. She lost the man she's loved for the last nine—"

Lillian returned with a stack of folders, full of papers, and extended them to Madison. "Here it is. All of it. I'm trusting you to bring him justice and hold whoever did this responsible." Lillian grabbed a tissue from a nearby box and sat back on the chair she'd been in before. "He kept notes on everything. Probably a hazard of his profession. Maybe he knew they'd kill him one day, and that's why he entrusted me with all of this? Though he made me promise not to ever look at it unless something happened to him. Well, I upheld that promise, and now, well, I want no part of it." Her chin quivered, and a fresh batch of tears fell.

What Madison now held on to was probably what the mob had been searching for at Douglas's house, and the reason the office had been tossed.

Lillian waved a hand toward the files. "I hope it gives you everything you need to nail 'em." The woman's wildfire was gone, replaced by palpable marrow-deep grief and anger.

Madison nodded. "We'll do all we can. You have my promise." The commitment slipped from Madison's mouth without much thought, but she'd stand by it. They would find justice for Emanuel Douglas and bring this woman restitution and, while they were at it, set out to right as many wrongs as possible that were committed by the Russians. "Do you have someplace you can go?" Madison asked.

Lillian blinked rapidly, and tears seeped from her eyes and down her cheeks. "What? Run? No, I'm not going to do that."

"These men are dangerous; I don't have to tell you that. They didn't find what they were looking for at Douglas's house"—Madison indicated the files in her lap—"but they will figure out where to come for them. It's only a matter of time."

"I'm not running. I just can't do it." Lillian crossed her arms.

"You are not safe here," Madison pleaded. "Let us get you set up in a safehouse."

"No! This is my home. Besides, you said you were going to catch whoever did this. You come through on your promise, I'll have nothing to worry about."

Madison's stomach clenched as she and Terry walked away from Lillian Norton's house. "I have a bad feeling about this."

"What are we supposed to do? We can't make her leave."

"I know, Terry." She'd still ask Higgins to keep a watch on her house. Just the thought of that sweet woman in the hands of a Russian killer made her want to vomit.

On the count of three, pull the trigger…

She took a deep breath and tried to focus. Her heartbeat was thumping in her ears.

We simply call it roulette when we play. The Russian part would be redundant.

Sweat dripped down her back.

"Maddy?"

Then a hand on her shoulder.

"Don't touch me!" Her loud voice brought her back to the present. It hadn't been the hand of a homicidal Russian, it was Terry's. His eyes showed empathy.

She could sense the unasked question—*Maddy, are you all right?* She was happy he didn't verbalize it, because at this moment, she wasn't sure she could lie. She cleared her throat. "We have to get back to the station and read these over." She brushed past him toward the car.

"Not tonight we're not, and…"

"What is it?"

"I realize it's a fresh murder case, but if I don't take this weekend with Annabelle, I might be the next victim. I'm sorry."

He and his wife were going through a lot. "Okay, I understand."

"Thanks, Maddy."

She nodded and called Higgins before she pulled away. He assured her he'd drive by a few times during his shifts and check on Lillian Norton. That still left her alone at night.

CHAPTER FORTY

"The bodies are piling up." That was Richards's greeting when Madison and Terry walked into the morgue Monday morning.

The weekend had passed with excruciating slowness with Terry taking the days off and Madison doing her best to respect his wish. It didn't stop her from going in and getting started on the files Lillian had handed over, but she hadn't landed on anything too implicating yet. Very disappointing.

Emanuel Douglas had essentially written a journal about his dealings with the mob. The pages were full of speculation. But surely, information they could use against the Russians had to be in there somewhere.

Sergey and Anatolli each lay on a stainless-steel gurney.

Seeing their lifeless bodies was surreal, like she was walking in a dream world. It was as if her mind didn't really want to accept what she was seeing, but their deaths didn't change an awful lot—not really. She was still determined to bring down the Russian Mafia. She would think that with them gone, these two shouldn't hold power over her, but the recollections of her time in the torture room with them was still ever clear.

She could swear their chests rose and fell with breath. Sergey's face came alive, and she could hear his voice. Anatolli's voice, too, was resurrected in her mind, his cackle audible.

"This must be rough for you," Richards said.

She looked up from the bodies, and the ME's brow was compressed, forming wrinkles that otherwise were not there, and Terry was watching her with concern.

"I'll be all right," she said.

"You don't have to be here for this."

"I realize that." She gave him a pressed-lipped smile, but she needed to be here, to know for absolute certain their hearts no longer beat—that they were no longer a threat to her.

"I will proceed then." Richards started by saying that given where both men were struck, it would have been instantly fatal. "Alive one second, gone the next," he added.

The fact that they'd left the world so easily wasn't fair. All the men Sergey and Anatolli were responsible for torturing and killing—likely a countless number.

Richards started on Sergey and then moved on to Anatolli. Even in death, Sergey was the leader.

The autopsies took longer than Madison had expected, but there were a lot of bullet fragments that Richards had to pluck out of their skulls.

When Richards finished with both men, he snapped off his gloves. "Unfortunately, because the bullets fragmented, it's hard to tell the type by looking at their present state. These will, however, go to the lab to be analyzed."

"Thank you," she said.

"You're very welcome."

"And Douglas and his maid, when—"

"At this point, I'll be starting this afternoon. But I can have Cynthia update you on their findings if you'd like. There's no reason you have to come back for their autopsies."

He must have read her mind. Normally, she'd make sure to attend every autopsy, but she couldn't bring herself to attend that many so close together. All the loss of life was on her shoulders. If only she had left the Mafia alone. "I'd appreciate that." Her phone rang, and it was Higgins. His message made her legs go weak. She ended the call but held on to her phone with a tight grip.

"Maddy...?" Terry took a step toward her. "What is it?"

"Lillian Norton was murdered."

CHAPTER FORTY-ONE

"I'm warning you, it's messy." Officer Tendum stepped to the side to let Madison and Terry into Lillian's house. The young officer looked pale. It wasn't his first dead body, but he was far from a veteran.

"Who found her?" she asked him.

"A friend. They were supposed to go to a local art showing. She came to pick up the victim—"

"Lillian Norton." She tensed, hating enough that Lillian's killer had taken her life; she wouldn't be surrendering her name too.

"Okay… She came to pick up *Lillian* and found her. She swears she never touched anything. She called it in, and Higgins recognized the address. Said you had asked him to keep an eye on her."

"I did drive by several times." Higgins stepped up to them. "Nothing looked unusual."

"It's okay, Chief." Madison put a hand on his shoulder and pulled out his nickname to tamp down the stark direness of the situation. He was carrying the burden for Lillian's death, but in that he was not alone. She put a hand to her hip and tilted out her chin. "Neighbors see anything—*anyone*—suspicious?" She looked at Higgins, but he deferred to Tendum.

"One woman said she noticed a large man with blond hair walking down the street Friday evening. Never saw him before—or since—apparently."

"Friday? It's Monday now. She remembered him?"

Tendum hitched his shoulders. "He stood out to her."

"Okay, so he was just walking or was he here at Lillian's house?" Madison asked.

"Just walking."

Madison wasn't getting her hopes up that this large man with blond hair factored in yet—but he was a new presence in the area, so she couldn't entirely ignore the possible weight to this lead either. But it wasn't like it would be easy tracking the mystery man down with that vague description. "Did this woman notice if he had a vehicle?" She was thinking maybe they'd luck out with a plate number.

"Nope."

Madison didn't say any more and took one step through the threshold, then came to a dead stop. The smell arrested her instantly—blood and a lot of it. She briefly wished for the job that would have her outside cordoning off the crime scene rather than being the one immersed in it.

"She's in the living room," Tendum prompted.

She didn't need direction on where to find Lillian's body. The smell would lead her there, but the trick was getting her legs to move. She shut her eyes for a second, trying to summon strength from a deep part inside of herself.

"You all right?" Terry nudged her elbow with his.

She forced herself to look at him and pushed out, "Yeah, I'm fine." And she was until she caught sight of Lillian Norton. Bile rose in Madison's throat, but she swallowed it back down. Cynthia was there, camera in hand, but stepped back to make room for Madison and Terry.

Lillian was laid out on the couch. One arm extended over the edge and reached for the floor, the other raised over her head, the wrist bent backward at an unnatural angle. But it was the collective image that had Madison's stomach churning. Blood covered her entire body and a good portion of the couch and floor. It was as if a can of red paint had been dumped.

Bile rose in Madison's throat again and she turned away, as the odor combining with the sight was all-encompassing.

"Wow. Looks like she was stabbed dozens of times," Terry said, stepping toward the couch.

Cynthia got in there and snapped off some photographs, then lowered her camera. "Agree." She glanced at Madison, but she was too busy coaching her stomach to calm down to talk just yet.

Terry bent his head this way and that. "Hard to say with the mess, but there doesn't seem to be any obvious markings on her wrists or arms."

"So she wasn't restrained while she was attacked." Cynthia frowned.

"Whoever killed her knew what he was doing," Terry said. "A professional." He looked at Madison, and she managed a nod.

Cole Richards entered the room then, along with his assistant. Cynthia stepped back from the body and confirmed she was finished.

Richards passed Madison a look that said, *See, the bodies are piling up...*

Then again, that could have been her conscience plaguing her. *"You are probably why my Manny is dead."* Madison never should have left Lillian alone.

Guess the other autopsies would have to wait too. Richards got on his haunches and examined Lillian. A short while after, he offered, "Preliminarily, I'd peg time of death as a couple of days ago."

Madison laid a hand over her stomach. Could the large, blond man who the neighbor had seen Friday night been Lillian's killer? If so, that would place him in the area around the time she and Terry had left Lillian Norton's house. Had they led the killer right to Lillian? Had he tortured her all night? "Any way of narrowing that down?" she asked.

"I'd need to do more testing back at the morgue before answering that question. But I would say it's possible her killer took his time with her." He pointed with his gloved finger toward the various stab wounds. "And before you ask, once I've had some time to spend with the body, I'll also be able to confirm which was the fatal blow."

"We've got to find this son of a bitch." The obvious, but a declaration of her ardent intent, nonetheless.

"You've certainly got that right," Richards said. "Whoever did this is cold and calculated. I can tell by looking at some of the wound locations that her attacker seemed to stab her methodically."

Madison glanced at Terry. The only thing that would have made Lillian a target were the files she'd given them. She and Terry had brought this fate upon Lillian. Madison turned to Terry, stared blankly into his eyes. "He killed her because of us, because of the information she handed over."

Terry barely nodded.

She held eye contact with her partner. "And if he killed her to get to Douglas's files, that means there's something in them the mob doesn't want to get out. We've got to get back to the station and really dig into them." *Make her death count for something...* As if anything could compensate for a life.

Madison and Terry spent the next hour going over the paperwork Lillian Norton had given them. Nothing yet.

Madison opened another folder as Terry returned from the bullpen with coffee.

He extended her a mug and slipped into the chair across from her. "Find anything solid yet?"

She glanced at the coffee, prepping her mind and mouth for the assault. It wasn't called "mud brew" without good reason. She was quite sure if a spoon was left in it for long enough it might disintegrate, but the coffee did have holding power, and that was what she needed to see her through.

She took a sip, still recoiled. "There's a lot here."

"Just nothing we can use."

She tapped a folder she'd read. "It's obvious that Douglas felt very strongly about the Russians being involved with Lexan's murder. And, yes, I realize that's not proof. Rather just conjecture."

"Admitting that is a good first step." He smirked at her, and she looked for something to hurl at him but came up empty.

"Very funny." She sobered. "But what isn't is that Douglas mentions other lives were taken by the mob. Unfortunately, no names or locations for the bodies, not that I've found as of yet anyway. Nothing verifiable."

"I can't imagine Dimitre being happy about the allegations."

"Yeah, but to kill three people to get to these files, I'd say there has to be something more concrete that we're missing." She fell silent, brooding.

"It's written all over your face, Maddy. None of their deaths are your fault."

It was hard to breathe, as if something heavy were sitting on her chest. "If it wasn't for me—"

"No. You're not responsible for any of this. You didn't kill anyone. Dimitre did. His hit man did. All you're guilty of is doing your job."

She balanced his words, his defense, his objection. "Thank you."

"Now don't get all soft and gooey on me."

"Me? I wouldn't dream of it." She would have punched his shoulder if he were closer. Her gaze dipped to her coffee, and she pushed the mug away. Turned out she wasn't that desperate. She scanned the page in front of her. "Oh, I think I have something now. A dump location." She could barely get the words out as her head swam with the lead she'd uncovered. She paraphrased what Douglas had written. "Douglas followed them out to a ravine, and they 'took care of someone.'"

"*Someone.* I see why you're excited." He rolled his eyes.

"Would you…stuff it?"

"That's a new one."

"There's only one area where there's a ravine around here. We're going to that spot now."

Terry pointed at the clock on the wall. "Don't you have an appointment?"

She glanced at the time and growled. Time had certainly gotten chewed up. It was going on two thirty. Dr. Connor would be expecting her in thirty minutes. "It will have to wait. I have a job to do. Hey, how do you even know about the appointment?"

Terry opened his mouth, closed it, opened it.

"Huh. I see, the sergeant. He wants to make sure you babysit me. I don't need a babysitter."

"Regardless, part of your job right now requires that you go to the shrink. Speaking of, you better get going or you'll be late."

Shrink… such a dirty word. She angled her head to the side and pierced Terry's eyes, but he held his ground. "Fine," she huffed and shot to her feet. "Don't go to the ravine without me. I mean it. Whoever it is has been buried for who knows how long already. Another couple of hours won't hurt them."

"You sure? I could go alone and check it out."

She narrowed her eyes at him. "You won't if you want to live another day."

Terry mocked terror and wiggled his hands.

She laughed. "Just read the rest of the files while I'm gone, gather whatever you can so we can use it to nail the Russians."

CHAPTER FORTY-TWO

Connor was in her chair, hair pulled back into a soft chignon and showcasing a warm smile. "Good day, Detective."

Madison pretended not to notice the doctor's discreet glance at her watch—a silent reprimand as Madison was five minutes late. She sat on the couch and leaned forward, her hands on her thighs, prepared to get up and leave at the slightest provocation. She shouldn't be here in the first place. Shrinks were for other people. After all, the only reason she was here was because she was required to be.

"Last time we touched on your relationship with your partner," Connor said. "How are things between the two of you now?"

"Everything is fine." Maybe if she rushed this along, she would get out sooner than the allotted time.

Connor wrote something down on her pad. "How would you describe *fine*?"

And it begins... The dance of give and take, the personal prodding, the relentless eye contact, and the analyzing of her body language. Madison sat up straighter, let her arms fall to her side, and leaned forward a little more to imply she was open to conversation and comfortable. Even if the truth was the opposite. She wanted to get on with obtaining evidence against the mob. Sitting here was like being bound with chains.

"Detective?" Connor prompted.

Madison smiled softly and shrugged. "Fine is just that. We're communicating and working well together."

Connor bowed her head slightly to the left. "I'm happy that things are *fine* with you."

Madison withered at the doctor's placating nature, and she didn't understand why she was making such a big deal of the word *fine*. *It's just a damn word!*

"So just to clarify, to you, fine is a good thing?" Connor raised an eyebrow, making Madison think of a schoolteacher putting their student on the spot.

"I think fine is fine. I don't think there's a need to overanalyze it." She squirmed. "And I really don't think I need to waste any more of your time. As I said, everything is going fi—good." Gratefully she'd stopped herself from saying the cursed word yet another time.

Connor rested her pen-holding arm on her chair. "I'm here to help you, Detective. You may not think you need to talk to someone. In fact, most people don't think they do, but psychology has been proven to be quite effective."

"Sure. I can see how it might help some, and I didn't mean to insult your profession. It's just that I have a job to do too. Just before coming here, there was a lead that I'm eager to follow up."

"By all means, pursue it when your session is over." Connor's tone balanced the line between reprimand and warmth. The silent reminder Madison was under orders to be there wasn't missed. Also the fact that Connor wouldn't be signing off until she was satisfied that Madison had spilled all her feelings.

Kill me now! Madison exhaled deeply and then proceeded to run through the events of that day at the warehouse as best she could remember. Parts she didn't—whether or not she went in with her gun raised, whether the Russians had fired at her when she arrived—she left out. When she'd finished, she said, "There's nothing else to say."

"How are you sleeping at night?"

She'd shared all that, and Connor countered with an unrelated question. Madison tried to tamp down her irritation before she spoke, not wanting it to transmit in her voice. "Just fi—good." She really needed to eradicate the word *fine* from her vocabulary—at least when talking to Connor.

"I think we still have more to talk about."

"Because I was going to say fine again?" Madison shoved out, and the doctor's eyes narrowed slightly in offence. "Listen, I don't have anything more to say." The walls were closing in on her, and she wanted out of there—now! She had things to take care of. "Can you just sign off for me? As I said, I have told you everything."

"I'd like to poke more into what prompted you to go to Sergey at the warehouse."

Is she even listening to me? Madison clenched her hands. "I would think that part would be clear by now."

Connor gestured for Madison to continue, as if it would amuse her.

"I wanted answers," Madison said through clenched teeth.

"Sure, answers, about that lawyer, Lexan. But why after so many years? Why at all? Why not just wait things out long—"

"Longer?" Madison snapped and shook her head. There was no way Madison was dredging up her family history and the connection to the mob, but she had something to say. "The mob's already had too much freedom—for too long. It's time for them to be held accountable."

"Already tried and found guilty." Connor poised her hand under her chin contemplatively.

"I know they're guilty—of far more than I'm sure I even realize."

"Yet you have doubts."

Madison's eyes snapped to meet hers. The truth reflected back at her—the reality that, yes, she entertained doubts from time to time. Lexan could have made other enemies, but his failure to defend Dimitre had landed the don in jail. He'd never seen the inside of a prison cell before that, as all previous charges were dismissed.

"Well," Connor prompted her.

"There are a lot of things to consider."

"You feel responsible."

"Responsible for?"

Connor swept her hand in front of her. "For all of it. For rushing into that warehouse, for putting your life in danger, for harming the relationship with your partner, for jumping to conclusions? Possibly for their deaths?"

And there it was—Sergey's and Anatolli's executions. She figured it would come up eventually, but that didn't make it easier to discuss. Madison's earlobes heated with rage. "I was doing my job," she hissed. "Their deaths are not on my head."

"Is that how you truly feel, Detective, or is there more to this picture?"

Madison had to look away and bite her tongue before she lashed out at this woman and the situation between them became irrevocable. She had to keep Connor on her side just long enough to get cleared. "There is only one thing I feel guilty about," Madison eventually volunteered.

"This isn't about guilt."

Her earlobes went from hot to blazing fire. Responsibility/guilt—she detested wordplay. Regardless, she found herself cooperating anyhow. "I should have pushed harder years ago and got the answers I needed about the Lexan case, but the next case came up, and then the next. Before I knew it, the Lexan case had gone cold. Reduced to file storage like the man never existed, as if his life meant nothing."

"You feel *responsible* for that."

"Of course I do." The confession hurled from her lips, followed by silence that ricocheted between them. When Madison dared to look at Connor, she was smiling.

"I think that will be it for today." Connor closed her notebook.

The woman must be unbalanced. She'd pushed and pushed, and Madison had cracked, and now it was session over? "We're finished now? So I can leave feeling guilty? Guilty over something I had no control over?"

Connor stood and came over to her. "As I said, Madison, it's not about guilt. I'd like to see you again."

"You've got to be kidding me." There went any hope of wrapping this up sooner rather than later.

"Here." Connor scribbled on an appointment card and extended it to Madison. "You keep working with me like you did today, and you should be free of me after a few more visits."

"A *few* more visits?" Madison swallowed back frustration and anger, and she still hadn't reached for the card. "I don't understand why you can't just release me now. I've told you everything." How many times did she need to stress that point?

"I believe we made some real progress today, but there's still a way to go. Now, I'll see you in two days, Wednesday at two o'clock." Connor pushed the card toward Madison.

She snatched it and stuffed it into a pants pocket. Why were things always worse leaving the doctor's office than when she'd arrived?

CHAPTER FORTY-THREE

The drive back from Connor's allowed Madison time to think—not that she wanted time with her thoughts. They stirred up more guilt and anger than she cared for. Logically, the Russians' crimes weren't her transgressions. She was no more responsible for their actions than she was those of a random terrorist.

She didn't have time to deal with all this personal mumbo jumbo, and that was one reason why she'd be making a stop before heading back to her desk. It would be a trip into the hornet's nest, but she was determined not to be the one who got stung.

She stopped in front of Sandy Taylor's desk. She was Chief McAlexandar's receptionist, and her desk barricaded the double doors behind her that led to the chief's sanctuary. "I need to speak with the police chief," Madison said.

Sandy called him, hung up a few seconds later, and shook her head. "He said you'll have to make an appoint—"

"Not happening." Madison rushed past Sandy to McAlexandar's office.

Sandy sprung to her feet. "Detective Knight, you can't…"

Too late, Sandy, too late. Madison had opened the door and stepped inside. McAlexandar was behind his desk.

"Knight, I'd say what a pleasure, but we both know I'd be lying."

Sandy shoved into Madison's side—the two of them wedged in one doorway. "I'm sorry, sir. She barged right on in here."

He dismissed Sandy with a wave of his hand. Sandy left but closed the door a little harder than necessary behind her.

"I need to talk to you."

"As I gathered," McAlexandar stated drily. "And obviously you're not going to leave until you do. Let's get this over with." He leaned back in his chair and gestured to one across from him.

She remained standing, one leg jutted in front of the other, and crossed her arms.

"Fine, stand. I don't care. What is it?"

"The Russians." She had always been direct, why stop now? She had to give him motivation to acquiesce to her wishes. To do so, she had to provide clear motivation. Potentially risky.

He leaned forward, his thumb tapping the back of his pinkie ring on his other hand. "What about them?"

"You're on their payroll."

McAlexandar laughed so hard his frame rocked. "You must have hit your head in that warehouse."

She solidified eye contact and hardly dared to breathe. "Did I?" Asked with genuine seriousness.

The chief's face reddened, and he wagged a pointed finger at her. "You better have your shit together to make an accusation like that."

Why was it every time she was around this man she wanted to reach out and strangle him until the blood drained from his face and the life force left his eyes? "Or what? You'll have me fired. Good luck. I'll fight it."

McAlexandar resumed his relaxed posture and leaned deep into his chair, resting his clasped hands in his lap. "You don't have anything on me, Detective."

"I'm quite sure that you tipped off whoever shot Sergey and Anatolli." Apparently, she was going down this rabbit hole, but it served a couple of purposes. One, she could work this to get her own wish—excused from seeing Connor. Two, his reaction would be telling as to whether he was in bed with the Russians. So far it was damning.

"Whatever you dream up. But do you have any proof to back up your wild claims?"

"I will get it."

"How nice of you to provide me with fair warning."

"I like my enemies lined up in front of me."

"Keep your enemies closer, Detective." His face took on sharp angles as he latched eyes with her. "What people fail to realize about that phrase is that it is unwise advice. See, with your enemies close, they know your weaknesses too, and they can take you down."

"Do I look afraid?" She held eye contact with him until he guffawed. "I'm glad you think this is all so funny. I'm coming after you, Chief, and you won't know when or how, but know that I am coming."

"You little twit," he spat. "Do you have any idea who you're talking to?"

"What are you going to do, call in the Russian hit man?"

His cheeks burned red. "Don't talk to me like that ever again."

She was definitely hitting the truth bull's-eye. "Why? Are you going to tell me I have no idea what you're capable of? Because I have a good feeling I do."

"You're judging me? You take the law into your own hands, storm into a warehouse that belongs to the fucking mob." He pulled down on his jacket. "As a result, half the city needs to be shut down because *you* acted recklessly."

His verbal assault had her reeling—and speechless.

"You have nothing to say to that, Detective? Yet I'm just supposed to look the other way while you do what you want? It's a joke. It really is. Here I am, put in this position. One of life's cruel jokes."

"One you put yourself in," she shoved out. "The only reason you want me off the job is to protect your own interests. It has nothing to do with anything else, so don't even pretend that it does."

McAlexandar's jaw slid askew, and he glared at her. "I think it's time for you to leave."

She slapped Connor's card on his desk. "Get me cleared."

She stormed out of the room, a part of her not believing she'd just spoken to the man like that. But she wouldn't be cowering in the corner anytime soon either. McAlexandar certainly wouldn't mention this visit to her sergeant, and she just might get out of seeing the shrink so she could get on with life. After all, she wasn't one to sit back and wait for things to unfold on their own.

With Madison gone, McAlexandar opened his desk drawer and took out the bottle of Scotch and a tumbler. The Mouth, as he referred to her, had the ability to turn a man of sobriety into a raging alcoholic. And he had no stake to that claim, so he was really doomed. But he didn't get to where he was because he backed down, and he certainly wasn't going to allow a loud-mouthed detective to bully him. At the same time, he should probably watch his steps. Just a little.

CHAPTER FORTY-FOUR

Instead of going to her desk, Madison checked out a department car and called Terry to meet her in the lot. "Are you ready to go?"

"I'll be right there."

True to his word, less than two minutes later, he was getting into the passenger seat. At least the passing time had allowed her to calm down.

"I didn't check out the ravine by myself. I waited for you," he said, clicking his belt into place.

"Good choice."

"The sergeant's looking for you, by the way."

He always was, and she doubted it had anything to do with her pitstop at the chief's office. "I bet he is. But when isn't he?" She put the car into gear. The only ravine in the area was about a thirty-minute drive, most of it city traffic until they hit the outskirts. She came to a red light. It was going to take even longer if they kept hitting these. "Maybe I should turn the lights on."

Terry looked over at her. "If a body's there, it's not going anywhere. No rush. Didn't you basically say that to me before running off to your shrink?"

She hated the sound of having a shrink and sure hoped the chief would take care of it. She glanced at the button for the lights. Terry was right. There wasn't a rush. "Did you arrange for Crime Scene to meet us there, help us take a look around?"

"Uh-huh." Terry looked out the window.

"I've been doing a lot of thinking," she said.

"'Bout time."

"Hardy-har."

"Hey, that's my line. Yours is *shut up*."

She heard the smile come through his voice but didn't turn to face him. Just then her phone rang, and caller ID showed it was Sergeant Winston. "Shit!"

Terry leaned over and must have caught the screen. He smirked with obvious delight. "You'd better get it."

"Son of a bitch."

"Lovely vocabulary." Terry's facial expression soured.

She smirked, basking in the tit for tat. *My swearing is what he gets for being a brat.* Her phone rang for the fourth time. One more, and the call would be shuffled to voicemail. She took a deep breath and answered.

"Knight, where the hell are you?" he pushed out.

"What do you mean?" She slid her focus to her partner. "Didn't Terry tell you where we were going?"

Terry mouthed, *Hey*.

"Yes, and never mind where you are."

"Then why did you ask?"

"It's the reporter. He wants to do another piece on you."

"Why?" Her life was getting out of control and fast. She didn't need a nosy reporter prying into her business.

"Why he cares, I don't know, but this could be good PR for the department."

What he really meant was it could be good PR if she stuck to an assigned script. "I don't think—"

"He's meeting you at Piccolo Italia at eight o'clock tonight. Don't be late. Oh, and, Knight, make sure he picks up the tab." He ended the call before she could respond.

"Unbelievable," she muttered and tossed her phone into the console.

"Why do I sense the earth stopped spinning?"

"Funny, because to me it's never spun faster and, I would add, it's off-kilter." And if it wasn't enough that she had to play nice with the reporter, he wanted to meet at the restaurant she and Blake used to frequent. She pounded her palm on the steering wheel—and just like that she was back in the torture room and full of fear and trepidation. Why were these flashbacks happening, and how could she make them stop?

CHAPTER FORTY-FIVE

Madison parked the department sedan at the side of the road, and the Forensics van pulled up behind them. Cynthia and Mark got out and went rooting in the back of the vehicle. Mark emerged with what looked like a metal detector, and Cynthia slipped a camera strap over her head. They both carried evidence kits.

The gravel crunched beneath their steps as they approached Madison and Terry.

Cynthia kept her sunglasses in place as she spoke. "Richards is on standby if we find any remains."

"Okay," Madison said and turned her gaze to the ravine.

The overgrowth was mostly shades of brown, with the odd clump of green grass. The blades rustled in the breeze, providing a contradictory ambience to an area that Madison suspected was a dump site for bodies—plural. Even though Douglas only mentioned one victim in reference to the ravine.

"According to Douglas, they took the body *down* the ravine. It's probably located at the base, next to the river." Madison took the lead down the hill, careful of every step. The ground was spongy, and small twigs were strewn everywhere. Low branches also served as a hazard.

It didn't take too long to reach the bottom, and gratefully no one was injured in the descent. "Spread out. Look for anything that stands out as strange and could indicate a shallow grave." Madison took in the area, her eyes keen and scanning. Her gaze settled on the contraption in Mark's hand. She nudged her head toward it. "What do you propose to do with that?"

"This?" Mark lifted the apparatus in response. "It's possible the body has metal on it. Rings, a watch, belt buckle, you name it."

So it was a metal detector... "Good thinking." At the mention of a watch, she thought of James Calin's, the one in the warehouse. Would they find his body out here? Madison continued taking in the area, and the four of them spread out. She went straight, Cynthia and Mark right, and Terry ventured left.

There was a mound of tall, green grass next to the river, and it stood out against the otherwise bland landscape. Decomposing flesh made good fertilizer, as much as she hated to give it much thought.

Madison lowered to her haunches and pointed. "I think I found something."

"Here too," Mark said over the soft pulsing *bleep* of the machine.

She rose to full height. "We better get Richards down here."

"Before we get way ahead of ourselves here…" Terry squatted near Madison and started clawing at the earth with his hands.

"Wait," Mark called out.

Everyone looked at him. Being the youngest person in the lab, he was usually more reserved. He proceeded, speaking in a softer tone. "This is more than just a metal detector. I should have told you, I guess. It allows us to get imagery of what is beneath the ground as well."

All of them went over to Mark.

"Here." He pointed to the screen when they were all close enough to see.

Madison couldn't make out anything discernable. "And we're looking at?"

"There is a body down there." He angled his head left then right. "Without a doubt."

"You are a genius!" Madison slapped him on the back, and Mark momentarily lost his balance.

"Thank"—he righted himself before falling—"you."

"How far down is he?" Terry asked.

Mark indicated a reading on the screen. "Five feet."

Madison pulled out her cell phone and called in Richards. There was work to do.

CHAPTER FORTY-SIX

The scene was scoured for a couple of hours, and when the sun had completely disappeared, lights were brought in to illuminate the ravine. In all, four bodies were found. While Madison had anticipated more, she figured the Russians likely had several dump locations just like this one. What was certainly interesting was bullets were found with each set of remains, which were mostly skeletal. The Mafia had probably been confident all the evidence was buried for good.

"These are not hollow-point bullets like those used on Lexan," Cynthia said, pinching one in her fingers. "If they were, they'd be flowered, the metal would be bent back to resemble petals."

"Okay, but are they the right caliber—a .22? They could have been fired from the same gun." The weapon used to shoot Lexan had never been conclusive, and it was believed that a silencer may have been used that affected the grooves and striations—basically fingerprints for guns—enough to hinder running down gun type.

"So you think the mob's hit man has been hanging onto a gun from eight-plus years ago?" Terry asked.

Madison shrugged. "It is possible. They believe themselves to be untouchable. They also never expected this site to be found. And they did what they could to prevent that from happening."

"Short of digging up the remains to get rid of the evidence."

"They could have, but it wouldn't have been easy. Based on the various states of decomp, these bodies weren't all dumped at once." Madison looked back at Cynthia for an answer to her earlier question. "Are they .22 caliber?" she repeated.

"They are, but further analysis needs to be done before it can be confirmed if the bullets tie back to the same type of weapon, let alone a specific one," Cynthia responded. "By the way, the autopsies did get done on Emanuel Douglas and Sonia Pike, the maid."

"Lillian?"

"Not yet. But it was a .22 caliber that took out Pike. Rest assured all bullet fragments will be run through extensive ballistics testing."

With a natural pause in the conversation, Terry asked Madison if they could talk. They walked to a clearing.

"Yeah?" she said.

"Those men who testified that you went in with your gun drawn…"

"They're ancient history. Why bring them up now?"

"They're ancient history? Ah, okay."

"Go on."

"I did some looking into them while you were at the doctor's office. I was curious how they might look for our Mafia hit man. Neither one is large or blond—that's if Lillian Norton's neighbor saw the killer. Both men have clean records. Not so much as a parking ticket. Both are also family men, Maddy, with a wife and two kids. Now, I wonder why they would lie. I want to believe you. I'm on your side, but—"

"You're on my side, *but* you're essentially accusing me of going in there with my gun drawn looking for a confrontation?" Just when she thought the negative repercussions from the events in the warehouse were behind her, Terry had dredged them back up.

"I never said you went in firing rounds."

The pulse of adrenaline reverberated through her head. "The lack of forensic evidence proves that. The fact that I didn't go in there armed at the ready is something you'll have to take my word on."

Terry ran a hand down his face and wrapped it around the back of his neck.

"Listen, you said they're family men. Isn't that enough right there to prove they could have been manipulated? They have something to lose—not just their own lives, but those of their loved ones. Dimitre's behind bars, but that's not stopping him from calling the shots."

"It seems literally." Terry rubbed the back of his neck.

She continued. "Douglas, his maid, and his lover all died because of this site." She gestured to take in the area. It was alive with activity. Every qualified technician was pulled in to help. There was too much ground to cover and too little time.

"Or it seems *likely* to be the case." He held up his hands. "Devil's advocate."

"Uh-huh. Well, you can be sure we'll tie this back to Dimitre."

"So we have—say—ten victims. Lexan, Sergey, Anatolli, four pulled from this ravine so far, Douglas, his maid, and his lover. There are various MOs involved—shooting, stabbing, strangulation. Also different weapons are employed—a handgun or more than one, a sniper rifle, a blade, and bare hands."

"Dimitre has a lot under his employ. Maybe we're looking for more than one someone. I'm thinking maybe one of those *family men*—actually, what are their names?"

"Donald Barnes and Gregory McDonald."

"Donald and McDonald?" She snickered, able to pull out some levity.

"Listen, I didn't name them."

"All right, fine. Maybe Barnes and McDonald aren't as innocent as it might appear on paper."

"From what I could tell, there's nothing to indicate either of them would have a background in sniping."

"You considered them suspect at one point. Otherwise you wouldn't have dug into them. Do either of them own a gun that fires .22 caliber?"

"I can check and see."

She nodded, then turned, watching Richards and his assistant loading one set of remains onto a stretcher. An anthropologist wasn't available for collection; they'd process the remains from the morgue.

"I did some other digging too," Terry said to her.

"Someone was busy."

"Hardy-har."

"All right. What else?"

"I dug some into Mason Freeman."

"And?" Dread creeped over her skin.

"His father had dealings with Dimitre a long time ago. Freeman's father passed away a few years back, but the records show he was in business with Dimitre for a brief stint until they parted ways."

She wasn't sure how she'd missed that. But the answer came to her immediately. She'd been so focused on the mob being behind Lexan's death, she hadn't honestly considered Freeman—not really. "Parted ways? Is that possible? Usually, you're in the mob for life."

"Exactly what I was thinking."

"How did you find out all of this?"

"Let's just say I've been working on this for days while you've been off here and there, going to doctor's appointments and such."

He made it sound like vacation. "Seriously, Terry?"

He laughed.

"Well, speaking of my being off here and there, I've got to go. I have that dinner date with the reporter. But tomorrow morning, you and me, we're going to talk to Barnes and McDonald. And Freeman."

CHAPTER FORTY-SEVEN

When Madison arrived at Piccolo Italia, King was seated, a bottle of red wine on the table and a glass half-full in front of him. He was wearing a blue dress shirt with the top two buttons undone and black pleated pants. He was reading on a tablet and didn't notice her approach.

"Mr. King," Madison said as she took the seat across from him.

"How nice of you to join me." King moved the tablet beside his place setting.

"I didn't have much of a choice."

"And here I was going to say you look nice."

She conducted the obligatory glance down at her attire. She had just thrown on a long-sleeved shirt and a pair of dark-blue jeans. She dressed it up with a black blazer, but no jewelry, no refreshed makeup, and certainly no eye shadow. "You're being more than generous, but thank you." She reached for the wine bottle.

"Let me." He retracted his hand when he caught her eye. "Ah, yes, you like to do everything yourself."

"Well, I am more than capable of pouring my own wine."

King laughed, and she found herself smiling, realizing how her words might have come across as if she were a lush.

"I don't mean it like that. I don't drink a lot." She snapped her mouth shut before she rambled on anymore. The purpose of tonight was public relations—what she wouldn't do for her job. She took a sip of wine, followed by a deep breath. "My sergeant said you want to know more about—"

"Welcome to Piccolo Italia. My name is Marianne, and I'll be your server this evening." A dark-haired woman in her early twenties stood at the side of their table. "Is there anything I can get for you?"

Madison shook her head. Her original plan was to have what she often did when she came here with Blake—fettucine alfredo. Now, she found herself more interested in spending some time with the wine. "Just a few minutes, please," she told her.

"Certainly." The server left.

Madison took a long sip of the red. She let the wine coat her tongue and appreciated its oaky flavors as they overtook her palate. Blame that ceremony and observation on Blake too. She took another sip, this one a quick mouthful and swallow—more her style.

"I take it the wine meets your standards."

She nodded. "They have a nice house red."

"They do."

"What is it you want to know about me?" The question tumbled out, but as much as it was nice to just sit, she wanted to get the unpleasant business of an interview over with. She had enough to process from the day without this stacked on top. First, Connor made her aware of the guilt—nay, responsibility—she carried around with her. Second, the four sets of remains found in the ravine. Maybe she should just view this meeting with King as a reward at the end of a hellish day. She could do worse than dinner at a classy restaurant.

"What makes Madison Knight tick?" he asked.

But maybe this would be as painful as sitting across from Connor. She did give King props for not dancing around his intentions. "Tick?" She laughed and took another drink of wine. *Was sharing one bottle going to be enough?* Though she should slow down, or she could say something she'd come to regret.

"Well, the public knows you're one determined cop, that you're even willing to put your life on the line, but who are *you*?" He tapped a hand on his chest, and it made Madison recoil. It was bad enough Connor wanted in her head, now she had King on the same quest. "When Detective Madison Knight doesn't have her badge and the gun, who is she?"

"I have a dog." Hershey, speaking of, was a soft ball of fur when she'd dropped by the apartment to get ready. She cared for his needs before heading back out, but it was tempting to stay home with him. She lifted her glass to her lips again, but this time didn't take a drink. She lowered it, thinking she really needed to slow down before the alcohol loosened her lips.

"You have a dog." King took a draw on his wine and tapped on his tablet. "That's good. People will soften toward you immediately. Everyone loves dogs."

That was her, always worried about pleasing other people. Screw it. She sipped her wine.

"Could you send me a picture of the dog? Oh, and his name? Hers?"

"Him. Hershey," she pushed out, uncomfortable and on the spot even parting with such surface-level information.

"Like the chocolate bars?"

"Yep."

"Huh. You must love your chocolate."

"You could say that."

"And the picture…of Hershey?"

She nodded. "I'll send you one."

"Excellent." King sat back, smiling, obviously pleased with himself. He took a quick swig of his wine, and his face became serious. "What about your personal life? What's it like? Do you have a Mr. Knight or a boyfriend?"

Madison's instinct was to bolt, and she shifted in her chair. "I'm here only because I really have no choice. No one has the right to make me dig into my feelings but my shrink, and that's—" *Shit!* His eyes lit, and since when had she adopted Connor as her shrink?

"You see a point in psychology."

She settled back into her chair instead of leaving. Blame it on the wine. "Can we talk off the record?"

"The entire point of this evening is so that it's *on* record."

"Listen, I just really don't know what you want from me. I have a dog, I love Hershey's bars." *Speaking of, it has been a while since my last one.*

"Which we've covered. Tell me about your family."

She let out a deep breath. "I have a strained relationship with my mother. My younger sister is perfect. She's married, has three daughters."

"Good. I can use all of that. Any romantic relationships at the moment?"

"Wait," she blurted out. "Don't publish that I have a strained relationship with my mother."

King met her eyes. "It would make you relatable and—"

"Garner sympathy? No. Don't print it."

King studied her and prompted again, "Romantic relationships?"

"None, but I'm happiest that way."

"Fair enough. Moving on… When you're not at work, what are you doing?"

"Is that a trick question?" She caught a glint in King's eyes.

He grinned. "You're one of those people who don't know how to relax, aren't you?"

"I'm relaxed right now." She took another draw of wine, and it went straight to her head. It was time to order. Where was their server? She looked around. No sign of Marianne.

"You like your wine." King nudged his head toward her wineglass.

"Please, don't put that down." She rolled her eyes. "I'm complicated, all right. I'm wired twenty-four seven. If there's something to do—and there always is—I'm doing it. It's just how I'm programmed. Work is what makes Madison tick." *Ack.* She had to stop drinking. Not only was she providing too much in the way of personal things, but she was also referring to herself in the third person. "I should really get going."

"You haven't eaten dinner, and they have a nice brie appetizer."

Appetizer? Apparently, the reporter had plans of dragging this evening out as long as possible. "Another time." It was a dismissive pleasantry. She had no intentions of seeing the man again. And if there were a God, he'd make that prayer come true.

"There is one thing we didn't touch on, Detective. Your grandfather, his murder. The real reason you became a cop and have a thing against the Russian Mafia. I want to discuss that with you."

She'd like to discuss how he even knew about her family's past. Had he done his own digging, or was his source Chief McAlexandar? Still, what would he gain from being King's informant on this matter? The answer presented itself immediately. It could discredit her in the public eye. Madison leveled her gaze at King. "My mother has a saying. It's nice to want and not always get. Good night." She stood, sobering due to the direction of the conversation. Her stomach grumbled in protest. That fettucine alfredo would have been divine, but she'd get another wish granted: time at home with Hershey and maybe a Hershey's *bar*.

CHAPTER FORTY-EIGHT

Madison went into the station the next morning with a Starbucks cup held firmly in one hand and a Hershey's bar in the other. She pulled the wrapper back and took another bite. Heaven. Every. Single. Time.

Terry greeted her from his desk by lifting his mug in a toast gesture.

Sergeant Winston came beelining straight for her in large strides. "How did it go with the reporter, Knight?"

Apparently, there was no chance of having a little space bubble when she first got in, and she was just there to pick up Terry. They were going to talk to Barnes and McDonald to get a feel for them. Neither of them might be the hit man they were after, but they could know his identity and where to find him—assuming they'd come out with that information.

"Knight," Winston prompted.

She waved her arm holding the Hershey's to get Terry moving. "Let's go." She then popped the last of the chocolate into her mouth and threw the crumpled wrapper into the trash bin. She took a few steps in the direction of the parking lot.

"Don't walk away from me, Knight," Winston bellowed.

She faced him. "We can talk about the reporter later. Right now, there's something Terry and I need to take care of."

"Terry filled me in this morning. He was here early," the sergeant said.

Good for him. She studied Winston, trying to gauge if the chief had told him about their interaction—not that it would have been a smart move for the chief—but Winston wasn't giving any indication he'd heard.

"We *will* talk." With that, Winston walked away.

Madison turned to her partner. "Where to first—Barnes or McDonald?"

"Barnes owns a Ruger SR22 that fires .22 caliber."

"Makes the choice an easy one."

Barnes lived in a quaint, middle-class neighborhood in the west end, which catered to families with young children. There was a public school close by and a couple of parks within a few blocks. Barnes's house was a brick bungalow with a large front yard. A wishing well took up prime reality in the middle of the lawn—tacky, but to each their own.

Madison and Terry walked up the path to the front door.

"Who knows if he'll even talk to us. Golden's probably told him to keep his mouth shut," Terry said.

"How was that anyhow?"

"What? Dealing with Golden?"

Madison nodded, loving how Terry could read her mind.

"Oh, just peachy."

Madison laughed at his sarcasm. "Yeah, I bet. I probably should have known better than to ask."

"Probably."

She narrowed her eyes at him and then went to knock. Before she could, the door opened. A woman in a green T-shirt and beige pants was standing there, squinting in the morning sunlight.

"Mrs. Barnes?" Madison asked.

"Yes?"

She held up her badge. "I'm Detective Knight, and this—"

"Knight? You're the detective who went into my husband's work with her gun and started shooting. Get off our property now." She pushed her door to close it, but Madison stuck her leg in there to stop it. "Step back," the woman barked.

Terry touched the sleeve of Madison's shirt, and she drew her leg back—reluctantly. The door was slammed shut.

Terry faced her. "You can't do that."

"I just did, and I don't need a lecture from you." She raised her hand and knocked.

"Seriously?" the woman yelled from behind the door.

"Stiles PD, and we have questions. We're not leaving until we talk with you." Madison turned and crouched down as if she were going to sit on the top step.

"Blasted hell!" The door *whooshed* open. "I'm going to call your boss if you keep up this harassment. Now leave," she hissed.

Madison took in the woman's demeanor. There was evident anger, but there was something else. "Who are you afraid of, Mrs. Barnes?"

She crossed her arms and shook her head. "Why do you think I'm afraid of anyone?"

"You're trembling."

"I'm chilly." She rubbed her arms.

"Were you threatened? Was your family? We can protect you."

"You're only interested in protecting your own ass. You don't care about us, about Don, about the kids. You care about your career. Well, he's not going to lie and retract the truth." The angles of her face sharpened. "Now get off my property."

The door slammed louder than before. This time, Madison would leave. But she'd be back. She never even had a chance to say her husband's supposed eyewitness account was meaningless.

"If I were you, I'd expect a call by the time we hit the car." Terry pressed his lips and hooked his eyebrows.

"Good time to put my phone on silent then." She went to do just that, but it rang before she had a chance. She looked at the caller ID. Maybe it was best to get this over with. "Detective Knight."

"Well, well, I'm surprised you answered. Maybe you never saw your caller ID."

"What do you want, Mr. Golden?"

"Oh, you're going with formalities. How have you been?"

"Stuff it. Why are you calling?"

"I heard you showed up at my client's house, Donald Barnes. His wife is livid, Madison."

"You can call me Detective Knight." Madison couldn't understand what she'd ever seen in Blake now. Her mind traced back to their intimate encounters and how he could be affectionate. She didn't miss Blake so much as she found herself longing for a man's touch. Troy Matthews's face popped into her head, along with his words, *If you wanted to be in my arms, Madison, all you'd have to do...* She was slowly driving herself crazy because she'd cut him off!

"You can't talk to these men, Mad—Detective Knight. They are protected by representation."

She could tell him this had nothing to do with the warehouse, but she wasn't going to tip her hand at all with her real interest in Barnes and McDonald.

"You hear me? Stay away from them. I don't want the next call to be from McDonald's wife."

Madison hung up and got into the car, where Terry was already in the passenger seat. She yanked on the belt and did it up. "Ol' McDonald had a pig—and that was his lawyer. The nerve of that man."

"What bothers you more—the fact that Golden's on Dimitre Petrov's payroll or the fact that you used to sleep with him?"

She glared at him. No words were needed.

"We going talk to McDonald?"

She shook her head. "Not just yet. We'll see Mason Freeman now."

"You're backing down because of Golden? You don't usually let anything stop you."

Matthews's nickname came to mind—Bulldog. Hopefully, he would come up with something else. She shook her head at that thought. Why did he need one for her at all? "Since when is being thorough a bad thing?"

"I never said it was. But when you put your life or the lives of others in danger, it is."

"Oh, we're back to that. Are you sure you want to talk about this?" She took a deep breath and gripped the steering wheel.

"Yeah, I guess I do." Terry undid his belt and positioned his body to face her. "Tell me the truth. I'm your partner. Did you go in with your gun pulled?"

She studied his eyes. He analyzed hers in return. Maybe it was time to speak the truth. "I don't know."

"You don't know?" He mocked laughter.

"Terry, I'm being serious here. I don't remember. I think it was just the entire experience. My mind's shut that part down."

"But it didn't shut down the part about being tortured, did it? I see how you disappear on me."

She took a stymied breath and directed her thoughts to her first steps into the warehouse. She shared what she remembered. "The girl from the front left after I asked for Sergey. Next thing I remember is Anatolli came up behind me and put a gun to my head." Tears filled her eyes, and she rushed to blink them away. "Never mind. I don't have to explain myself to you, or to anyone." She put the car into gear, pressing the gas pedal a little too hard. The car lurched forward as it accelerated.

He straightened and did up his belt. "I'm not asking you to explain yourself. Just tell me what happened. I'm your partner."

She stiffened. "You say that like we're married or something. You live your life, I'll live mine."

"All right. If that's how you want it, then that's how it will be." He turned to face out the window. His tone indicated he was offended by her reaction.

"Terry." She hadn't intended to hurt him, but she was beyond frustrated at not being able to remember everything from that day clearly. She also hated to think he didn't believe her when she said that was all she recalled, like she was withholding for some reason.

"Nope, that's okay. You keep it all bottled up, and someday when you explode, I hope I'm nowhere around you."

She shoved her head against the neck rest of her seat. She didn't want to be around for it either.

They drove to Knockturnl in silence. Madison was slipping into the darkness and hated to think she was suffering from PTSD. That happened to other people—not her. Besides, she'd lived through hell and had emerged from its flames with only the odor of smoke on her clothing. She was fine. Right? Or was she? And then she couldn't help but consider that things could have turned out a lot differently than they had.

On the count of three, pull the trigger.

She pinched her eyes shut. When she opened them, instead of seeing the cityscape around her, she was back inside the torture room. It was so clear.

The flavor of blood is all I can taste, all I can smell.

Sergey's pacing in front of me while Anatolli holds the gun against my forehead.

Terry shoved her arm. "Madison? Maddy?"

"Yeah?" Groggy, like she was being torn from a dream.

"Madison!" Terry yelled and reached for the wheel.

The car had veered into the left, oncoming lane. She made the correction.

Holy shit! She'd been driving when she blacked out. "I'm… um… I'm fine." She rubbed a sweaty palm on her thigh.

He looked at her lap, back at her eyes. "Please do us a favor and pull over."

She did as he asked.

He shifted his body to face her more directly. "Can you be honest with me for once? You're obviously not fine."

She glanced over at him. There was a softness in his eyes that begged her to release her ego and open up to him. If she did though, she would become vulnerable. But she thought back to what Dr. Connor had said about Terry. He had a lot going on in his life, and it wasn't fair to gamble with hers when his was chock-full of uncertainties. She also had the promise she'd made to herself to consider—but it was too hard to let go. "I really am fine." She said the words, avoiding his gaze, while inside she screamed for help.

CHAPTER FORTY-NINE

The young Britney Spears lookalike smiled when they came through the doors at Knockturnl. "Mr. Freeman is back, but I'm afraid he's in meetings all day."

"I'm sure he will find a few minutes for us," Madison said.

Britney glanced at her computer monitor and back at them. "He's in a fifteen-minute window right now. I can try him." She pressed a button on the headset she wore. "Detectives are here to see you, Mr. Freeman." Her eyes shifted between them. "Uh-huh, okay, will do." She disconnected the call. "He'll be down. In the meantime, if you want to make yourselves comfortable..." Britney gestured to a conference room in the corner.

Madison and Terry did as Britney suggested, and a few minutes later when Mason Freeman entered, he didn't look much different than Madison remembered from years ago—still handsome with blond hair and blue eyes. His skin was kissed by the sun, though, likely from his recent trip to Jamaica. Another discernible difference was the life experience reflected in his eyes. Now, he was both a father and the owner of a successful company—something he wasn't the last time she had spoken with him.

"Detective Knight, it's been a long time." He shook her hand.

The general easiness of his greeting made her uncomfortable, and she questioned his reason. "We have some questions for you," she said firmly, unswayed by his kindness.

He dropped into a leather swivel chair across from them. "Let me guess. This is about Bryan Lexan. Jessica said you were by the house, but I thought we answered all of your questions years ago." He cocked his head to the right.

"Some new developments have come up."

"I saw the assassinations on the news."

Madison played the art of silence. Often it made people uncomfortable and eager to fill the gap. She didn't think Freeman was necessarily behind Sergey's and Anatolli's murders, but she couldn't ignore Freeman Sr.'s connections to the Mafia that Terry had uncovered either.

Freeman looked from her to Terry, back to her. "You think I had something to do with that?"

"Did you?"

"Of course not. I had nothing to do with Bryan's death either."

She found it interesting that he'd rushed that out. Something else also struck her curiosity. "Jessica told us about a threatening letter she saw."

"Well, if she saw something, she never told me about it." A subtle flicker in his eyes destroyed his claim.

"So you've never heard of this before now?" she pressed.

"No."

"Apparently, it was a letter given to Bryan Lexan weeks before his murder."

"As I said, I know nothing about it and have nothing to do with it." Freeman leaned back in his chair.

"Your claim to innocence years ago was that you didn't have a motive. You had the girl."

"That's right."

"You also provided us with an alibi for the night of his murder."

"Yes, I was with Jessica."

At the time, Madison hadn't given much thought to the fact that they'd alibied each other out, but she had been fixated on Dimitre Petrov—an oversight she needed to correct. Not that she gave the mob a pass, but she wasn't so sure how innocent Freeman really was anymore. She leaned forward, inching her way into Freeman's personal space. "We have questions about your father's business dealings."

"What about them?"

"Our research has led us to discover that your father was in bed with Dimitre Petrov."

"Okay," he dragged out. "What does that have to do with me?"

"So you don't deny the relationship?"

"I don't see your point in bringing all this up. Besides if my father was friends with Petrov, it would have been for a good reason. Doesn't mean my father was a criminal, and I'm not going to sit here and listen to you destroy his name and reputation. My father was an honorable man, Detective."

Madison studied his face. He was aware of his father's affiliation with the mob, but not necessarily the details. She switched the subject back to the letter. "Why didn't Jessica mention this letter to the police before now?"

"You'd have to ask her that question." He twisted his wrist to check his watch and jumped up. "I've got a meeting. I trust you understand."

"Actually, there is one more thing." Madison put the envelope from Dimitre's letter on the table and shoved it toward him.

"What's this?"

"An envelope. Do you recognize the stationery's design?"

"Detective, I've been cooperating—" He lifted the stationery from the table, flipped it over, and then put it back down. "It's the same style we have here, less the name in the top right-hand corner."

"So you admit to having this type of envelope?"

Freeman took a seat again. "Where are you headed with this?"

"A piece of this envelope was found in the driveway where Bryan Lexan was shot. Do you know how it got there?" Madison asked.

"No, why would I?"

"Well, you had reason to hate Bryan Lexan. He misled Jessica, hurt her deeply, as I recall. When Lexan had staged his death, he broke Jessica's heart, and it was no secret that around that time you carried a torch for her. Maybe you wanted him out of the way?"

"Jess wasn't going back to him. She got to see Bryan for the lying, selfish bastard he was. I really have to go." Despite his words, he didn't make an effort to get up. "And surely you can't really suspect me of killing Bryan because of an envelope? Hundreds or thousands of companies would use that style. And what about the Russians? From what I remember, you were convinced the mob was behind Bryan's murder. Why are you coming back now and trying to upset my life…Jessica's? She doesn't need this. Neither do I. If you need anything further from us, you can do it through a lawyer."

Freeman got up and headed to the door. "I trust you'll see yourself out."

Madison settled behind the wheel and started the car. They never even got around to asking about a Mafia hit man and if Mason Freeman could point them anywhere. "We still need to answer why Jessica held back about that threat all this time. That's not sitting well with me."

"We might never know. You aren't really considering that she had something to do with Bryan's murder now?" Terry scrunched up his face. "Freeman was right. You've always thought it was the mob. Why are you second-guessing yourself?"

Freeman was right. "Bryan had put Jessica through a lot," she ruminated. "When I had to deliver the news of his death—the one that turned out to be fake—she was devastated. After he was murdered for real, Jessica didn't seem as upset."

"You blame her? Guy hurts her, rises from the dead, only to wind up murdered—for real. A part of her might have even thought he deserved it."

"Huh." There had to be more to this. To start with, Jessica and this supposed threat that came from the Russians. This was despite the letter having no signature. And why bring it up now? Then, Mason redirecting the conversation to the Russians. It also entered her mind about Dimitre bringing up his visitor with the bowler hat. What if... "Dimitre sent us looking for the guy with the bowler hat."

"Okay. Seems like a random thing to say right now, but go ahead."

"Not random at all really. He was, in effect, telling me that he knew about Lexan's staged death. After all, Darrell Kinton was who supplied the cadaver."

"All right, so it's proof Dimitre knew about Bryan's attempt to disappear. Kinton could have been double-dipping—working for both Lexan and Dimitre—as we considered before."

"Yes, but I think there's more to this. Both Freemans did their best to steer us back to the Russians. Jessica by randomly bringing up this written threat."

"Mason by bringing up the mob just now," Terry interjected.

She nodded. "Trying to remind me they are who I suspect. An effort to steer my attention away from them again? But somehow Dimitre found out Lexan was still alive. Someone had to have told him. It wasn't going to be Sergey and Anatolli." She paused there, raised her eyebrows, curious if her partner was patching this all together.

His eyes widened. "Oh. You think Jessica or Mason tipped off the Russians about Bryan Lexan actually being alive?"

"It could make sense. It would also explain Dimitre's feeling wronged by Sergey and Anatolli. If they told him Lexan was dead and then Dimitre was informed that he'd just faked his death and was still alive..."

"Dimitre would have felt like an idiot."

"Yep. Dimitre found out his men originally lied to him. He only let them live until now for one reason. They ended up making things right." She never should have doubted for a second the Russians were behind Lexan's murder. "But when I came poking around again, he saw it as time to sever his connection with them. Permanently. I do think Freeman told Dimitre that Lexan was still alive. Not that I can prove that. Yet. I also believe he either confided in Jessica about this or she suspected. Hence her bringing up the letter and the Russians."

"To take our attention off Mason."

"Yeah."

"And Mason's motive? As you've pointed out, he got the girl."

"Could have been more to it. Mason could have wanted revenge for all that Bryan had put Jessica through with staging his death. Also maybe he did fear that with Bryan being alive, Jessica would forgive him and end things. By telling the Russians that Lexan was still alive—assuming he did—the mob would get what they wanted too."

"Win-win."

"Yes. Freeman got Lexan killed; he just didn't pull the trigger himself."

"All hypothetical."

"Also logical and plausible. It even explains why Sergey and Anatolli were killed."

"Wow."

"Uh-huh. Dimitre didn't want the past resurrected but…" A ripple of guilt sliced through her. "Their time was up. Question is, did Sergey and Anatolli take care of Lexan themselves, or did the mob hire someone else? Is it the same hit man we have running around trying to clean up the mess now?"

CHAPTER FIFTY

Later that afternoon, Madison stormed into the lab, Terry following her. "We need some answers, Cyn."

Cynthia folded up a sweater she had been examining and put it back into an evidence bag. She made some notations on a logsheet and looked at them over the top of her glasses. They were perched halfway down her nose, but instead of making her look old, it gave her a studious appearance most men would term sexy librarian. "What do you think I am? An answer machine?"

"I'm hoping so." Madison smiled at her.

"Well, Sam's processing the bullets taken from Douglas's maid, the two Russians, and the dump site remains."

Samantha Reid was another employee in the lab who specialized in firearms and ballistics.

"*And?*"

"Patience, woman. As I said, *she's processing*, as in still working on it. As soon as I hear something, I'll let you know. You have my word." Cynthia went to her computer and turned it off, then grabbed her jacket.

"Where are you going?" Madison asked.

Cynthia grinned. "I have a date."

"It's only three in the afternoon."

"Happy you can tell time at your age." Cynthia winked at her. "I'm leaving early, but I'll be back tomorrow. I've just been pulling a lot of overtime lately and need a break to blow off some steam." With that, she waved goodbye and left.

That evening, Madison was still irritated that Cynthia had bailed that afternoon. Rationally, she also saw that her friend needed time out of the lab. And not everyone was a workaholic.

Madison considered going to the Cracker Jack but shook off the notion. She was just hoping Matthews would show up again. Silly really. She didn't have time to develop a relationship, and even the thought of anything serious with the SWAT guy was laughable. Romance didn't last—*ever*—not in her experience anyway.

She had ended up buying a bottle of wine and taking out an order of Chinese food before heading home. She took Hershey out and fed him, then poured some wine and dished out food for herself.

She ate quickly—with a fork from her utensil drawer, throwing out the chopsticks that the restaurant had tossed in the takeout bag. She'd never gotten the hang of using them. She took a sip of wine and shoved another forkful of food into her mouth when her landline rang. She chewed unreasonably fast and swallowed roughly. A large piece of celery attempted to go down the wrong pipe and had her coughing. Tears filled her eyes.

The phone kept ringing.

"I'm...coming," she squeezed out through the hacking fit. *As if the caller can hear me...* The choking episode calmed down, and she answered.

"I need to talk to you." It was Cynthia, and she'd just blurted out the words.

Madison buzzed her friend in, and mere seconds later, Cynthia was entering Madison's apartment. She threw her arms around Madison, nearly upsetting her wine.

Madison backed up. "Whoa. What's going on?"

Cynthia's eyes went to the glass. "Wine? Excellent." She took Madison's glass and gulped it down, handed it back empty. "Pour me some?"

"Ah, sure." Madison poured some more for herself and got a glass for Cynthia. She gave it to her friend. "What's wrong?"

Cynthia blinked rapidly, then sucked back some wine. At least a quarter of the liquid was now gone. Add that to the half glass she'd drunk of Madison's in five seconds.

"Why would you assume something's wrong?" Cynthia's voice was squeaky, and she walked to the living area. "Hey, Hershey. Hey, buddy."

"Cyn?" Madison followed.

Cynthia raised her glass to her lips again. Another quarter of the wine disappeared.

"You should probably slow down. Just a little."

Cynthia met Madison's gaze.

"Or not," Madison said under her breath. "Did you come over here to get drunk?" An obvious throwaway question, but she was getting frustrated that her friend wasn't talking, just drinking.

Cynthia laughed. "Well, no time like the present." Another tilt of the glass. Appeared to be only a sip this time.

Cynthia dropped onto the sofa, and Hershey padded over to her feet. She rubbed his head, and he closed his eyes in doggy ecstasy.

Madison stood in front of Cynthia, blocking her view of the television. "Talk to me."

Cynthia's shoulders sagged. "Can't we just watch some TV?"

Madison turned it off. "You drank my wine. I deserve something here. What's going on?"

"All right, I'll talk. Maybe we could go out, have a drink."

Madison's eyes skipped to her glass as if to say, *We already are*.

Cynthia drank some more wine. Seconds passed.

"Cynthia?" Madison prompted.

"And nothing stronger around here? Say whiskey or—"

"Cyn."

"Lou asked me to marry him."

"He…*he*…*he* what?" She collapsed onto the couch beside Cynthia.

"He asked me to marry him. Yep." More of Cynthia's wine disappeared. She lifted her glass toward Madison. "I hope you have more."

"What did you say?" Madison was having a hard time gathering her thoughts, let alone finding her voice.

"I didn't say—" She took another mouthful of wine.

"Here, give that glass to me before you pass out and never get to what you said in response."

Cynthia pulled the glass out of Madison's reach. "I didn't say anything." Her eyes pooled with tears. "I just got up and left the restaurant. Just like that. He could still be sitting there for all I know. Oh my God." Cynthia leaned forward, and Madison swooped in to take her wineglass. Cynthia rested her face in her hands and spoke from behind them. "I do like him."

"Not exactly a secret."

"But me, married? Madison, we're not even living together, even if we spend a lot of time at my place— I need a cigarette." She started patting her pants pockets.

"Not in here you don't."

"Great, then we'll go out. Drinks are on me."

"You can't just run away from this."

"Why not? What would you do, Maddy?"

Run like freaking hell! But she couldn't very well say run when she just told her friend she couldn't.

"Well?"

"I don't let relationships escalate to that point." She blew out a breath, relieved that she'd dodged all responsibility in this conversation.

"Guess you don't. You end relationships so you don't have to face this question." She jabbed a finger at Madison. "You're the smart one. Yep, you are. If only I could keep myself away from this man."

Madison smiled.

"Oh no, don't do this to me. You're supposed to be on my side."

"I'm your best friend, Cyn. I want what's best for you. Is Lou the best thing for you?"

"Oh God." She reached out to take her wine back from Madison. "I don't know." She put her lips to the glass.

Madison went to take the glass again, and Cynthia snarled. Madison held up her hand.

"Do you love him?" The question knotted Madison's stomach. She took a draw on her wine.

"When you said yes to Sovereign, did you love him?" Cynthia countered.

"Ah, jeez." Madison rubbed her head. She really hated talking about all this touchy-feely stuff.

"I mean it, Maddy. Did you love him?"

"I thought I did."

"But you must have. You still have strong feelings for him."

Madison shrugged. "What does any of this matter, or have to do with you guys?" She was going for a diversion.

Cynthia rushed a hand to her left temple. "This stuff hits you fast with an empty stomach."

"You have been pounding it back." Madison laughed at the scowl on Cynthia's face. "Hey, no judgment here. I have some Chinese food if you want some."

"Sounds great." Cynthia stood, wavering, and went to the kitchen counter to serve herself some food.

Madison's apartment was open concept, and she watched Cynthia from the couch. "You don't just like him, you love him." Again, with the mention of love, nausea swirled in her gut. Not because she was jealous that her friend had a relationship in her life, and not because she'd be left alone when Cynthia ran off and got married. Things always changed, regardless of protestations to the contrary, but the subject just made her uncomfortable.

"Oh, what is love anyway? I mean, really?" Cynthia stabbed a fork into the container of chicken balls and put two on her plate.

"You're asking the wrong person."

Cynthia settled back onto the couch and balanced her plate on her lap. "Am I though?"

"Why would you ever think I'm the right person to talk to about love?" Madison laughed. "I'm a commitment phobe."

"Are you? Or do you just know what you want? You're secure in who you are."

"Look who's talking. What is this relationship doing to you?"

"See, right there. I never let a guy get to me like this before. I'm not thinking straight." Cynthia stuffed some chow mein into her mouth and spoke while dabbing at the corners of her lips. "When you were engaged to Sovereign, where was your head at then?"

"Obviously outer space." She smirked, trying to make light of the deep feelings she'd had at the time. Right now, she was tired of talking about Sovereign. She'd given him enough of her life already. All this talk about love though, maybe she'd say yes if Matthews asked her on a date. She'd keep things between them casual and distant.

"Hello?" Cynthia snapped her fingers and laughed. "You there now?"

"Very funny." Her friend had a way of reading her too well. Madison added, "I just think relationships are complicated."

"That's not an answer to my question."

"Fine. How did I feel about Sovereign back then?" Madison paused to give her the impression she was giving the question actual thought when she didn't have to give it any. "I was insanely in love. I thought the world revolved around us and our relationship. Until things blew up."

"He was an ass for cheating on you."

"Say that again."

"But you recently kissed him, and he hurt you a long time ago. Would you consider getting back with him?"

"Hell no."

Cynthia knew that Madison and Sovereign had kissed not long ago, but Madison had never told her friend that he'd proposed just that recently. *Look into my eyes and tell me you don't love me anymore.*

Madison emptied her glass and reached for Cynthia's. "Want more?"

"Absolutely."

CHAPTER FIFTY-ONE

The next morning, Madison met up with Terry before heading to the lab. Mark was passing Cynthia a file folder when they arrived.

"Morning," Terry said.

Mark gave them a wave on his way out.

Cynthia took her glasses off and set them on the table. She ran a hand down her face. "Gawd. Already? I can barely see straight, and my head is spinning. I should feel guilty for last night. Mark, Samantha, and Jennifer were here until about two in the morning. The good news is we have some results." Cynthia held up the folder Mark had given her. "They finished analyzing the bullets pulled from Sergey and Anatolli."

"You get anything from the sniper's perch?" Madison asked.

Cynthia stifled a yawn and met Madison's gaze. "Straight to business even today, I see."

"I thought you'd prefer that," Madison shot back. She still hadn't heard what her friend decided about the proposal.

"Huh. Well, we found a strand of hair with a skin tag. Jennifer ran that, and there is DNA."

Jennifer Adams worked in the lab and specialized in serology and toxicology.

"A single hair? It could be anyone's, from any time. What?" Terry shrugged when both women looked at him. "I'm just stating a fact."

Madison shot him a glare, but said to Cynthia, "Any match?" Really a throwaway question. Getting DNA results never happened quickly.

"Do I really need to answer that?"

Madison shook her head.

"It's never that easy." Terry dropped into a chair beside Cynthia.

"And the bullets?" Madison asked, craving leads like her next chocolate bar.

"The sniper used hollow points, much like the ones pulled from Bryan Lexan, though a different caliber obviously. They were fired from a rifle—type not yet known."

Madison reached for a chair, mulling over one particular piece of information Cynthia had just delivered. "It's possible whoever shot Lexan also shot Sergey and Anatolli."

"That might be a stretch, but whether it was the same person or not, in those three cases, hollow-point bullets, as I said." Cynthia opened the file, and her eyes scanned down the page. "As we touched on the other day, the bullets pulled from Douglas's maid were *not* hollow points. Same as the ones pulled from the ravine victims. But in these cases, they were all .22 caliber."

"Like with Lexan," Madison said. "Any luck tracking down a gun type?"

Cynthia met Madison's gaze. "The grooves and striations confirm the same make and model of gun was used to kill Lexan and the maid."

Madison's legs weakened. "I didn't think you could determine the gun type used to kill Lexan."

"I couldn't until now, but by comparing the markings from the bullets that killed Lexan to ones we have now, there are some similarities."

She swallowed roughly. "We do have the type now, then?" She was having a hard time giving herself over to acceptance after all this time.

"We do. Now, that same gun *type* was used on the victims in the graves, but the bullets came from a different weapon than what was used on Lexan and Pike."

"What type are we looking at?" Madison pushed out, tapping a foot. They finally had a real lead.

"A Ruger SR22."

"You said…" Her stomach tossed. "An SR22? A Ruger?"

"Yes. Now, I had Mark run a search for registered Ruger—"

"Donald Barnes has one," Madison spat.

Cynthia's shoulders sagged. "Way to steal my thunder."

"Sorry." Madison lowered herself into a chair before she fell down. "Blame Terry."

"Sure, throw me under the bus," he pushed out.

Madison narrowed her eyes at him and went on. "Barnes is one of the guys who claimed I went into Homeland Logistics with my gun drawn, and here he owns the same gun type responsible for all these murders."

"Yep. Looks that way." Fatigue was quickly eating away at Cynthia's best features.

There was no way the gun model match was a coincidence. "So much for an innocent family man," she tossed out at Terry. "Barnes could be a mob hit man."

"All right," Terry said, "but do you think a professional gun for hire registers their weapons?"

"Guess we'll find out. We've got to get a warrant secured for that gun immediately." After all this time, was she finally going to close the Lexan case?

CHAPTER FIFTY-TWO

The search warrant came through for Barnes's Ruger SR22 and all his .22 caliber ammunition. It was around noon, and she and Terry were on the way to the Barnes residence now. They probably should have brought SWAT along to serve the warrant, considering Barnes was armed and suspected as being dangerous, but they didn't. They did bring backup though.

"I can see Barnes killing Sonia Pike, those people in the ravine, even Lexan," she said. "But we still have someone out there who killed Sergey and Anatolli. Then there's Douglas and his lover, Lillian Norton. If the same person is responsible for all of them, we're certainly looking for a killer who is versatile."

"As any professional killing machine should be."

Madison looked at Terry, curious how he made something so heinous sound comical.

Terry shrugged. "What?"

She shook her head and parked across the mouth of Barnes's driveway. A squad car came in behind—Higgins and Tendum.

Terry banged on the side door, and he and Madison both prepared to draw their weapons.

Barnes's wife opened the door and sighed heavily at the sight of them. "I told you to talk to our lawyer." She went to close the door again, but Madison nudged her foot in the opening, pushed the warrant through, and followed.

"Wait! Where do you think you're going?" The woman snatched the warrant. "You can't do this to him. He hasn't done anything wrong."

"Legal, ma'am, I assure you." Madison brushed past her and onto the small square landing that had one staircase going to the basement and one to the main level. "Is your husband home?"

"He's out."

Mail sat on the stairs going to the main level, as if the envelopes were just taken from the box and deposited there with no interest in the contents. At a quick glance, most of them appeared to be bills—no wonder they were cast aside. Madison went up and entered the kitchen. Dirty dishes lined the counters, and clean ones sat in a sink drying.

Terry wedged his way into the house, and Barnes's wife trailed him.

"Do you know where his Ruger SR22 is?" Madison asked. "It would save us the trouble of ripping the place apart."

"I should probably get Mr. Golden here to take a look at this." She waved the warrant.

"You can do as you like, but we'll be getting started." Madison put on gloves and went to the nearest cabinet door, opened it, and then moved onto the next. They could hit up the regular spots where people stored their guns, but it was possible they'd happen upon something else in the execution of the current warrant that could advance the investigation.

Terry followed her lead on the other side of the kitchen.

"Fine," the woman huffed out.

Madison stopped opening cupboards. Terry kept going and pulled some items out and put them on the counter.

"Stop! Please. I'll get the gun for you."

More like it. "Take us to it," Madison told her.

The woman flicked on a light at the top of the stairs and led them into a back corner of the basement. She pointed to an unlocked gun cabinet. "It's in there."

"All right. Stand back. Let me get it," Madison said.

Terry stayed with the woman at a distance while Madison opened the locker. The SR22 was right in front of her. Madison took it out, turned around to thank the wife for her cooperation, and found Donald Barnes standing there, holding a Glock aimed at them.

Madison tightened her grip on the gun. She could tell it was loaded due to its weight.

"Let my wife go!" he barked.

Madison made eye contact with Terry, who was facing her, his back to Barnes. The man's wife was tight to Terry's side. If her partner turned around too quickly, it could spook Barnes into pulling the trigger.

Madison held up her hand to stay Terry's movements. "Mr. Barnes, there's no need to worry. We'll let her go. Detective Grant is going to step to the side."

"He stays where he is!"

Terry's eyes disclosed mortal fear, but she hoped he could read her eyes—they were going to make it out of this alive—all of them.

"Come here, Dawn. Get beside me now." Barnes's arms were unsteady, the gun swayed. The sweat on his brow, the shiftiness of his eyes, panic laced each element of his being.

His wife shuffled over to him. Her face had paled considerably, and tears were streaming down her cheeks. "Why are you—"

"Shut up, Dawn. I mean it. I will kill them. I will." His eyes were bloodshot. Madison looked closer, and his pupils were dilated.

She was getting a really bad feeling. It was possible that Barnes had come from another part of the basement, but also just as likely he came from outside. If the latter was true, what happened to Higgins and Tendum? She hadn't heard gunfire, but her gut was acid. It was due to the Glock he was holding. Standard Stiles PD issue. Coincidence? "Where are the other officers, Mr. Barnes?"

"Mr. Barnes. Mr. Barnes." He parroted her. "So fuckin' proper."

"Where are they?" She lifted the SR22, pointing it squarely at him. "Are they safe?"

"They will be okay. They will be." Barnes's chin screwed up, his face contorting as a wave of emotion was laid bare over him.

Will be... Madison went cold. "What did you do?" she seethed. "Tell me, Mr. Barnes. We can work this out." Her heartbeat pounded in her ears. Adrenaline was pumping through her system, fine-tuning all her senses—sounds, sights, and smells all came into clear focus.

Barnes smelled of marijuana and whiskey. The basement was musty. She heard Terry's breathing, and her own, as if each inhale and exhale existed in a world of its own.

"Work this out?" Barnes scoffed. "You want to put me in prison. I won't go."

"Please, Don." His wife touched his shoulder. In an instant, he swung out his arm and connected with her, and she slammed to the ground.

Madison squeezed the trigger. The bullet found purchase in Barnes's shoulder, but he squeezed off a round. The gun jerked to his side with the recoil, altering the trajectory of the round.

A deafening report. Then eerie silence.

Dawn's hand went to her chest, and blood oozed between her fingers. Shock played over her features. Her eyes glazed over, and her mouth opened. No words came out. She collapsed onto her side.

Barnes dropped beside his wife. "No. No!" he wailed.

Terry turned around, pulled Barnes from the floor and away from his wife.

"I...killed...her," Barnes cried. "What have I—" The rest of his words disappeared, and he became silent as Terry cuffed him, read off his Miranda rights, and led him upstairs.

Madison could barely breathe. Was this what she had signed up for? Death?

In a flash, she was back in time to the warehouse. There had been a noise that she went to investigate. Then the rest filled in with stark clarity. Her chest heaved with relief from the recollection. She had only drawn her weapon when provoked.

Her gaze went to Dawn. There was nothing they could do for her. The bullet entered her chest right where her heart would be. The light in the woman's eyes had extinguished, leaving them wide open and vacant like unseeing marbles. She was gone. But if not for the visual confirmation, there was this emptiness to the room that announced a life force had left, not to return.

All of this could have been prevented. If only. But she'd just been following a lead. She swallowed the emotion, trying to tamp down the guilt. She talked herself back from the ledge, back from the point where she wondered if this job was worth the long hours and the sacrifice. Her dedication to this career stripped away her humanity one fiber at a time. She forced herself to recall the solved cases, the ones where justice was brought to the victims and closure provided to their families.

Then she snapped back to the present. Higgins and Tendum.

She ran outside. Sirens were ringing through the air and getting louder. She found Tendum sitting on the ground next to Higgins, helping hold him up. Blood was pooled all around Higgins, and it appeared he'd been struck in the chest.

At first, the shock had her feet cemented to the ground, but she pushed through. She ran, her legs about as effective as steel bars. She didn't want to know if… She couldn't finish the thought. She closed the distance between herself and Higgins, fearing the entire time that her friend, her mentor, may be dead.

She dropped to her knees in front of him, careful to avoid his blood. He appeared so still, but he was breathing. "Come on, Chief." Hot tears fell against her cold cheeks. "You will pull through. Chief, I want to hear more of your stories. Do you hear me?" She lowered her forehead to his and closed her eyes. When she opened them, she faced his wound straight on and caught the soft rise and fall of his chest. She couldn't lose him, not like this, not ever if she could help it.

An ambulance pulled to a stop, and paramedics hurried toward them. She stood and backed up to provide them room to work.

"Please save him." She'd plead on her knees if it would make a difference in whether or not he survived. To Higgins, she said, "Chief, we'll be talking about this over a drink. Everything is going to be fine."

Higgins's eyes fluttered shut.

"What the hell happened?" she barked at Tendum.

Tears were running down his cheeks. "He...he got my gun."

Madison was speechless and angry. At Tendum and Barnes.

She stormed over to Terry where he was with Barnes, who was also waiting for medical attention for his gunshot wound. She yanked on Barnes and started patting him down just to make sure there weren't any more surprises.

"What are you doing?" Terry reached out to stop her, but she kept at her search.

"What does it look like I'm doing?" Standard procedure dictated perps be searched before being loaded into a cruiser or ambulance.

"You cops are fuckin' stupid."

Rage filled Madison's vision, blinding her. Images flashed, the actions she wanted to take, the consequences. Was it worth it? Her attention trailed over to Higgins. Paramedics had put him on oxygen and were securing him onto a stretcher.

"You don't know anything." Barnes cackled.

She punched a fist into Barnes's injured shoulder, and it had him howling and buckling to the ground. She shrugged under Terry's shocked expression. "He wasn't cooperating." She met her partner's gaze, daring him to challenge her. He said nothing.

She hurried back to Higgins and the paramedics. "He's going to be okay, right?"

"Time will tell."

"I'm coming with you." She passed a glance at Terry to make sure he heard her.

Tendum came to the back door of the ambulance as the one paramedic swung the doors shut. "We're full," the paramedic said.

Madison caught the young officer's face in the crack before the door shut, and it was probably a good thing. She might kick his ass for letting Higgins get shot. But Higgins had to be okay. He had to be.

CHAPTER FIFTY-THREE

Somehow the sirens weren't as loud inside the ambulance, but they served as background noise that underscored the severity of the situation. The paramedic worked on Higgins, trying to staunch the blood flow and keep him awake. Machines beeped, and an intravenous was established.

In the front, the driver was talking excitedly to the hospital, letting them know they were incoming. "Gunshot wound to the chest…"

Pulling in air was like sucking back nails. Madison remained speechless on the way to the hospital, afraid that if she said one word, somehow she would jinx Higgins's survival.

He opened his eyes briefly, but they fluttered shut again.

The paramedic continued to work animatedly over him.

Madison wanted to reach for Higgins's hand, but she had to let the paramedic do his job to save her friend's life. She had to think positively, no matter how hard it was while seeing him like this.

The ambulance slid to a stop under the overhang for Emergency as if it were a jet plane that had just careened to a graceful stop on the runway.

The back doors flung open, and the two paramedics had Higgins unloaded and wheeled into the hospital in seconds. She stood there, watching after them, lost and helpless. There was nothing more she could do other than pray, and she and God weren't all that close.

Flashing lights caught her eye, and a cruiser pulled up and parked. Tendum got out and jogged toward her. "Is he…?"

"What are you doing here? Don't you think you've done enough already?" There was nothing this young recruit could say to bring Higgins back to her, nothing that could retract the bullet, nothing that could reverse time and consequence.

"This wasn't my fault."

Madison's earlobes heated with anger. "It was your gun. A man's life is on the line *and* a woman is dead because you let a perp take your gun."

"It all happened so fast." Tendum clenched his jaw and ran a hand through his hair. "I…I couldn't do any—"

"You could have taken him down with Higgins's gun. You're to stop the threat, even if that means you shoot to kill."

"It wasn't that simple."

"It's always *that* simple. You didn't do your job. You froze. And because of that, Higgins may die."

Tendum turned and vomited on the walkway. He ran the back of a hand across his mouth. "He shot Higgins. He held the gun on me."

She shook her head, disgusted. "You're obviously not cut out for this job. If I were you, I'd think about what I was going to put in my resignation letter. If you don't quit, you can bet I will make your life hell. And if you pray, Tendum, you better have started, because if that man doesn't make it—" She pointed to the hospital, the rest of her words not forming aloud as she went into the cool, bright light of the waiting room.

CHAPTER FIFTY-FOUR

Hours passed. Terry and a myriad of officers were at the hospital, bursting the waiting room beyond its legal capacity. After all, a brother in blue had been shot in the line of duty.

Barnes had been treated and hauled downtown, and even if his SR22 didn't match the previous homicides, he was at least responsible for the murder of his wife and for shooting Higgins. He'd live the rest of his life behind bars.

She glanced over at Terry periodically. She should come clean about how her memory had returned, but now wasn't the time or place. She would tell him though. At least she could answer the question that had haunted her for days about who pulled their gun first in that warehouse.

She bolted to her feet. "This is crazy. Why hasn't any—"

A doctor came through the swinging doors dressed in a teal-blue uniform with a mask dangling around his neck and resting against his chest. He appeared to be too young to carry the responsibility of life in his hands. He looked all of twenty-six, not much older than Tendum, who sat slumped in a chair, resting his head in his hands.

The doctor approached and glanced at Madison and Terry. He settled on her when Terry took a few steps back.

"Is Mr. Higgins's wife here or significant other or family member?" he asked her.

"He's not married and doesn't have any living blood relatives," she told him. Higgins had never married. He had dedicated his life to the Stiles PD. He dated women but always considered himself "on the market." He liked things that way. Maybe that was another reason Madison was drawn to him. He couldn't commit in romance either. "I'm as close as you can get to being his family. Detective Madison Knight."

The doctor nodded. "Mr. Higgins…"

He kept talking, but she focused on his body language. He wrung his hands. His shoulders hunched. Madison swallowed roughly.

"…it's going to be touch and go for a while." His eyes probed hers as if he sensed she'd drifted.

"So, he's going to make it?" Her voice came out small, and the words thrashed about in her chest, hope battling to win out over pessimism.

"The next twenty-four hours are going to be critical. He needs his rest, but if one of you wants to go in for a short visit, in about twenty minutes, then that should be fine."

Reserved optimism, but she'd latch onto it. Otherwise, she'd go over to Tendum and strangle him. She laid a hand over her heart. Higgins was going to make it. The tough dog had come out the other side of a bullet. Relief tugged the corner of her mouth, but uncertainty reined in the emotion and prevented its full formation. "Thank you, Doctor."

"You're welcome. I'll send a nurse out for you shortly." He walked away.

Madison spun to face Terry. Worry had added years to his appearance, or was she reflecting back at herself through his eyes?

She glanced over at Tendum. He made a motion to get up, but Madison held up a hand to keep him there. She went to him. "He's going to be fine." She wanted to add, *no thanks to you.*

Relief washed over Tendum's features, and his blue eyes became a little brighter. "Thank God."

"He's still not in the clear, but I'm able to go in and see him in a few minutes."

Tendum straightened. "I didn't mean for any of this to happen."

Terry brushed her elbow as he stepped beside her. "Things happen, Officer, things outside of our control, but first and foremost, we keep our brothers safe. You got that?"

Madison picked up where Terry left off. "Sounds like a recruitment speech, but it's the truth. We're a family. I mean, look around this hospital, it's a sea of blue. Brothers and sisters come together when one has fallen."

"You think I've failed the brotherhood." Tendum's voice was low and fractured.

He let a perp get close enough to grab his gun. He'd failed to act in the heat of the moment. He didn't deserve the badge. Yeah, he'd failed the brotherhood, but she bit back from saying it out loud. She had made her thoughts clear when he first arrived at the hospital. Instead, she said, "I'll leave that for you to figure out." She walked toward the mass of hallways branching off the emergency area like tentacles. She just needed to put space between herself and Tendum.

Footsteps tapped behind her on the tile flooring.

"You were a tad harsh on him."

She stopped walking and faced Terry. "Higgins might die, and I'm supposed to take it easy on Tendum because I might hurt his feelings?" She sniffled, and tears stung her eyes. She did her best to blink them away.

"I realize you really care for Higgins," Terry said softly, stepping on delicate ground, "but his getting shot wasn't Tendum's fault, and you know it."

"Do I? It was his service weapon."

"Sometimes—"

"Don't say sometimes things happen. An officer is fighting for his life. One other person never had the opportunity. It all could have been prevented." She resumed walking—not sure why or where she was even going. But it was difficult to stay still, as if that somehow represented giving up.

Terry pulled back on her shoulder.

She let out a deep breath, crossed her arms, and turned around again.

"It's not his fault," he repeated.

A nurse called out her name. "Detective Knight?"

Madison hustled toward her.

"This way." She led Madison down a hallway and stopped outside room 113.

"Thank you."

"Don't mention it. The doctor said to keep it brief."

Madison nodded and went inside, her mind prepared to see her friend, fallen and broken. Reality was much, much worse. On both sides of the bed, tubes from machines fed into his arms—blood and a clear liquid that was probably pain medication. Higgins's eyes were shut as she approached.

"Reggie." His first name slipped off her tongue, her natural response to seeing him this vulnerable.

He slowly opened his eyes. "Mad—"

She put her hand on his arm. "It's okay, Chief. Save your strength."

He looked at her.

She feared smiling in case emotion overtook her. She needed to be strong for him, for herself. "We've got the guy who did this."

He blinked slowly.

He was so pale, and his eyes were clouded. She preferred to replace the current reality with how she saw him—a fighter, an amazing cop, and an even better human being. She squeezed his arm. "You're going to come out of this, my friend." Sorrow fractured the last word, but she dared to continue speaking. "Now, you're just going to have something to brag about—Superman, the Man of Steel."

"Don't forget to tell that to the ladies." He winked lazily.

Madison laughed. "I'll be sure to. Remember when you were my training officer?"

"How could I forget? You were so stubborn. And I wondered where they got you from. You were a girl."

"You noticed, huh?" Madison laughed. She was still the only woman in the department—despicable but true.

"Right away. I took a lot of flak for it."

"You did, but it was the 1950s around PD before me. I brought you guys into the twenty-first century, though the department could definitely use more women."

"You've done so much more than change the landscape." He shut his eyes for a few seconds.

She turned away as tears threatened to fall. Maybe it was okay if this man saw her emotion. She had cried at the scene, but he'd been out of it completely. She faced him again. "You were inspiring. You still are. I'm the cop I am today because of you." One tear snaked down her cheek, and she wiped it away.

"Thanks, but that's all you." Higgins lifted his hand, dismissing the compliment. But he'd always been modest and never required praise for his hard work.

"Well, the doctor is feeling confident in your recovery." She might have slanted the news a bit, but it was best he thought positively.

"Of course. Do you really think a bullet could keep an old dog like me down?" His eyes found hers. "I'm Superman." His smile drained from his mouth, and his eyes closed again.

It was time for her to go. "You get some rest." She leaned over him and kissed his forehead. Another rogue tear fell as she did so.

CHAPTER FIFTY-FIVE

Madison and Terry were back at their desks at the station. The action she'd taken against Barnes was ruled a good shot—meaning it was justified and equal force in response to the situation. They tried to interrogate Barnes but were stonewalled by a request for his lawyer.

"I remember how everything took place at the warehouse," she began, figuring now was a good time to tell him that her memory had returned.

He looked over at her, as if to say, *Go on*.

"The girl at the front closed shop and left, but there was a noise in the back that I went to investigate." She paused there and studied his eyes. Would he judge her for this or understand? "I did have my gun, but it wasn't drawn. You do know where I was?" The implication being that it was a mob business front and perceivably dangerous.

He nodded, pardoning her action.

She continued. "When I went through the doorway, I didn't see anything, but I was about to go up the stairs when Anatolli came on me from behind and fired. I pulled my gun, and then Sergey showed up at the top of the staircase. I was wedged between them." She took a heaving breath and went on. "I pulled my trigger. Anatolli pulled his."

"His bullet must have gotten Sergey."

"Mine went into the wall, so that would make sense."

"And you got lucky."

"I guess. I'm not sure how I managed to escape Anatolli's first bullet. Thankfully, I dropped in time." Tears beaded in her eyes, but she willed them away. She needed to get a grip before she completely fell apart. She sniffled and jutted out her chin. "But you have my word that I will never intentionally put my life at risk like that again."

Seconds passed. Terry just looking into her eyes. Eventually he blinked and dipped his head, accepting her promise. With that behind her, her thoughts turned to Higgins in that hospital bed.

"I'm sure Higgins will fully recover," Terry said as if he read her mind.

"He's too stubborn not to." She stopped there, hesitating to say what she had in mind. "There's one place I've got to go, Terry, and you're not going to like it."

"Don't even say it. We can't be running to the prison—"

"Let me tell Dimitre that we have Barnes and that we're onto his assassin."

"But we're not. Barnes has lawyered up, and he's not going to say a thing. We don't even know if his Ruger was used in any murders."

"Dimitre doesn't have to know any of that."

"Okay, what exactly do you intend to accomplish by visiting Dimitre?"

"I—" Her cell phone rang, and she held up a finger to Terry as she answered. A few seconds later, she was thanking her caller and ending the call. "That was Cynthia," she told Terry. "She said that Richards concluded Lillian Norton had been tortured for a number of hours and that TOD was between four and six Saturday morning." That man the neighbor had seen was likely Lillian's killer. Madison sure hoped she and Terry hadn't led him to Lillian, but now all she could do was move forward. She opened her email on her computer. "Also, look at this."

He came around to her desk.

She clicked on the attachment. "Cyn sent this over. Hand impressions from the person who strangled Douglas."

Terry leaned over to see the photo. "Big hands."

"Yeah. And the bruising makes them look even bigger, but Cynthia estimates our guy would be…" She read the short message. "Six foot eight. Holy sh—crap!" She amended to the PG version under Terry's eye.

"A Russian giant."

"Say that again." She was only five foot five. The guy would tower over her by fifteen inches! Seeing Dimitre and possibly coaxing this guy out of hiding was a *very* bad idea. And after she'd just promised Terry she wouldn't risk her life again. But this wasn't too risky, was it? She'd be ready.

"You still think seeing Dimitre is a good idea?"

She peered into his eyes, trying to read his mind. Did he know her true intention when it came to the Mafia boss? "I don't see what other choice I have."

"Okay, well…" Terry walked off in the direction of the coffee machine, and Madison's phone rang. She answered to Chelsea.

"A reporter called me," Chelsea said. "He called Mom too. He's nosy, Maddy. Why is he prying into your personal life?"

"He's a reporter, that's what they do." Madison had this horrible suspicion about why King was harassing her family.

"You haven't answered my question. What's going on? Why is this man asking about Grandpa?"

"What did he ask you?"

"If I knew the real reason you became a cop. He also inquired if I was aware of the connection between our family and the Russians. What is he talking about?"

She wasn't ready to go there with her sister yet and wasn't sure if any time would be right. "I'm sorry, sis, I'll tell you. Just not right now."

"Maddy, you can't leave me hanging like this. Please tell me."

"Trust me. I will. Please be patient."

Seconds passed.

"Fine," Chelsea pushed out. "But I told him I didn't know anything, and that's the truth. I'm kept in the dark like mushrooms."

Despite the context, Madison found herself smiling, as she'd just thought of that cliche the other day. "I love you, Chels, but I've gotta go." She hung up, enraged. That reporter needed to learn boundaries. Due to him, she'd need to tell her sister the whole truth about their grandfather's murder sooner rather than later.

CHAPTER FIFTY-SIX

Madison sat across from Dimitre Petrov at the prison. "Sergey and Anatolli didn't kill Bryan Lexan on your orders."

Dimitre's cheeks twitched. "I told you I didn't kill him. I even wrote to you to say as much."

It finally snapped in place for her on the way here. Just as he had told Madison about the man with the bowler hat to let her know he was aware Lexan had faked his death, his letter to her had been for the same purpose. No one could claim the Russian mob boss communicated clearly. He intentionally spoke in riddles to toy with people. "Sure. Not the first time, when he faked it. Not that you knew that right away. When you did make that discovery, that's probably when you wrote me your claim to innocence."

Dimitre was smiling at her as if impressed that she'd unraveled that much.

She went on. "But he tricked you, and your men lied to you, made a fool of you."

The smile disappeared. "Ridiculous."

"No. You found out about Sergey and Anatolli's betrayal."

His eyes temporarily skipped to a place behind her.

"But eventually they did take care of Lexan, didn't they? I mean, otherwise Sergey and Anatolli would have been long dead by now."

Underlying amusement lifted his cheeks, but his eyes remained dark.

"I just don't understand why you waited so long to get vengeance on your men, to claim back your power."

"You know nothing."

Madison sat back in her chair. "Are you certain of that?"

"Ah, I see what you are doing. Setting trap. I will not bite."

"You don't have to bite anything. Your guard, Jacob, has been fired. We know you bought him off. And the warden is suspended, pending an investigation." She circled a finger in the air to take in the room. "This little resort you live in"—she slapped her hands together—"is over."

"You are bullshitting me."

"Am I?" She held eye contact with him, and after he glanced away, she stood.

"Detective."

She faced him.

He spoke a few words in Russian. She was quite sure that he'd just made an oath to have her killed. Everything was working according to plan. She just hoped when the Russian giant came for her, she'd be ready.

CHAPTER FIFTY-SEVEN

On the way home, Madison stopped by to see Higgins at the hospital, and he was already improving. He'd be just fine and end up with bragging rights about dodging a bullet.

Connor had left her a voicemail and was unmistakably ticked off. She said she couldn't be bought or coerced into signing off on a patient's release from her care. Apparently, McAlexandar had reached out to the shrink. She told Madison she expected a call back to rebook another appointment.

Madison took the elevator in her apartment building up to her floor and rested against the wall. It was only seven thirty, but she was exhausted. Regardless, minutes from now she'd be riding back down with Hershey.

The car chimed its arrival, and she sauntered down the hall, struggling with freeing her keys from her jeans pocket as she went. She slipped it into the lock and twisted. But the door was already unlocked.

Shivers laced down her spine. *Hershey!*

She stormed into her apartment.

In the light cast through the windows, she made out Hershey's silhouette on the couch. But he wasn't alone. Another larger-than-life form was next to him.

She went cold and slowly reached for her gun.

"How nice of you to join me, Detective. I've been waiting." He flicked a finger toward her holster. "Now I wouldn't be pulling my gun if I were you." He turned on the lamp on a table next to him, and Madison's eyes worked to adjust to the brightness. When they did, she saw a large blond man—possibly the same one seen in Lillian Norton's neighborhood—and he was holding Hershey under his right arm. Her Lab let out a small wince of excitement at her being home. "Ah, no need for that either." He put his hands on both sides of Hershey's head and rustled up his fur. "Cute dog you have here. But I've never seen the purpose of dogs. They are so…fragile. It would only take one twist, and your little hush puppy would be in doggie heaven."

She stepped toward him. "You sick son of a bitch! I'll kill you myself, I swear it."

He pulled a gun and held it to Hershey's head. "Your gun on the floor. Now."

Hershey barked, his keen senses kicking in and alerting him to the threat.

Madison did as he'd directed and studied the weapon he held. A Ruger SR22.

"There. Was that so hard?"

She needed to get Hershey away from him. "This doesn't need to involve the dog."

"Oh, you have a sentimental attachment to him. How cute." He petted Hershey's head, but the dog's barks were sinking into a growl.

"Hershey, it's okay. Come here, buddy. Come here." Madison lowered to her haunches. Maybe she could grab her gun and jump up and shoot this man between the eyes. It sounded good, but there was the possibility she'd miss or act too late.

"You tell him when it's okay to come and go? Like he's a slave? Does he answer to a bitch? No good man should. Right, Hershey?" He mussed the top of the dog's head again.

"Get away from him. I mean it."

"Or what? What are you going to do? Talk me to death?" He laughed.

Hershey managed to slip from the man's reach and came scurrying across the room to Madison.

She hurried to grab ahold of him and took him down the hall to her bedroom. She closed him inside.

Footsteps came heavy behind her, but before she could turn and defend herself, the man had grabbed her by the hair, his fingernails digging into her scalp.

A cry escaped her throat.

He dragged her into the living room. Her body arched backward as she tried to keep pace with him. He tossed her onto the couch as if she weighed nothing. For the first time, Madison had a real sense of the man's proportions. He *was* a giant among men, and certainly to her!

"You put your nose where it doesn't belong." He came at her with the agility of a running back.

"You're not going to get away with this." She lifted her arms to cover her face, and he dropped down over her. His massive structure surrounded her without effort. She struggled beneath him, and her power ebbed as waves of defeat pulsed through her. But she couldn't give in. This was a fight for her life.

He held up his gun, pointing it at her. "Do you want death to come quickly or nice and slowly?"

Her head was still throbbing from his pulling on her hair, and it was hard to think clearly. She was left with pure instinct and the will to survive. She thought of bringing up her knee, but it would only send him jutting forward—his head into hers, and she would risk him firing his gun in the process.

Think! Think! Think!

"We have time before you go out. You want a goodbye present?" His face lit into a sneer. He lowered down over her and ran his tongue from her chin to the side of her eye. "You have never had it so good, bitch." He leaned back, placing his gun on the coffee table her grandmother had given her.

At this moment, with her life flashing before her yet again, she remembered what her grandmother had told her. *Madison, we hold it over men in three ways: looks, brains, and the ability to see things through.*

He was unlatching his belt.

Madison's focus kept drifting to the table and the gun he had forfeited in a rush to pleasure himself—and violate her—but she couldn't get caught looking at it. Her best chance at survival was to play along and distract him. "You are a big man."

"Don't worry. It will only hurt a little bit." He laughed, and she felt him growing against her.

She couldn't go out like this. She wouldn't. She refused. She reached out and touched his chest and swallowed the bile that rose in her throat.

His head was still angled down to work on his zipper, but he raised his eyes upward to look at her. He gripped her hand and squeezed it so hard she thought her wrist would pop.

"Please. I just want to see all of you." More bile shot into her mouth, and she pushed it back down. "I love a man's chest," she went on.

"You are into this?" He stopped moving.

"Please. Just let me see you."

Seconds passed. What was he thinking? Was he onto her tactic? Willingness made these types uninterested. But she was also hoping for a pocket of time in which he was distracted so she could snatch the gun.

"You first, sweetheart." He put his hands on her lower abdomen, and she almost reached for the gun then, but it would have been premature. It wasn't time. Yet.

He found the base of her shirt and ripped the material up her torso until she lay exposed, her breasts screened off by her bra alone.

Her stomach was curdling, and she was calling on what her grandmother had taught her. She would prevail. She would endure. She would survive.

His hands wrapped around her back and unclasped her bra. "I could just strangle you with this."

She had to place herself out of body. She closed her eyes briefly. When she opened them, she did her best to be seductive. "Now show me yours."

He sat back and lifted his shirt over his head.

She had a second, or less, at most. She wormed over, just enough to reach the gun, and pulled the trigger without thought. The bullet burrowed into his left shoulder.

He dropped his arms. His shirt was left bunched beneath his armpits. Crimson spread across his chest. There was a look of bewilderment etched on his facial features. His eyes fell heavily, and she heaved him off her. His head hit the coffee table on the way down.

Score one for Grandma!

The door to her apartment blew inward, and Terry and Matthews barged through, both with guns readied.

"Whoa! What the shit! Get out of here. I'm not even dressed. Crap!" Madison crossed her arms to cover herself and bolted off the couch. She wrapped herself with what fabric remained of her shirt.

"Didn't realize you were into the Russians like that," Terry said, keeping his gaze above her shoulders.

She narrowed her eyes. "Shut up."

"Watch out, man, that bulldog has teeth."

She glared at Matthews, but she found when her eyes met with the green of his, her breath hitched.

CHAPTER FIFTY-EIGHT

Two Days Later

Answers bring closure, and finally, after years, Madison had that. The murder of Bryan Lexan was no longer a cold case, but a *closed* one.

The Russian giant was Constantine Romanov. His last known address was in Russia, but he had an apartment in Stiles. Before now, he had held no criminal record in the United States. The same brand of hollow-point bullets used on Lexan were recovered from his apartment. The gun he had in Madison's apartment—a Ruger SR22—matched the one used to kill Douglas's maid, Sonia Pike, and Lexan. A sniper rifle was also collected along with bullets that matched what was used to assassinate Sergey Evanoff and Anatolli Belsky.

Constantine's hands were a probable match for the impressions on Douglas's neck, and they found a knife that was a likely match for what caused the injuries to Lillian Norton. The neighbor who saw a big blond man picked Constantine out of a lineup, so they could put him in the neighborhood. DNA from the piece of hair taken from the sniper perch was still awaiting processing, but it very likely would be a match for Constantine.

Additional good news was Constantine would pull through his injuries and have to account for the murders he'd committed. He'd be facing multiple sentences of twenty-five to life. The case against him was open and shut.

"So how did you know Constantine was coming after me?" Madison asked. She and Terry were at a table at Starbucks.

"I told you."

"You had a gut feeling?" She laughed.

He grumbled incoherently, then said, "I put two and two together when you told me you were going to see Dimitre."

"And you let me go?"

"Not like I can control you." He smiled.

"Uh-huh."

"I was also tipped off by the look on your face when you heard how big Douglas's killer was. You were obviously terrified."

"Me? Terrified? No way." She hoped she sounded convincing. "Moving on. Dimitre's prison transfer went through, so he'll have to start working on his relationships from scratch."

"It won't stop him for good."

"I know."

"You'll have a target on your back until you die."

"Wow, thanks for laying it out there for me, Terry."

"So there would be no sense in my getting another partner."

"Another partner?" Hearing him say it hurt more than her assumption that he'd been debating about it.

"I never did put in a request."

"All for the best," she said. "You'd miss me too much anyhow."

"Damn right."

She gushed inside and smiled. "I do have another question for you."

"Fire away."

"How did Matthews end up coming along? You know, to save my ass? Even though, I had things under control."

"You're kidding, right? I went to him, and when he found out you were in danger, he was on board. I think he has a thing for you."

A warm flush ran through her. "Think or *know*?"

Terry shrugged. "He told me on the way to your place."

"Hmm."

"What? I swear to you."

She smiled. Now she was terrified.

"So you wanted to talk," Terry prompted her.

"Ah, yes, I do." Madison was going to tell Terry her suspicions about the chief. She also wanted to come clean about her past and tell him why she held such animosity toward the Russians. She laid out her feelings about Chief McAlexandar to start. When she finished, Terry raised his eyebrows.

"You think the chief is bought?"

"Without hesitation—and here are the reasons why. It goes back to the Lexan case. Blood from an unknown donor was in Calin's apartment—as you probably remember, he was the one Lexan had call Jessica pretending to be a Russian mobster. Well, that sample got lost. Samples don't just go missing, especially with Cynthia in charge. Someone higher up messed with it. And, yes, I realize this is your first time hearing about this. My name to the newspaper—given to King by an unnamed source. I believe that was also McAlexandar. He was trying to discredit and get rid of me. Instead, his efforts backfired and made me popular for whatever reason." She waved a hand, though curious of the effects his next article would have—whenever it came out. "And the assassination of Sergey and Anatolli? The time and date for their preliminary hearings were to be kept under wraps."

"That can get out sometimes, but you think he provided that information to Dimitre, who then passed it on to Constantine?" Terry held his cup in his hands, but since she had started talking about McAlexandar, he hadn't taken a sip.

"Or directly to the killer."

"You think the chief is in direct contact with a"—Terry looked around and leaned across the table—"a Mafia hit man?"

"Why not?"

"Suppose it's possible, but some hard proof would be nice." He rubbed the back of his neck.

"My first tipoff that something was up—easier to see what looking back—was the media shouldn't have been at the courthouse that day either. Someone informed them too. Maybe to cover the origin of the leak? Again, I think that leak was the chief." Her phone rang. Caller ID told her it was Chelsea. She sent her sister to voicemail. She regarded her partner with seriousness. "I hope you will help me gather hard evidence." She moderated her tone of voice, not wanting to scare him.

"You want me to help you get the chief put in prison?"

"Sure, why not?" She tossed it out matter-of-factly, but she was serious. If McAlexandar was criminally inclined as she suspected, Dimitre probably compensated him handsomely to cover his tracks—and to undermine Madison's efforts. The chief hadn't counted on the fact that she couldn't be bullied into silence or into looking the other way. That made her his enemy, and she'd need all the help she could get. "There's something else I want to talk to you about."

"I'm almost afraid to ask." He smiled gently.

"You accused me of my thing with the Russians being personal. Well, it is." She took a deep, staggered breath. "My grandfather used to be a cop. He was shot down when he was out for dinner with my grandmother. They were celebrating their thirtieth wedding anniversary and his retirement. He died on the floor of a restaurant while my grandmother watched on, helpless. The boy who shot him was only fifteen." Her voice cracked.

Terry nodded like he understood, but there was a lot more to the story.

She went on. "He shot my grandfather because he was responsible for getting the boy's father convicted of fraud charges. But that was the base charge. The rest included money laundering and falsifying of tax documents. He worked for the Russian Mafia."

Terry let go of his cup. "I had no idea."

"Yeah, well this is why shutting them down is so personal to me. If that boy's father hadn't been mob and if my grandfather had never arrested him, he might still be alive.

His murder pushes me forward, and I've been determined to find him justice since I found out about it. As far as I'm concerned, they all belong behind bars."

"Found out about it? So you weren't around when he was killed?"

She shook her head. "I wasn't even born yet. My mom, she was twelve. My grandparents had her later in their lives." Madison offered the explanation to account for her mother's age and a thirty-year marriage. "It's a lot of the reason our relationship is rough. She lost her dad right when a girl needs her father the most—or at least that's how she puts it. And he was a cop, now I'm a cop. She'd rather I be doing anything else."

"She doesn't want to lose you too."

"Yeah. And as I said, I hold the Mafia responsible for my grandfather's murder, for leaving my mother without her father, my grandmother without the love of her life," she declared in all seriousness. "If it hadn't been for the mob, then the rest of this wouldn't have unfolded. At the time, Dimitre's older brother ran things. His name was Vlad, but he died years ago. It's rumored that Dimitre had something to do with his death, but as always, there is no proof."

"He killed his own brother to take over?"

"Well, it's rumored, like I said. The son of the Mafia accountant, Jimmy Bates, served his full twenty-five-year prison sentence and got out when I was seventeen."

"Don't hate me for saying this, but Bates was just a kid, acting out in defense of his father."

She shook her head. "I'm not sure it's that simple."

"You think Dimitre or his brother, Vlad, put the kid up to it?"

"Uh-huh, and I will shut them completely down—if it's the last thing I do." She paused and watched as her words sank into her partner's mind.

"All right, then." His lips twitched and gave birth to a smile. "Just don't scare me like that again." He wagged a finger at her, imitating the chief.

She laughed. "I promise." Her cell rang, and she put her caller to voicemail again. "What is it with my phone right now?" She silenced it and tucked it into her coat pocket.

Terry's face was somber. "I should probably confess something. I knew all of this about you, your grandfather, the mob."

"You knew? How? You just said that you had no idea."

He sank into his chair. "I had no idea until this morning's paper."

"Why counter with all these questions like you had no— *This morning's paper?*" Her head spun. "What? Today? Nice of King to give me a heads-up. God, that's why—" She pulled out her phone. Missed calls from her sister, mother, Cynthia, and Howard Buckley, the prison warden from Dimitre's previous institution.

She dialed through to her voicemail. She didn't have the heart to listen to her sister or mother right now and forwarded to Cynthia's message. She listened to hers and Buckley's. Seconds later, she hung up and filled Terry in. "Cynthia said the anthropologists in charge of the victims from the ravine were able to reconstruct their faces. One has been confirmed as James Calin. The other three men are still unidentified. Their bones confirm that gunshots were the cause of death for all four men. The markings on the bullets found in their graves match Barnes's SR22. He'll never see life outside of a prison again."

"Some more closure. Anything else?"

She smiled and nodded, then fell serious. "I also got a message from Howard Buckley, the warden at Dimitre's previous prison. He wants to talk to me about Dimitre. Says he has news I'll want to hear."

Madison arranged to meet with Howard Buckley at a deli located downtown. Terry offered to go with her, but she told him if Buckley was planning to come clean about something, he might be intimidated by them both being there and clam up.

She found Buckley sitting in a corner booth, with an untouched corned beef sandwich in front of him. She slipped in across from him. "So I'm here, what do you want to talk to me about?"

"You told me to call if I thought of anything."

"I did." Madison wasn't going to press the man to talk, thinking if she acted almost disinterested, he'd be more forthcoming.

"What I'm about to tell you is off the record." He dipped a corner of the sandwich into mustard but made no move to eat it. "I mean it, if you say I said it, I will deny it with my dying breath. Do you understand?"

"I do."

"You were asking about Dimitre's visitors and if I knew who would come and see him. Well, I know someone he'd talk to."

She remained quiet. Saying the wrong thing could be worse.

"We're talking about a very powerful man. Do you understand, Detective? He will kill my family, me. Heck, not that I care if he kills me if they're gone." He dropped his sandwich on his plate and wiped his fingers on a napkin.

"Yes, I get it. Dimitre is a powerful—"

Buckley was shaking his head. "Right now I'm talking about the man who Dimitre spoke with."

More powerful or equally so? She wanted to push him, but that approach wouldn't work with Buckley. She'd have to show some restraint. "Okay."

"I really shouldn't say anything, but I want a clean conscience. That's all I want. I want my family and me to be alive too, of course, but a clean—"

"I will not tell a soul. You have my word." She was out of patience—and willpower. "Who was it?"

"The Chief of Police," he blurted out.

It was one thing to have suspicions about the chief, and another to have them confirmed. "Patrick McAlexandar came in to see him?" she squeezed out.

Buckley shook his head and took a bite of his sandwich, then washed it down with a swig of water. "Like I said, he *talked* to Dimitre." Buckley's eyes went to his plate.

Call it a hunch: whatever Buckley had to say would betray someone else. "Whatever you say is between us, remember?"

"All right, Jacob, Dimitre's guard—Dimitre would always bum his cell for his communication, you know, to the outside world."

She nodded. "And he was sure it was Chief McAlexandar?"

"As sure as Christmas is December twenty-fifth every year." He leaned across the table. "Said he knew the voice sounded familiar, but when the chief made some press statement the other day, he knew for certain."

Press statement? That was news to her—not that she followed everything the man did. Maybe it was time to really start paying attention. "And Jacob told you this?"

"Yes, I swear to you on a stack of Bibles. And there was someone who had come recently to visit Dimitre."

"Who?"

Buckley's face paled, and he pushed his plate away. "I really overstepped even mentioning him. He's…he's…*ah*…huge. Had wild eyes too."

"Blond hair, built like brick shithouse?"

Buckley reached to the plate and picked at a fry, avoiding eye contact. That cinched it for her—Constantine had visited Dimitre in prison. Brazen.

Her phone rang.

"Off the record. Remember," Buckley said.

"You have my word." She slid out of the booth and answered her cell. "Detective Knight."

"This is Terry. Get back to the station right away."

CHAPTER FIFTY-NINE

Madison found Terry at his desk. "I've got news for you."

"I go first. I called you here, remember."

She gestured for him to proceed.

"Our Russian friend has disappeared."

"Constantine Romanov?"

"Yeah. Who else—never mind."

"What do you mean disappeared?"

"He managed to slip the officers watching over him and get out of his hospital room." He stood and let her have his chair.

She dropped into it. "You've got to be—" She stopped, glancing up at him. "Effing kidding me."

"I wish I was."

"There won't be any justice for all his victims. Including Lexan." The thought of that tore through her.

"Detective Knight? Grant? Come into conference room three." Sergeant Winston waved them over and turned around, leading them down the hall.

This was the largest of the conference rooms and could hold a couple hundred people. Inside, others from the department were already gathered. She and Terry must have missed a memo.

Winston gestured for them to take a seat. He stood at the front of the room and announced to everyone, "After years of service as Chief of Police, Patrick McAlexandar has stepped down. You're all here today to meet the new acting chief—"

Whispers filled the room.

"Please," Winston said with some impatience.

The room fell silent.

Madison glanced at Terry. Had McAlexandar stepped down because of her? Maybe. But she doubted it was remorse or guilt that had him doing so. She was quite sure she hadn't seen the last of him.

Her attention went back to the podium, her thoughts on a new chief. Likely it was going to be another power-hungry man who held no respect for women in the police force. He would look down on her, thinking she was capable of nothing more than bringing him coffee.

The conference room door opened, and a woman in a pressed pantsuit walked toward Winston. Her long, straight brown hair was pulled back into a ponytail. Bangs framed her face and provided an air of mystery to her. She had small, delicate facial features, and her makeup was applied modestly—a pale-pink lipstick and muted browns for eyeshadow.

"Please welcome Andrea Fletcher," Winston said, stepping back and initiating applause.

When the noise died down, Fletcher took the podium. "As you just heard, I'm your acting chief. Men, they can't have all the fun. I think it's time to shake things up." Her eyes searched the room and settled on Madison, as if she'd found her target.

After the announcement, everyone went to a nearby community hall to celebrate the appointment of the new police chief. Champagne would be brought in and the active police staff reduced to the non-drinkers and the beat cops.

Before heading over, Madison called Chelsea and laid out everything about their grandfather. She apologized to her sister that she had to find out some of this from a newspaper, but went on to field Chelsea's questions. Her sister handled the answers well. "I just wanted to protect you," Madison told her.

"I know that now. I love you, sis."

"Love—" Her sister was gone, and Madison headed to the gathering.

She found Terry right away and joined him.

"So do you think the chief knew you were onto him?" Terry asked Madison.

No question—not that she was going to tell Terry that she'd called McAlexandar out days ago. She simply nodded, but when she saw Cynthia across the room, she excused herself.

"That was quite the surprise," Cynthia said.

Madison peered into her friend's eyes, more interested in something else. "I never heard. What did you decide?"

Cynthia became quiet, and the energy coming from her was hard to read. "I know you'll be there for me no matter what—whatever I decide?"

"No question."

"Well, I hope you can stomach taffeta because I want you to be my maid of honor." Cynthia's face went from hardened lines to a full-blown smile, and she held out her left hand. A gold band circled her ring finger, a square diamond twinkling.

"You're…you are?"

"Yes. I'm getting married!" Cynthia threw her arms around Madison. "I'm so happy. I don't get it, but he makes me happy. Life's too short."

Madison was smiling, but her heart was fracturing. *Life's too short.* Wasn't that a statement and a half? If anything, recent events had taught her that truth.

Cynthia pulled back from the embrace. "Oh, and here he comes."

Lou kissed Cynthia, and then turned to Madison. "I take it she told you? I mean, I could hear the squealing from across the room."

"Squealing? Like I'm a pig or something?" Cynthia played cross and batted him in the chest.

Lou laughed. "Never. It was simply an animated discussion. My apologies."

"Isn't he terrific?" Cynthia laced her arm through Lou's.

Madison was truly happy for Cynthia. She remembered what it was like to live in that bubble of happiness and romance, but sadly, she also recalled how devastating it was when that bubble burst. She surveyed the room and saw Matthews headed straight for her.

Cynthia and Lou said their goodbyes and left.

Madison *squealed* in her head for them to come back.

"Hello there." Matthews was standing right in front of her.

"Hello." She laughed. Why did she laugh? Again, there was something about him that had this…*effect*…on her. She swallowed hard and wished she had gotten herself some champagne. The last time this man had seen her, she'd pretty much been half naked. She had to divert to small talk. "Quite the change for the department."

"Yes." He kept his eyes on her, his face expressionless. He was impossible to read. What was he thinking? Did she even want to know?

She cleared her throat. "I never thanked you properly."

"This sounds like it could be fun."

She swatted his arm and then lowered hers as soon as possible. This man would be her undoing if she allowed it. "You saved me from the Russians, then you saved me—"

"From another one."

"Yes. Although, *technically*, I had shot him before you guys busted in."

"Speaking of busts…"

She narrowed her eyes. "Don't even go there."

"I wouldn't dream of it."

Something in his eyes told her that he did, but it didn't bother her like she thought it would. "I never did hear the rest of your story, Hotshot, about how you worked under pressure."

"Hotshot, eh?"

"Hey, you call me Bulldog."

"I think out of the two nicknames mine is better."

"And whose fault is that?" She flipped his meaning so the implication was that the one she gave him was superior.

"In defense of bulldogs, they are rather adorable."

His flattery had her insides warming up. She allowed her mind to wander back to the warehouse, but instead of reliving the nightmare this time, she recounted the many promises she had made to herself. One was that she'd open herself up and love with all her heart. She took a deep breath, riding both excitement and nerves. But what kind of person was she if she couldn't keep a promise to herself? "Hey, bulldogs have all sorts of wrinkles. You're not saying I have those?"

"I wouldn't dare."

She smirked. He was smart and cute—*and* interested in her. Her mother would be thrilled. She shook her head.

"So you were saying that you hadn't thanked me properly," he said.

"I did. Yes."

"Is that you asking me out on a date?"

"Me asking you? No." Maybe it wasn't too late to run away, tail tucked between her legs.

"I'm surprised."

"What do you mean?"

"For an independent, forward-thinking woman, such as yourself, I'd think you'd know exactly what you want."

He was egging her on, but she wanted to lean into it. She stood a bit taller, sucked in her gut. She slowly let out the breath she was holding. Was she really going to do this? "All right. Would you join me for dinner tonight?"

"Dinner." He winced. "And tonight? That might be moving things along too fast."

She jabbed his shoulder. "It's just dinner I'm proposing, not marriage. It's a meal, not forever—" She clamped her mouth shut. She was prattling on like a rambling idiot all because Cynthia's engagement was messing with her head. "Just forget everything I said."

"What if I don't want to?"

Her legs went a little weak, and she fell speechless.

"I assume you're paying since you asked me," he added.

"Hmm."

"Is that a yes? You're paying?" His eyes took on further intensity.

"Sure, why not?"

The man was smooth—in more ways than one—and she loved it. They agreed on a restaurant and time.

"Now, I'll be at your place to pick you up at eight. Be ready on time and do get yourself gussied up," she said, playing up the stereotypical role reversal.

"Gussied up?"

She laughed. She would actually take the time to put on some makeup tonight, a spritz of perfume too—if she had any.

"I'll be ready. Will you?" He smiled as he caressed her shoulder.

She opened her mouth to speak, but no words came out. His touch sent shivers up her spine, and she wished his fingertips had lingered longer. She watched as he walked away, her heart racing, her mouth suddenly dry. She was really looking forward to their date, but there was something else she had to take care of right now.

She retreated to the streets and took out her phone. The call was answered on the second ring.

"Hi, Mom. It's me, Madison…"

Catch the next book in the Detective Madison Knight Series!

Sign up at the weblink listed below to be notified when new Madison Knight titles are available for pre-order:

CarolynArnold.net/MKUpdates

By joining this newsletter, you will also receive exclusive first looks at the following:

Updates pertaining to upcoming releases in the series, such as cover reveals, book descriptions, and firm release dates

Sneak peeks of teasers and special content

Behind-the-Tape™ insights that give you an inside look at Carolyn's research and creative process

There is no getting around it: reviews are important and so is word of mouth.

With all the books on the market today, readers need to know what's worth their time and what's not. This is where you come into play.

If you enjoyed *Just Cause*, please help others find it by posting a brief, honest review on the retailer site where you purchased this book and recommend it to family and friends.

Also, Carolyn loves to hear from her readers, and you can reach her at Carolyn@CarolynArnold.net.

Upon receipt of your e-mail, you will be added to her newsletter mailing unless you express your desire otherwise.

Keep on reading for a sample of *Deadly Impulse*, book 6 in the Detective Madison Knight series.

CHAPTER ONE

Apparently not even a dead body could stop traffic.
Madison scanned the three-lane, westbound stream of cars. All of the drivers had somewhere to be. Even now, only a few braked to gawk at the investigation on the side of the road.

Squad cars with flashing lights cordoned off the right lane, and the officers were diverting traffic over. This was the busiest intersection in Stiles. With a population of about half a million, seventy-five thousand people passed through this section every hour. Shopping plazas with franchise restaurants and grocery stores occupied two of the four corners; the other two had health care buildings, including one of the city's three hospitals, the largest of which was on the northeast side of the intersection.

Peace Liberty Hospital sat on acres of land with chain-link fencing running its perimeter. It was outside that fence that the deceased had been found.

Cole Richards, the medical examiner, was working over the body as Crime Scene Unit investigators Cynthia Baxter and Mark Andrews were busy taking pictures and collecting anything that might be evidence.

Cynthia headed up the crime lab. She was also Madison's closest friend. Her strong genetics gave her the sexy librarian look, and she had wielded that power expertly over men until she got involved with Detective Lou Stanford of the Stiles PD. Now she was engaged. Three months had passed since the announcement, and Madison still hardly believed it some days.

Mark was the only man on the forensics team and the youngest of its four members. Both elements served to make him the target of blame and teasing. All in good fun, of course, even if he might not think so at times. He had long, dark hair that he tied back into a ponytail at the nape of his neck. His hairstyle and other mannerisms had most of his colleagues curious about his sexual preference. To date, it remained an enigma.

Madison lowered her sunglasses and took in the scene. It was midday and mid-July, and the sun was beating down with nondiscriminatory heat.

The deceased was an elderly woman, her identity unknown and age estimated to be in her late sixties or early seventies. She had a short cut of gray hair and wore a T-shirt and a skirt. She sat in a wheelchair on the side of the road, her head dipped to her chest at an unnatural angle. That position alone would disclose to anyone paying enough attention that she was dead.

It was a sad state when people were too preoccupied with their busy lives to notice an elderly woman on the side of the road like that. As it was, people would have passed in good quantity before the jogger who had found her had come along.

His name was Erik Marsh, and he was sitting in the back of a squad car providing his statement to the officers who had arrived first on scene. She and Terry would talk to him shortly. The people who found a body were always the first suspects.

The woman's chair was on the grass beside the sidewalk, placing her closer to the fence than the road. Based on her thin arms and frail frame, she would have needed help to get there. A wooden board strapped to the back of the chair read, PUT AN END TO ABORTION.

"Protesters in this area are not uncommon, but what makes an older lady come out and sit in the hot sun with a sign strapped to her?" She asked the rhetorical question of her partner, ruminating on what brought the woman to this point.

Her partner, Terry Grant, was three years younger than she was and her total opposite. He loved running, and his hair was always perfect—rarely were one of his blond hairs out of place. Madison, on the other hand, hated mornings, so she stuck with a wake-up-and-wear-it cut. While she had a hard time making commitments, Terry was married to his sweetheart of just over five years. Annabelle was pregnant with their first child and due any day.

Madison continued. "Not to mention, why would she get involved in such an issue? Her child-birthing days are behind her."

"She could have faced this issue earlier in life, or maybe a family member had? She could have been trying to keep things the way they used to be."

"When was abortion legalized?"

"In most states, 1973. That would make her somewhere in her late twenties, early thirties, if she faced the issue herself." Terry pulled his phone out and poised a finger over the screen. Despite Madison's desire that he take notes on a lined pad, like other cops, he was adamant about embracing technology. His hardheaded determination was paying off, though, as his texting speed was improving.

"There's no way she came alone. Someone must've brought her here. But was she dead when they dropped her off, or did she die sitting in this heat? My grandmother always wore a hat on a hot day." She paced a few steps and brainstormed aloud. "I don't think this woman chose to come here."

"Good deduction," Cole Richards stated matter-of-factly.

It was the only way Richards talked to her these days. Madison's friendship with him used to be one based upon mutual respect, but things had changed when she questioned his ruling on a prior case. From there, she had dug into his personal past. If she could go back and change things she would.

Richards continued. "Her forearms show bruising to indicate she was in a struggle, but the cause of death still needs to be determined."

Madison's gaze fell to the woman's wrists, marred in hues of purple. Heat surged through her, the fire of adrenaline blending with rage.

Richards's dark skin pinched around his eyes as he squinted in the bright sun. "Based on the coloring of the contusions, they happened around the time of death."

"And when was that?"

"I estimate time of death between twelve and eighteen hours ago. Her body is in full rigor."

"You can't narrow it down any more than that?" Madison asked.

Richards shook his head. "Liver temp will be off given the heat. I'll know more once I get her back to the morgue and conduct a full autopsy."

"When will that be?"

He shrugged. "I'll let you know."

Madison nodded. "So you don't think she died here?" She hoped his answer would instill some faith in humanity. Surely if she'd been here for that length of time, someone would have seen her before Marsh.

"Again, I'll let you know."

"What about lividity? Doesn't it tell you anything?" Terry asked.

Lividity was the settlement, or pooling, of blood in the body after death. If it showed in the woman's buttocks and the backs of her thighs, she would have died in a sitting position. But that would've only told them she'd died in her chair, not her actual location.

"I'll let you know once I conduct the autopsy. As for *where* she died, I will leave that up to you to determine." Richards signaled for his assistant, Milo, to come with the stretcher and body bag. Sadness always soured Madison's gut when the black plastic came out, ready to wrap the dead in its dark cocoon.

She turned to face the road. "Protesters against abortion are nothing new around here, but I have a hard time accepting that she was a regular. Why would a woman her age get involved with such a controversial issue?"

"No idea. All I care about is finding out what happened to this poor woman." He put his phone away, seemingly done with taking notes.

Madison watched as the woman was sealed inside the bag. Memories of her grandmother rushed back and made her more determined to figure out all that happened to this woman. Her grandmother had been the greatest influence and supporter in Madison's life. She had died of brain tumor a couple of years ago and had left everything to Madison, overlooking Madison's mother and causing the already-existing rift between them to grow. Madison had turned down marriage and children for law enforcement, and that didn't sit well with her mother.

Madison gestured to the twentysomething man dressed in spandex who was talking with an officer and running a hand through his hair. "First, we'll speak to Marsh over there. After that, we'll show her picture to hospital personnel and see if they recognize her. If she was a regular protester or a patient, maybe we'll get an ID."

Terry opened his mouth to speak, but before he could get any words out, Cynthia called over. "Maddy," she said, holding up the protest sign in her gloved hands. "You might want to see this."

Madison and Terry stepped closer to the chair, and she followed the direction of Cynthia's pointing finger. There was an imprint on the wheelchair: PROPERTY OF PEACE LIBERTY HOSPITAL.

"We found it when we removed the sign," Cynthia said. "It looks like there is a serial number on it, too. VG235. The hospital does loan out chairs, and I bet they track it and match it to patients by those numbers."

Madison's heart sped up. Maybe this case would be an easy one to solve. In the least, having an ID was a good start. "Have Marsh brought in. We'll get to him soon."

CHAPTER TWO

"The serial number VG235 was assigned to Elaine Bush." Jackie, the nurse behind the emergency room desk, looked over the glasses perched on her nose.

"We're going to need her address," Madison said, just as a page went out over the intercom. It was in hospital code, but Madison understood every word. A patient was missing from the psychiatric ward.

Jackie listened to the announcement and then asked, "Do you have a warrant?"

Madison was aware of the blood heating in her veins. She swore she could sense every cell as it moved through her. Her earlobes warmed, too. She didn't have the patience for a nurse on a power trip. Terry stood beside Madison, quietly letting her take the lead.

The nurse accompanying Jackie kept glancing over. She had registered several patients in the time they had asked a few questions. The scowl on her face indicated she wasn't too impressed having to handle the workload by herself. The waiting room was full to capacity with people of all ages, sporting all sorts of injuries.

Jackie must have sensed her coworker's attitude. She quickly glanced over at her and shrugged. She looked back at Madison. "I don't understand why you need—"

"Elaine Bush's body was found outside of your hospital an hour ago," Madison said.

"Help me! He's going to die." A woman in her thirties ran to the counter, dragging a man behind her. Blood poured out of a head wound.

Madison averted her eyes but not before she noticed the rebar projecting from his skull. And…all that blood.

The bile rose in her throat, and her legs became unsteady. She set her hands on the counter for balance. Her head was spinning slightly.

"Here." A nurse ran over, placed the man in a wheelchair, and carted him off. This left behind the hysterical woman, tears streaming down her face, her arms flailing in wild arcs. A second nurse at the desk calmed the woman down enough to obtain her insurance information.

When Madison looked back at Jackie, she tilted her head to the right. She wasn't fazed by what had just transpired. Of course, for an ER nurse, she had probably seen similar, or even worse, before.

Jackie's eyes drifted to Madison's hands. "You don't like blood, do you?"

Madison lifted them from the counter.

"You're a cop and you don't like blood?" Jackie chuckled. "How do you—"

"Never mind me. The woman in the wheelchair didn't die of natural causes." It might have been a push on the facts, but it was justifiable. The woman had bruising on her wrists. There had clearly been a struggle. The circumstances were strange, at best.

The grin on Jackie's face melted. She touched her neck, which had turned blotchy from nerves, a telltale sign for some people. "You're telling me she was murdered?"

"It hasn't been ruled out." Madison held eye contact. The pause allowed the smells of the hospital to permeate her sinuses—antiseptic cleaner and the fragrance of flowers, the smell of sickness and death. To think life was also brought into the world in this place…

"All right. One minute." Jackie pushed her glasses up her nose and put her attention back to the computer monitor. "Miss Bush lives at— That's odd."

"What?" Madison asked.

"There's a note on her file. The wheelchair, VG235, must have been reassigned. She ended up with another one."

"What do you mean? I don't understand."

Jackie drew her eyes from the monitor to meet Madison's. "According to Elaine's record, when they went to get her chair upon checkout, it wasn't there."

"It wasn't there? You're telling me it disappeared? It seems a lot goes missing around here," Madison said, remembering the announcement over the speakers.

Jackie's eyes glazed over in brief confusion, and then she pointed to the ceiling. "You understood the code."

Madison nodded.

"I don't know what else to tell you about the chair. It's missing as far as we're concerned."

"Well, we found it along with a dead woman."

Jackie's blotchy skin was now a bright red. "From my end, there's no way to know who she was if the chair had been missing." Her words came out low, in an almost apologetic tone.

"We're going to need Elaine Bush's number," Madison said. They needed to confirm, without a doubt, that Elaine wasn't the one in the chair.

"Certainly."

The other nurse glared over at Jackie. "Watch what you're doing," she said.

"Keri, a woman is dead."

"Still." The other nurse shook her head and went back to another patient.

"Here you go." Jackie handed Madison a piece of paper with Bush's phone number scribbled on it.

Madison dialed it immediately. After three rings, a woman answered, identifying herself as Elaine Bush. After confirming some information with the woman, Madison hung up the phone.

She stepped away from the counter, gesturing for Terry to come with her. "The woman in that chair was not Elaine Bush."

"So we find out who she was."

She nodded. "Unfortunately, it's not going to be quite that simple. I'd wager she didn't die where she was found, all things considered."

"You want to make a bet?" There was a spark in Terry's eyes. It wouldn't be the first time they made bets during an investigation. The regular was twenty dollars. While she'd like to claim she won the majority of the time, it wasn't necessarily an honest assessment. But she wasn't in the mood.

"No, I don't want to make a bet. I want to find a killer."

"Come on, I could use the extra money with the baby coming."

She sighed. "Fine."

"The regular amount?"

"Sure, why not?"

"You say the lady died elsewhere, and I say she died where she was found." He extended his hand to seal the wager with a shake. She complied, and he was all business when he pulled his hand back. "Let's go to the abortion clinic, see if they recognize the woman. You didn't actually think it would be as easy as providing them a chair number and getting an ID, did you?"

"I had hoped."

"Zip-a-dee-doo-dah, zip-a-dee-ay. My, oh my…" A man in a white hospital gown was skipping down the hall, a few orderlies chasing after him.

"It seems they found their missing psych patient." Apparently, Terry had understood the code, as well.

Madison rolled her eyes at his obvious statement. "Nothing escapes your grasp, does it?" She headed toward the elevator, hiding her smirk.

CHAPTER THREE

"How does a wheelchair just go missing?" Madison asked Terry as they shared an elevator up two floors to the abortion clinic.

"I can only imagine the traffic going through this place in a day. It might not be as hard as you think."

"A hospital employee wouldn't stand out pushing one."

"Like I said, Maddy, I don't think anyone would. You saw how crowded that waiting room was and the number of people who were being helped by the other nurse at the desk."

Her phone vibrated, notifying her of a text message. It was from Cynthia. Richards booked the autopsy for first thing the next morning. Madison shared this information with Terry, and although he nodded, his eyes seemed distant—a common occurrence these days.

Doctors had told Terry and Annabelle that their baby could be born with spina bifida, but they strived to stay positive.

"Are you thinking about the baby?" Madison asked.

"I'm thinking of *him*, yes." He gave her a slick smile. Despite ultrasounds not revealing the baby's sex, Terry was convinced it was a boy.

"How is Annabelle these days?"

"She's excited, nervous. She wants him out." He laughed, but the expression quickly deflated.

"Good. And I bet." Madison was thirty-five and didn't have a mothering bone in her body. If she thought pregnancy through to birth—all the bodily fluids and the blood—it made her squeamish and just sealed the fact she would likely never have a family.

"So if you get to ask about my life…" he teased.

"Oh, no, you don't. My relationship with Matthews is off the table."

"Matthews? Sounds rather formal and cold."

Troy Matthews was head of SWAT for Stiles PD. She'd known him for years, but it wasn't until a recent case that their friendship had turned into something more. Despite her initial resistance, some things cannot be stopped. The draw she had to him was one such thing. He was an alpha male and, as such, attracted women in droves. He was into working out and ripped. But he was serious-minded and interested solely in her—or so he kept trying to convince her.

Madison took a deep breath thinking back to last night—their bodies entangled, moving together… She had to wish the images from her mind. At least for right now. They were on a case.

"I can tell by the flush of your cheeks, things are heating up."

"Oh, shut up." She punched him in the shoulder and then smirked. Her relationship with Terry would never change. He was like the younger brother she'd never had.

"By the way, you're looking good these days," he added.

She narrowed her eyes, tempted to punch him again.

"What?" He lifted his shoulders, hands palms out toward her. "I just noticed. I thought women liked this type of acknowledgment."

But she wasn't "most women." She wasn't worried about what men thought of her. After being betrayed by her fiancé in her early twenties, she'd been somewhat bitter for the better part of a decade now. It didn't help that he—Toby Sovereign—was also a detective and currently working with

Stiles PD. The greatest tragedy was how she held what he had done to her against all men who had entered her life—up until now. She still dated, of course, but she never allowed anyone to get too close. No, her heart was hers and hers alone. With that state of mind, though, the loneliness was also hers alone. She had both Cynthia and Terry to thank for helping her to see that life was too short to sit around and mope. Even Troy deserved some of the credit.

"You must be working out," Terry said, breaking her train of thought. "Does Troy have you on a program?" Terry snickered, evidently amused with his innuendo.

"Would you just—"

The elevator dinged, interrupting as it announced their arrival on the second floor.

She stepped out first. Not that she'd admit it to Terry, master of the treadmill, who ran ten miles every morning, but she *was* exercising. And eating healthier. Before her shifts, she'd walk Hershey, her chocolate lab, at a brisk pace for an hour. Thanks to the obedience classes she was able to fit in every other Saturday, he was a pleasure to walk. She had started with one block and kept building herself up.

She hated to concede that the new lifestyle had anything to do with Matthews—Troy. She still slipped sometimes, but it was beginning to get easier to refer to him by first name. She was doomed. Whenever she sensed the trepidation setting in, the hesitancy over accepting their relationship, she'd blurt out *Matthews* to establish focus again.

But life had taken her through a lot in recent months. She had almost died at the hands of the Russian Mafia and came close to being raped by one of them, too. Faced with the muzzle of a revolver to her head, she had promised herself that she would forgive past hurts and try to love again with a full heart. The latter was really tough. It equated to vulnerability, the very thing she always did her best to avoid.

The elevator started to close, and Terry was still in it. She stuck her hand out to hold back the doors. "Are you coming?"

"Yeah. I guess so."

There was a small waiting area in the clinic with three patients waiting for their turn. One woman was by herself. The other two had someone with them—one a man, the other seemingly a female friend.

Madison and Terry approached the front counter. The blond receptionist's smile faded when Madison held up her badge.

Then she brought up a photograph of the dead woman on her phone and extended it to the nurse. "Do you recognize this woman?"

She leaned forward and squinted as if she needed glasses but refused to wear them. "I do."

"Do you know her name?"

"No. Sorry." She sat back in her chair and Madison noted her name tag: MARY ELLEN.

Mary Ellen had just looked at the picture of a dead woman she recognized, and there was no evidence that the news shook her.

"She was found outside the hospital perimeter."

"Someone killed her? That's why you're here?" Tears beaded in her eyes as if everything was just sinking in.

"You knew her, but you don't know her name?" Madison was struck by the conflicting responses and emotion. First, no reaction, and now she seemed distraught. But Madison could relate to how the woman was feeling. Not that she ever cried at a crime scene. It was bad enough that she hated the sight of blood and had vomited in front of Troy Matthews once because of it. But there had been exceptional circumstances.

"I pass the protesters on the way home in the evening," Mary Ellen replied, "and I have seen her out there before."

"Was she normally in a wheelchair?"

Mary Ellen shook her head. "Even though I work in here and she stands against abortion, she was inspiring. Here was this delicate, gray-haired woman, standing tall for what she believed in."

"She was out there on a daily basis?" Terry asked.

"Come to think of it, she hasn't been out there in some time."

Madison glanced at Terry. It was likely that whoever left the woman outside the hospital knew that she protested abortion.

"'Some time'?" Madison prompted for a precise answer.

"A couple months, I think."

"Was she ill? Did she have an operation?"

"I'm sorry, I don't know."

"Did you happen to notice the sign she held?" Madison asked.

"Yeah, it said, 'Put an end to abortion.' Simple and direct."

"A wood sign, painted lettering?" Terry inquired.

"Yes." Mary Ellen's eyes squeezed shut and then opened again. "What does that have to do with anything?"

"She was found with that sign strapped to the back of a wheelchair," Madison said. She thanked Mary Ellen for her insights, and after they spoke to some other nurses, Madison and Terry headed back for the elevator. It was apparent they were missing key aspects to this case already. No ID on the woman. No apparent motive. Was she disposed of because the family couldn't afford burial? Had her death been an argument taken too far? It likely wasn't elder abuse, as Richards had said the bruising happened around the time of death. She factored in, as well, that it was possible the person who left her there was the one who found her. Remorse could have set in afterward.

"We need to see what Marsh has to say," she said. Part of her expected Terry to defend the man's innocence, how he probably just happened upon the older woman. "You have nothing to say?"

"Nope. I agree with you."

"You what?" Terry was rarely in quick agreement, and while it was an obvious next step to what was before them, he'd been overly accommodating since her recent situation with the Russians. In some ways, she'd rather he go back to his regular, snappy nature that had her defending herself at most intervals along an investigation.

Also available from
International Bestselling Author
Carolyn Arnold

DEADLY IMPULSE
Book 6 in the Detective Madison Knight Series

She sees his face all the time—eyes open, eyes closed, it doesn't matter. When no one's around, she lets herself sink into her fear. He came for her once; he could come for her again.

When **a sixty-eight-year-old woman is found dead outside the hospital in a wheelchair with an anti-abortion sign strapped to its back, Detective Madison Knight expects it to be an open-and-shut case.** On the surface, there are no signs of foul play, but the deeper she digs, the suspicious death turns into a homicide. Just as the victim is identified as Faye Duncan, **two more bodies turn up—Faye's niece and a homeless man.**

Madison doesn't buy that a serial killer is on the loose, despite the conviction with which her ex-fiancé and fellow detective try to convince their superior. She sees the vagrant as sadly nothing more than collateral damage in a much bigger picture—but what motive for murder could span generations?

As **Madison wades through all the secrets and lies, she uncovers some shocking and heartbreaking truths. She had trust issues before, but this investigation will remind her of the cost—sometimes fatal—of trusting the wrong person.**

Available from popular book retailers or
at CarolynArnold.net

CAROLYN ARNOLD is an international bestselling and award-winning author, as well as a speaker, teacher, and inspirational mentor. She has several continuing fiction series and has many published books. Her genre diversity offers her readers everything from cozy to hard-boiled mysteries, and thrillers to action adventures. Her crime fiction series have been praised by those in law enforcement as being accurate and entertaining. This led to her adopting the trademark: POLICE PROCEDURALS RESPECTED BY LAW ENFORCEMENT™.

Carolyn was born in a small town and enjoys spending time outdoors, but she also loves the lights of a big city. Grounded by her roots and lifted by her dreams, her overactive imagination insists that she tell her stories. Her intention is to touch the hearts of millions with her books, to entertain, inspire, and empower.

She currently lives near London, Ontario, Canada with her husband and two beagles.

CONNECT ONLINE
CarolynArnold.net
Facebook.com/AuthorCarolynArnold
Twitter.com/Carolyn_Arnold

And don't forget to sign up for her newsletter for up-to-date information on release and special offers at
CarolynArnold.net/Newsletters.

Made in the USA
Las Vegas, NV
07 September 2024